REMEMBER MY FACE

A WILLIE CUESTA MYSTERY

JOHN LANTIGUA

Arte Público Press
Houston, Texas

Recovering the past, creating the future

Arte Público Press
University of Houston
4902 Gulf Freeway, Bldg 19, Room 100
Houston, Texas 77204-2004

Cover illustration by Brian Dumm
Cover design by Mora Des!gn

Names: Lantigua, John, author.
Title: Remember My Face: a Willie Cuesta mystery / John Lantigua.
Description: Houston, Texas : Arte Público Press, [2020] | Series: Willie Cuesta mystery |
    Summary: "Willie Cuesta, former Miami Police Department detective turned private
    investigator, is relaxing at a beachfront hotel when he receives a call from an immigration
    attorney about a case. He's reluctant to leave the view—of the sea and several bathing
    beauties-but Willie can't afford to turn down work. He agrees to travel to central Florida to
    search for Ernesto Pérez, an undocumented farmworker who has disappeared. His family
    is worried sick because, though he had been calling and sending money home regularly
    to Mexico for years, he hasn't been heard from in three months. In Cane County, Willie
    discovers a healthy agricultural industry, a large migrant population picking the crops and
    a heavily armed, anti-government militia. Willie quickly discovers Pérez isn't the only
    undocumented worker to go missing; several have disappeared, though their illegal
    status means no one has bothered to investigate. As he digs into the case, several
    suspicious characters surface: Narciso Cruz, who is responsible for smuggling in the
    undocumented workers willing to do the backbreaking labor for minimal pay; Quincy
    Vetter, a local landowner who has imposed his anti-government sentiment county wide;
    and Dusty Powell, a drug dealer who has contributed to several heroin overdoses in the
    area. And there's the very beautiful daughter of a farm owner who wants salsa lessons . . .
    is someone setting him up? When people he talked to start turning up dead, Willie knows
    he's onto something big—and dangerous. But is it related to the local drug business? Or
    the anti-government lunatics? When his investigation leads to a piece of property near
    the Everglades, Willie Cuesta finds himself playing cat-and-mouse with several armed
    men intent on putting an end to the case—and him!"—Provided by publisher.
Identifiers: LCCN 2020026600 (print) | LCCN 2020026601 (ebook) | ISBN 9781558859074
    (trade paperback) | ISBN 9781518506284 (epub) | ISBN 9781518506291 (kindle edition) |
    ISBN 9781518506307 (adobe pdf)
Subjects: GSAFD: Suspense fiction.
Classification: LCC PS3562.A57 R46 2020 (print) | LCC PS3562.A57 (ebook) |
    DDC 813/.54—dc23
LC record available at https://lccn.loc.gov/2020026600
LC ebook record available at https://lccn.loc.gov/2020026601

20 22 23   4 3 2 1

*For my family—children, spouses,
granddaughters—with love.*

CHAPTER ONE

Willie Cuesta lay on a chaise lounge on Miami Beach staring out to sea. It was late afternoon and many of the people near him had turned their lounges around so that they faced west, working overtime on their tans. They were sun worshippers, while Willie was more of a sea worshipper. His favorite time at the beach was twilight, when he could watch the fading light slowly turn the water from bright aquamarine to gorgeous shades of jade and then to a dusky steel blue. And he liked tracking the ships as they made for deep water too, wondering just where they were heading—the Bahamas, Barranquilla, Barcelona?

Willie reached into the small cooler next to him, pulled his open beer out of the ice, and took a taste. The chaise lounge belonged to a seaside hotel called the Caroline, where Willie sometimes did undercover event security. He wasn't on duty at the moment, so he could sip a beer. He wore a shirt imprinted with palm fronds over a bathing suit so that he blended in with the crowd. It was an arrangement that worked well for both him and the hotel's owner. Willie got a nice place to drink a beer during his off-hours and the hotel could count on a private investigator—a former Miami PD detective—to be on the scene, just in case trouble erupted among the beach-blanket set. So far, calm sailing.

He uncrossed his ankles and re-crossed them the other way, his bare feet dangling off the end of the lounge. He was just over six feet, slender, angular. His hair was jet black and swept back, his face long with prominent cheekbones, his eyes a light brown with flecks of green, often narrowed in a squint. Part of that was the sun, but it was also the world around him, which required careful scrutiny. His

1

old police colleague, Fanny Cohen, called him the Cuban Clint East-wood. "Except he's cold blooded and you're hot blooded, and you're not all that tough."

He took another sip of beer, watched a pair of particularly lovely ladies sashay along the surf line, and then his cellphone sounded. On the screen appeared a local number he didn't recognize. He assumed his business voice.

"Cuesta & Associates, Investigations and Security." Truth be told, there were no associates, only Willie, although he did hire free-lancers like Fanny from time to time. Would-be clients didn't need to know that.

"Is this Willie Cuesta I'm speaking to?" a woman asked

"Yes, it is. How can I help you?"

"This is Abbie LeGrange. I'm an immigration attorney here in Miami. You were recommended to me by another attorney, Alice Arden. I believe you've worked with her. She said you might be able to assist me with a case."

She spoke in the clipped tones of someone who charged by the hour. Willie charged by the day, but he answered in kind.

"Yes, I know Alice. I've handled a lot immigration work for her. And, yes, I might be available for an assignment, depending on what it is."

"Can you come to my office at six p.m.? I'm at 2020 Biscayne Boulevard."

Willie's eyes narrowed. He wasn't wild about moving, having to abandon his seaside reverie, unless he smelled a paying assignment. He took a pull from his beer before replying.

"You'll have to give me at least a hint what this entails. No sense wasting your time and mine if we're not a match."

Ms. LeGrange hesitated, but only briefly. "Let's call it a miss-ing-persons case. Missing persons plural."

"Missing persons? Have you gone to the police?"

"My client can't go to the police."

Willie frowned. "Why not?"

"That is not something I want to discuss over the phone."

Willie soaked that in. Working for people who couldn't or wouldn't go to the authorities could mean a lot of things. Maybe they were *malditos*—bad guys. On the other hand, they might just be people who didn't want police poking around their personal business. Lots of folks fit that description.

"Just who is it that's missing? And what do you mean by plural?"

"As I said, I'll explain it all when we see each other. I think it will be worth your while. I can't afford to waste my time either, amigo. What do you charge?"

"Well, that depends on what I have to do."

"Fine. We'll talk that over when you get here too."

Willie crunched the numbers of the conversation. Truth was, he couldn't afford to turn down work, or even the possibility of work, not at the moment.

"So, I'll see you at six?" the attorney asked.

A pelican had landed about fifty feet offshore and was preening itself. The two lovely ladies he'd noticed earlier had taken seats in the sand nearby, also preening themselves. But duty called.

"I'll see you then. Text me the address, please."

"Will do."

He disconnected, drained his beer, tucked the empty bottle back in the cooler, got up, slipped into flip-flops and trudged across the sand in the direction of the hotel to change clothes. The hotel guests who had already retired to their rooms had draped their bright beach towels over the railings of their balconies. They hung like semaphores. Were they signaling calm seas or rough sailing? Willie would find out soon enough.

CHAPTER TWO

The drive over Biscayne Bay to the mainland at that hour went against rush hour traffic, or at least most of it. Willie had changed into a sports jacket and slacks and erased all evidence of the one beer from his breath. He rolled down the window, let the wind rip through his hair and took in the Miami skyline, with its apron of aquamarine water. Always a treat.

He turned onto Biscayne Boulevard, heading north. The Biscayne Corridor, as they called it these days, was in the process of gentrification. For decades it had been a gauntlet a few miles long peopled to a large degree by hookers, male hustlers, dope dealers and the clientele from outside the area who came to do business with them. Much of the commerce had transpired in rundown motels with nautical names like the Seven Seas, the Sun n' Surf, the Ocean Breeze. If those walls could talk their tales would be tawdry, to say the least.

Then the real estate boom of the early 2000s reached the corridor. That new construction slowed some during the Great Recession, but now it had spurted again, growing like a long, thick vine up Biscayne Boulevard. Shiny new office buildings and condo towers had been built. The streetwalkers and dealers were rousted, migrating farther west, where the streetlights were still dim. Small legitimate businesses and Latin families that had been there for years were also being squeezed out. Along the way, the media revealed that many of the luxury condos had been purchased by corrupt officials and criminal elements from other countries, using the purchases to launder dirty money. As one of the displaced prostitutes put it, "That neighborhood has gone to hell."

A few of the old storefronts were still there, and one of them was the law office of Abbie LeGrange. It was an extremely narrow space,

4

half of a subdivided structure it shared with the equally cramped check-cashing venue next door. It was so narrow that the letters in the word "IMMIGRATION" stenciled on the murky front window had been arranged in an arch so they would all just fit.

Willie parked right out front and pushed open the glass door of the office. The small reception area was wood-paneled, furnished with a gray metal desk, flanked on each side by various gray metal filing cabinets. Sitting at the desk was a matching gray-haired lady. She was flipping through a file but looked up at Willie.

"Can I help you?"

"I'm Willie Cuesta. I'm here to see Ms. LeGrange."

She brightened. "Oh, yes. Abbie is expecting you. Go right in."

Willie rapped once on the closed wooden door. The office he walked into was exactly like the one he was leaving—paneling and gray metal—except that the woman sitting behind the desk was a generation younger than the one outside. In fact, so strong a facial resemblance existed between the two that Willie stopped, glanced back at the smiling secretary, then at the attorney. It was as if he had somehow stepped into an earlier epoch of the very same life. The younger woman must have seen that reaction many times.

"Yes, she's my mother," the attorney said before Willie could ask. "This is a family business."

She stood, stuck her hand across the desk. "Thank you for coming. I'm Abbie LeGrange."

Willie closed the door behind him and shook her hand. She was about thirty-five, with thick auburn hair and her mother's light blue eyes. She wore a navy-blue suit and a white blouse with a bright red silk kerchief tied about her neck. Willie figured if you were trying to help people stay in the USA, dressing in red, white and blue was an effective subliminal message. He wondered how many different ensembles she had that employed the same color scheme.

She indicated another woman sitting in a chair at the far end of the desk, shifting the conversation into Spanish. Her American accent was barely noticeable.

"With me is Señora Cecilia Pérez. She is my client, and we are hoping you can help us. The case involves her family."

Ms. Pérez was about fifty years old, her face a beautiful bronze color and her black hair pulled back in a tight bun, streaked with just a few strands of gray. She wore a simple, high-cut black dress and black shoes, but draped over her shoulders was a brightly striped shawl, the kind that Mexican weavers were famous for. A small, gold cross hung from her neck on a thin chain. But what most attracted Willie's attention were her eyes. They were deep-set, almost black, the gaze in them both intelligent and grave. She simply nodded at him; no glad-handing from Ms. Pérez.

Willie took an empty chair, crossed his legs. "You said over the phone that this matter involves a missing person, or persons."

Abbie LeGrange swiveled in her high-backed vinyl chair, opened a file, removed a photograph and slid it across the desk to Willie. It depicted a young Latino man, probably in his late teens, posed with books under his arm, outside what appeared to be a school building. He was a slender, smiling, good-looking kid, with straight black hair, café au lait skin and dark eyes. The gaze in them was lively, mischievous.

"That is Ms. Pérez's nephew," Abbie LeGrange said. "His name is Pedro Pérez. That photo was taken several years ago in southern Mexico, which is where they are from. He is now twenty-one years old. Cecilia says he looks essentially the same."

Willie glanced down at the photo again. "He looks like a smart boy."

Abbie LeGrange nodded. "Only not as happy these days as he was back then. He's had a bit of a rough ride."

"How so?"

That led her to dip into the file again and slide another photo towards Willie. This one was older. It showed the same boy at least five years younger. This time he was in the countryside, posed in front of a neat, white stucco house with a roof made of aluminum siding, the sort of place many rural Latin Americans lived in. With him were two little girls and a handsome, stocky, bronze-skinned, mustachioed man who looked about forty. The man wore a cowboy hat, a Western style shirt and jeans. The moustache was neatly clipped, the clothes scrupulously clean. His gaze was serene.

"I take it this is a father showing off his beautiful children," said Willie.

"That's right. The older man is Ernesto Pérez. He's seen there with Pedro and his two younger sisters. For years, Ernesto worked his own small farm in Mexico, where he grew mostly coffee. He wasn't wealthy, but he was able to work independently and make the money he needed to provide a good life for his family. Then the workers who picked the coffee started leaving Mexico and coming to the US to work, where they could make more money. That happened to many of the growers in southern Mexico. With no one to work the harvest, their coffee crops just rotted on the plants and they had to shut down. I've had lots of clients come through this office who once worked coffee in Mexico."

She shook her head at the demise of the industry, then went on. "Ernesto suffered the same fate. For a time, he went to work as a foreman on larger farms growing other crops. That didn't work either. He didn't like the way he and other employees were paid and treated by the owners of those big spreads. Not long after that photo was taken, he left Mexico for the US to find work to feed his children, just as many other men have done over the years. That was seven years ago. Read the back."

Willie flipped the photo over. Scrawled in black pen and block letters were the words in Spanish, "*Para que recuerden mi cara.*" So that you remember my face. He turned it over again.

"He came here to Florida. Is that it?"

"Right again. He was smuggled across the border with a group of other Mexicans, through the Arizona desert, then cross-country. His older sister, Cecilia here, had already arrived a few years earlier, was living in Miami, and he stayed with her when he first came. But then he took a job picking tomatoes, working the harvest all through Florida and farther up the East Coast."

On investigative trips through Florida, Willie had sometimes seen workers in the fields. You spotted them bent over double, picking whatever they were picking, along long rows of plants, often under a blaring sun.

"Not an easy gig," he mumbled.

"No, but what he was doing was learning the tomato business. In time, the skills he'd developed running his own farm became apparent and he became a foreman in the harvesting crews. He was still illegal but made better money. He lived frugally and sent home more than enough to feed his family and keep his kids in school."

She leaned forward and tapped the photo of the boy with books under his arm.

"Pedro even got to go to the university, something unheard of in his family."

She glanced at Cecilia Pérez, who nodded back with obvious pride in her nephew.

"Then things got even better for Ernesto, or at least he thought they had," the attorney said.

"How's that?"

"He was offered a year-round manager's job on a farm here in Florida. He made even better money and no longer had to migrate from state to state to work. He was talking about bringing his family to live with him. Everything was going great."

She stopped and swiveled in the chair momentarily, as if watching her story head off in another direction.

"And then?" Willie asked.

She swiveled back. "Three months ago the flow of money suddenly stopped—as did the weekly phone calls home."

"Why was that?"

"Because Ernesto Pérez disappeared."

"You mean he stopped contacting his family?"

She shook her head. "No, it wasn't just that his family lost contact with him. From one day to the next, he disappeared. Even the people he worked with didn't know what had happened to him. They said he simply vanished from the farm where he had been working. Cecilia and her husband went up there, contacted the employers and also a friend of his. The man's name is Andrés Colón and he was close to Ernesto. Even he didn't know what happened."

Willie glanced at Cecilia and she nodded somberly.

"Where is this farm?"

"It's in Cane County," Abbie said, "about four hours northwest of here, in central Florida. Lots of agriculture . . . sugar, citrus, vegetables. Do you know it?"

"I've heard of it. Never been there."

"Well, about six months after he got that job, he disappeared. As I said, that was almost three months ago."

Willie uncrossed his legs, re-crossed them the other way.

"I hate to say this, but how do we know that Ernesto didn't bump into a lady in a cantina one night and she convinced him to run away to California? They have farm fields out there too." Cecilia Pérez shook her head brusquely. "No, absolutely not. My brother would not do that. He would not abandon his wife and children. He is a serious man, a man of rectitude. If you knew my brother, you would never say such a thing. Never."

Her jaw was set, and her eyes were angry at Willie's speculation. She wasn't leaving any room for argument.

Willie cocked his head. "That leaves us with the possibility that something happened to him. I'm assuming that the local sheriff was contacted, along with hospitals and morgues."

"They covered all those bases and got nowhere," Abbie said. "But Cecilia's last conversation with her brother leads us to believe that someone may have meant him harm."

Willie turned to the Mexican woman. "What was this conversation?"

She was still peeved at him and spoke tersely. "As I've told you, my brother is a good man. He does not put up with disrespect, but that is not enough for him. He has the need to involve himself in the troubles of other people who he feels are being abused. He was like that back in Mexico. When he went to work for other growers back there, he didn't hesitate to confront those large landowners if he felt they were cheating workers. He was fired, and his life was threatened, too. Part of that attitude was a sense of fairness, but it was also just stubborn pride. It angered him to work for other people, especially people he couldn't respect. That was why, in the end, he had to leave there and come here."

Ms. Pérez appeared caught between admiration for her brother and the desire that he not be quite so admirable.

"Did he do that here as well?" Willie asked. "Get involved in other people's problems?"

She nodded somberly. "Yes, he did. We spoke by phone every Sunday. At times, he told me about migrant workers who were being mistreated by bosses or landlords or even by other Mexicans. He said, since he had been here in Florida longer than many of them, he knew better who to contact for help. The last time he called, he said he had heard of something very disturbing happening to laborers in the area where he lived. He needed to determine whether it was true or not, and then decide what he should do about it."

Willie squinted, as if trying to see the abuse she referred to. "He didn't say what it was, or who was responsible?"

She shook her head. "No, that was all he said. Mr. Cuesta, my brother never sounded afraid, but that day I heard fear in his voice. It was as if he didn't tell me what he suspected because he didn't want me to worry."

Of course, that hadn't worked very well. Cecilia Pérez was now very worried indeed. Willie took the other photo, of the boy, from the desk.

"If the father is the missing person, why am I also being shown a photo of the son?"

Abbie leaned her elbows on the desk. "Because about two weeks ago, young Pedro suddenly showed up at Cecilia's house in Miami. He had dropped out of school and borrowed money to be smuggled from Mexico. He told her he had come to either find his father or discover what had happened to him. She tried to talk him out of it, but he wouldn't listen to her. Then he left her home. We know he went to Cane County and made contact with Ernesto's old friend, Andrés Colón. We don't know where he went after that. He has a cellphone, but he isn't answering it. Cecilia and everyone else in the family are all worried sick about him."

Cecilia Pérez emitted a strangled sigh. "I am more than worried, Mr. Cuesta. Whatever happened to my brother, I don't want it to happen also to my nephew. He loves his father very much. He is young, doesn't know this country and will not know who he is dealing with. He may start asking questions, doing things that will put him in danger. We need to find him."

Willie held up the photo of the boy. "So, my assignment is to try to find *him?*"

Abbie nodded. "Well, yes, but we also want to know what happened to his father."

Willie understood now what Abbie LeGrange meant by "missing persons plural." They were hiring him with the hopes that he could deliver a twofer—two missing men for the price of one.

He took a few moments to digest it all. Yes, he needed the work, and his day rate was the same no matter how many people he was looking for. Also, Ms. Pérez was a woman who didn't appear to be rolling in money. She wouldn't be able to shell out twice over.

Willie wanted to help her, but she would have to understand that the likelihood of success was small. The very idea of searching for missing persons who were migrants was mind-boggling. He might never find either of the men, given the size of Florida farm country and the thousands and thousands of Mexicans out there. These were undocumented men who, given their legal situation, might not want to be found. They were the ultimate missing persons, needles in literal haystacks. Add to that the fact that rural Florida wasn't Willie's turf. He didn't have information sources among sugarcane cutters the way he did among Miami nightclub bouncers.

"I can use the work, but only if Mrs. Pérez understands the odds," he said and started to detail the difficulties.

Abbie cut him off. "I've explained that to Cecilia. As difficult as it sounds, she and the other family members want you to try to find them. What will you charge us?"

Willie's day rate had a range, depending on the assignment and just how well situated his clients were. He quoted Abbie LeGrange a figure at the low end of that range. Since he would have to work upstate, there would be travel expenses, but for now he would settle for a three-day retainer. That would irritate his accountant, who always insisted he get money for expenses up front. So be it.

Abbie wrote him the check.

"Cecilia and her husband run a small landscaping firm. They aren't broke, but they aren't loaded with money either. They're paying me, and I'm paying you. We can't afford you for too long. Please keep that in mind."

Willie said he understood. He got up to go.

"We will all be praying for you, Mr. Cuesta," said Cecilia Pérez.

It always made Willie nervous when people felt they had to pray for him. He thanked her nonetheless.

Abbie LeGrange stood up to bid him goodbye. In her red, white and blue outfit, he was tempted to salute her. Instead, he shook her hand and made for the street.

CHAPTER THREE

W illie went home to pack a travel bag. Then he phoned Fanny Cohen, who picked up on the third ring.

"Cohen here. Talk to me."

It was the same way she had answered her phone during her many years at Miami PD.

"It's me, Fanny. I caught a new case today and I'm hitting the road tomorrow morning. I figured I'd pick your brain."

"Come pick. You can drink a margarita with me on the balcony while you do."

He headed that way.

Fanny Cohen was a woman to be reckoned with, which many South Florida criminals had discovered over the years. By her own account, she was raised to be a Jewish American princess.

"But I failed at the princess part."

In her teens she had spent a year on a kibbutz in rural Israel, which included training with the Israeli Army. She learned that she was a crack shot.

"I would have stayed there for good if my parents had let me. I was the Jewish Annie Oakley."

After college, the family plans were that she go to law school. But much to her parents' dismay, Fanny was more interested in law enforcement on the streets than what occurred in courtrooms. She joined the Miami Police Department.

"When my mother saw me in the patrol uniform she almost had a stroke."

Fanny rose quickly through the ranks to become the first female, Jewish major crimes detective in the history of the force and had won enough commendations to wallpaper her house. She served for

12

almost three decades and retired early several years before in order to care for her beloved husband, Arnie. He eventually died of cancer. While on the force, she had served as Willie's mentor. Her long experience gave her invaluable sources of information. Of course her contacts in the Jewish community were strong, but Fanny was also possessed of fine instincts that she put to work in those communities where she wasn't connected by history—the Cubans, Central Americans, the Russian mob, the Italian Mafia.

"I'm a Jew. Given what we've been through, I can smell a bad guy at sixty paces no matter what language he speaks."

She was a tough taskmaster and second mother to Willie—his work mother. It was she who scolded him if his paperwork wasn't perfect. It was she who badgered him about his appearance, eating right, not drinking too much and not taking unnecessary risks on the job. It was she who had raised an eyebrow at a couple of his lady friends.

Most importantly, it was Fanny who had eventually convinced him to quit the force before he ended up behind bars himself. That advice had come after two cases Willie had handled. The first was that of a man who had beaten the three-year-old son of his girlfriend so badly the child was in critical condition. Willie was called to the scene, took one look at the little victim and something snapped. He launched himself at the perpetrator with his bare hands and, before other officers could drag him off, he had slammed the guy's head against a concrete wall repeatedly. It was only a miracle that he didn't crack his skull like an egg.

With no witnesses, his colleagues had been able to cover for him that time. In the report it said the perp had tripped trying to escape and fell down concrete stairs, somehow hitting every step with the exact same spot on his head.

In the second case, two years later, Willie had no such luck. That arrest involved a child molester who abducted an eight-year-old girl. Willie had interviewed the girl, seen her tear-stained face and blood-stained dress. He tracked the guy to a dive bar on North Beach and lost it the moment he laid eyes on him. This time he picked up a metal stool. His fellow officers pulled him off, but by that time the creep was bloodied, unconscious, in critical condition and had to be medevacked to the hospital. Civilian onlookers were at the scene, meaning Willie almost certainly would be suspended.

Before he had a chance to leave the police station that night, Fanny called him into an interrogation room, sat him down and locked the door, just as if she were questioning a perp. She was a fraction of his size—no more than five-four—pale, small-boned. Still, she dominated the face-off with her intelligence, the way she always did in that room.

"You can't do this job anymore, Willie. In this gig you can't control what cases you catch. You could change units, go to economic crimes or burglary, but those cases would probably bore you to death. And you never know what scene you might have to work in an emergency. If what happened this time happens again, not only will you get fired, I'll have to arrest you and send you to prison. I don't want to do that, but I will."

Willie shook his head as if trying to shake loose some part of his mind so he could dispose of it. "I don't know how this happens."

"It happens because you're a human being. Most people couldn't do this job for the same reason you can't. You can't handle seeing gratuitous cruelty. Some of us have a switch we can trip. It says, 'I'll put this guy in prison and make him pay not just with a few minutes of pain but for the rest of his life.' You don't have that switch, at least not in the worst cases. Someday, you're going to kill somebody."

Fanny had her eyes fixed on him, both stern and compassionate. It was a way she had. Her soulful brown eyes could read faces and situations the way most people read words on the page.

"You're a sunny boy most of the time, Willie. Problem is, you also have a tendency towards hurricanes way deep inside. Hurricanes are lethal."

Willie squinted. "What would I do? This is all I've ever done."

Fanny shrugged. "You could do what lots of guys do after here. You could go into corporate security, but, again, that would be deadly dull for you. I don't see you guarding office buildings for the rest of your life, taking orders from glorified office boys. You're too independent . . . not to say insolent. You should think about going into private work, become a PI. That way you can pick your cases. Some of them will be dreck, divorces, etcetera, but not all."

Willie knew she had thought it all out before sitting him down. She was right. The next time he crossed paths with a child molester or a woman beater, he could kill the bastard. Then he would end up sharing a prison with even more of them for a very long time. He had almost always followed Fanny's advice, and, after a few days, he did so at that juncture as well. He quit the force and the internal affairs investigation was quietly closed. He got his private license and became Willie Cuesta, PI.

As for Fanny, these days she taught classes in criminology at Miami Dade College, helped babysit her younger grandkids and did a lot of reading. But she was restless. So he availed himself of her expertise, bringing her in on his cases. She had even insisted on doing street work, including occasional surveillance in divorce cases.

"Sitting outside motels with my camera is as close to sex as I get these days," she quipped.

Willie didn't believe that. Fanny was still short of sixty and a vibrant, attractive woman. In fact, a retired cop from Key West had been paying her visits of late. Willie had refrained from asking too many questions.

She lived in an ocean-front condo on Collins Avenue on Miami Beach. The security guard at her building knew Willie and waved him right through. He took the elevator up twelve floors and found the door open a crack. Fanny was propped on a chaise lounge on the balcony overlooking the night ocean. She wore white Capri pants, a sky blue blouse and held a margarita glass. He poured himself one from a pitcher on the tray table and took the lounge next to hers. They toasted.

"What's up, Willie boy?"

So, Willie told her about the call from Abbie LeGrange and the meeting with her and Cecilia Pérez. Fanny took it in, irrigating the information with small sips of her drink.

"Not knowing where two different relatives are, that must be very tough on that family. Mexicans are particularly tribal. The whole tribe loses sleep when *one* member is unaccounted for. The women of that family, especially, must be delirious by now."

"Do you have any contacts up there in Cane County?"

That was the main question Willie had for Fanny. She had been a detective for so long and worked cases with law enforcement personnel all over the state that she knew officers in every corner of

Florida. She scrunched up her thin lips, searching her memory. Finally, she lifted an index finger.

"Yes, I do know an investigator. Bring me my Rolodex."

Willie got up, went to the desk in the corner of the living room and brought Fanny her old-fashioned rotary file. It was stuffed with hundreds of cards, all with names and numbers scribbled on them. She flipped through it now, stopping, reading, grimacing, going on. Finally, she plucked out a card with her pencil thin fingers.

"Ah hah! Here we go. I helped this gentleman on a case about a half dozen years ago. A meth dealer from up in those parts escaped a raid on his lab and they thought he'd headed down here. I found him shacked up with a local hooker in South Beach, drugged to the gills with a third-degree sunburn."

She handed Willie the card. Lieutenant Rory Camp of the Cane County Sheriff's Office. He copied the information into his notebook, then pulled out his phone and took a photo of the card as well.

"He owes me one," Fanny said. "Tell him I sent you. I'd love to go with you but one of my granddaughters has a violin concert. Attendance is mandatory."

Willie thanked her, drained his drink and was about to leave.

Fanny pressed him back down into the lounge. "I'm putting pasta on now. You're staying for dinner."

Willie started to demur.

"Don't argue with me," she said. "You're going to eat a decent meal before you go traipsing around the state. And while you're gone, you're gonna check in so I know some nasty farmer doesn't put a pitchfork through you."

Willie didn't argue. He poured himself another margarita and watched the stars glitter over the wine dark sea.

CHAPTER FOUR

B y seven o'clock the next morning, Willie was on US 75, known as Alligator Alley, slicing west through the Everglades. The sun was just up, dawn light kissing the tips of the tall sawgrass and illuminating the underbelly of the swollen cumulus clouds roiling above.

An old Latin ballad sounded in Willie's memory, about a crooner . . .

Traveling that trail through the tropics
The air around me all perfume and mist.

At one point, a spindly white heron took flight, crossing the road just yards in front of him. Its sweeping wings, moving as if in slow motion, captured that new daylight, which turned them whiter than snow. Willie watched the bird glide out of sight and wished him a good day.

Alligator Alley was a straight black ribbon across the state, with relatively little traffic. A driver could get lulled into drowsiness. What kept Willie alert was the fact that for much of the way drainage canals paralleled the roadway, and he figured the gators were waiting there for him to take a nap and veer into the water. His cousin Pablo, who traveled the road on business regularly, had put it best: "Those gators like Cuban food, Willie. You have to be careful."

About two hours into the trip, he turned onto a two-lane state road heading north. It ran along the western edge of the Everglades, bordered by sawgrass and scrub. Soon the wilderness gave way and he entered farm country. First, he hit sugar cane, stalks eight feet tall or more, with feathery pink tips that swayed gently in the breeze off the Glades. The cane eventually gave way to row crops, planted in lines straight as arrows that stretched towards the horizon on both sides of the road.

In the distance, Willie could see groups of pickers amid the rows of plants. They wore broad-brimmed straw hats and bright clothing, maybe so they could easily spot each other among all that green. They looked like scarecrows that had come to life and were scavenging the crop.

Willie was a city boy accustomed to a skyline dominated by the glass condo towers of Miami. Now, he became aware of the enormity of the sky over those fields. The clouds had cleared and it was now a blue dome dazzling in its clarity. He kept on expecting to see something, anything, rise up into it on the horizon. His gaze got lost in the distance. You could take the *muchacho* out of the city, but you couldn't take the city out of the *muchacho*.

Four hours after leaving home, he cruised into Cane City, the seat of Cane County. At the entrance to the town, on a wide grass median dividing the main drag, stood a concrete monument about twenty feet high that looked fairly new. It was carved in the shape of a sugarcane stalk. At its base was a bronze plaque with an inscription. Willie slowed to read it:

CANE COUNTY
FERTILE GROUND FOR FREEDOM

The sculpture wasn't exactly fare for an art museum, but it was certainly imposing. And it wasn't the town's only striking feature.

At first look, Cane City appeared to be a typical rural Florida outpost. The small business district, made up of aging one-story stucco buildings, was stretched neatly along the two-lane state road under that unbounded blue sky. It had the expected selection of small-town stores: groceries and gas stations, a few clothing emporiums, a couple of burger joints, a cellphone store and a nail salon. Digging in the dirt was rough on the nails. And, of course, plenty of churches—about one per block

As expected, the town also had a distinctly agricultural flavor. A John Deere franchise featured a large parking lot full of brand spanking new clover-green tractors. Another large store called BioMaster advertised agricultural chemicals: pesticides, insecticides, herbicides. A banner declared, "Everything you need to kill the enemy!" Serious business.

Willie saw a couple of gun stores, which wasn't unusual any-where in Florida, especially not in a rural area where you found hunters. What *was* unusual was that as Willie was passing one of those stores, a man dressed in civilian clothes and a cowboy hat walked out with a holstered handgun on his hip. A short distance later, Willie stopped to let a local citizen navigate a crosswalk and saw he was also wearing a firearm. In the next two blocks he counted a few more armed individuals, both men and women, and one of them, climbing out of a parked pickup, had an automatic rifle—an AR-15—draped over his shoulder. Willie wondered if they might be local plain-clothes law enforcement agents, but none of them dis-played any type of badge, and the weapons were all different.

You didn't see this every day in Florida. Lots of folks had con-cealed weapons permits, sure, but "open carry" was not legal in Florida, as it was in some other states. It seemed like the citizens of Cane County had not gotten the memo. But Willie wasn't a police-man anymore and, given how heavily armed they were, he wasn't about to stop to tell them. He kept going, hoping to get off that weaponized street as quickly as possible.

Luckily, a block later he located the Cane County Sheriff's Office. He parked and entered a small lobby paved with dark green tile. A single metal desk sat there, manned by a bright-eyed, female uniformed deputy. Willie asked for Lieutenant Rory Camp.

"Lieutenant Camp is now *Captain* Camp, second in command under the chief," she said with a touch of Southern accent. "I'll see if he's in. Who should I say is here to see him?"

Willie handed her his card.

"Please tell him I'm a friend of Detective Fanny Cohen, Miami PD."

While Willie waited, he gazed out at the stores across the street and the parking lot that served them. He noticed that the bumpers of numerous cars and the front windows of several businesses all bore the same distinctive decal. It featured a gold shield like a medieval knight might carry, crossed by two automatic rifles. Above that image were the words "Sovereign Rights Movement."

Willie recognized the name from the time he'd been a police-man and had studied extremist organizations operating in Florida. The SRM was a group that frowned on the intrusion of government—both federal and state—in local affairs. Willie figured the local popularity of a separatist outfit like the SRM probably accounted for the open display of weaponry within the county limits. Those kinds of folks didn't like anybody telling them where to wear their firearms, and they seemed to have sway in Cane County. Willie had known that he would miss home but hadn't anticipated it hitting him quite so quickly.

A minute later, Willie was escorted into a brightly lit corner office, where his hand was crushed in the powerful grip of Captain Rory Camp. He was an extra large, florid-faced man, probably six-five, two-forty, wearing a dark green sheriff's uniform bearing gold captain's bars and a wide black leather utility belt, from which hung a Glock. Behind his desk on the wall were photographs, some of a large woman who almost certainly had to be Mrs. Camp, as well as snaps of five children who were apparently their progeny. They were all large, both the boys and the girls, no matter what the age; they had probably been born large. All of them wore the same toothy, corn-fed grin as the captain. In the middle of those photos hung a 4-H calendar that depicted a prize brahma bull. It looked like the bull might be related as well, although it wasn't smiling.

Camp offered him a seat and settled his bulk behind the desk.

"How is my friend Fanny Cohen?" he said with a larger dose of Southern accent than the deputy.

"Fanny's retired now." Willie mentioned her husband's passing away.

Camp expressed his condolences.

"Fanny was a great girl to work with," he said.

Willie concurred. The idea of the Jewish Fanny Cohen and the good ol' boy Rory Camp collaborating on a case seemed highly unlikely on the surface. But Fanny had assured Willie that the big man was a tenacious investigator—no simple cracker.

"What can I and Cane County do for you?" he asked.

Willie told him the story of Ernesto Pérez and his sudden disappearance. "His sister told me he had been working at a place called Eccles Farms."

Camp pointed out the window. "About five miles farther up the road. Run by a fella named Homer Eccles."

"I'm told Pérez's family down in Miami filed a missing person's report on him at the time," Willie said. "Ernesto Antonio Pérez, age forty-eight. I'm wondering if anything ever came of it."

He copied the full name and date of birth on a notebook page, ripped it out and slid it across the desk to Camp. The big man turned to the computer on his desk, hit some keys, brought up a screen and typed in the information. He squinted at what came up.

"Yep, we have a missing person's report filed on a man by that name about two months ago." He used his right index finger to tap the screen. "It was filed by a Ms. Cecilia Pérez of Miami."

"No report by anyone local?"

He shook his head. "No, nobody."

"How about your John Doe file? You get any unidentified dead gentlemen over the past three months?"

Camp brought up a new file, turning the computer screen so Willie could see it. On it were individual color photos of three men, one white and two Latinos, all apparently between forty and sixty, all with faces that depicted considerable dissipation. Two of them displayed fresh facial bruises, and all had their eyes closed as if they were asleep. They weren't sleeping; the images were morgue photos and the men were dead.

Willie took out the photo of Ernesto Pérez. Camp glanced at it and back at the screen.

"Well, at least he's not here in this file. Why don't I copy this photo and pass it out to my patrol deputies again? Maybe they've seen him."

Willie said that would be good. He thought of also giving him the newer photo of the boy, Pedro Pérez, but held back. The kid was in the country illegally. The father was too, but he had a local work history and maybe people to vouch for him. Pedro Pérez had just arrived, and knew nobody. Willie couldn't be sure if they found him whether Camp and his people wouldn't just turn him over to immigration agents. Camp lumbered out to a copy machine, came back and returned the photo of the father.

Just then, his desk phone sounded. He answered it, listened to someone on the other end, scowling at what he heard.

"Okay. I'll be there in a few minutes. Wait for me."

He hung up, shaking his head wearily. "Drug overdose. Kid, nineteen years old, found dead in a little town called Sawgrass, about ten miles from here. Probably heroin. If it is, it's the second one in the last two months. Used to be the worst a kid could get into from there was some bad moonshine. You pumped the stomach and sent him home. Not anymore."

Willie nodded in commiseration. He knew small towns all over the U.S. had drug problems, in part because the towns didn't offer adolescents all that much to do. Drugs were a way to travel—virtually—out of town, except too often the trip was one way.

Camp got up and Willie did the same. As they did, a young male deputy with a big black moustache stuck his head in the door.

"The sheriff wants to see you before you go out."

Camp grimaced, and the deputy rolled his eyes.

"Tell him I'll be there in a minute, Williams."

The deputy departed.

"Problems with the powers that be?" Willie asked.

Camp sighed. "A political appointee, you don't have time to hear my problems with him."

"I noticed, driving in, that folks around here don't do much to conceal their concealed weapons."

"Oh yes, and that's just one of the state's laws that I've been ordered not to enforce here. We don't ticket locals for expired state registrations or licenses either. From now on, they'll register with the county. I'm told some businessmen will stop collecting the state sales tax. We're in the process of seceding from the state of Florida."

Willie winced. "Am I correct in assuming this is the influence of the Sovereign Rights Movement?"

"Exactly. In some parts of the United States, they raise a ruckus about some remote grazing lands. Here, they've taken control of county government. That includes the head of the county commission, plus my boss—the sheriff—and numerous new members of this department. Don't get me started or I'll get myself fired."

They walked out into the lobby.

"I'm looking for a place called Sunset Trailer Park," Willie said. "A friend of the missing man lives there." He was referring to Andrés Colón.

Camp gave him directions to the place, which was approximately two miles away. Willie handed him his business card with his cellphone number, just in case anything new arose. Willie held out his hand, then tried to pull it back, but it was too late. Camp squeezed; it hurt.

CHAPTER FIVE

W illie followed Camp's directions. He stayed on the state road as the stores petered out and the cane took over again. About a mile north, he found an isolated building that Camp had mentioned in his directions—the Seminole Outpost and Casino. Enclosed by a low stucco wall and featuring a spacious parking lot, it was a long, one-story structure made of thick, varnished logs, like an extra-large cabin built during the old Florida settler days. In the windows, Willie could see neon signs announcing "$$$LOTS, $$$LOTS, MORE $$$LOTS." Nothing too traditional about that.

The Seminole Indians owned the casino. They owned most of the casinos in Florida. The tribe enjoyed that privilege because of its status as a "sovereign nation." Willie wondered if the local "sovereign rights" radicals had been inspired by the Indians. Maybe, maybe not. The Seminoles were just out to make some money; the other local citizens were seemingly out to make trouble.

Willie gave the casino a pass right then, took his next left and went down a quarter mile until he saw a dirt road on the right. He took that through a couple of curves until he saw trailers.

What lay before Willie wasn't one of your more genteel trailer parks full of retirees from up north in shiny motor homes with all the latest conveniences. No Jacuzzis or granite countertops in this neighborhood. These were old, weathered, rectangular aluminum boxes, replete with rust and dents. Willie speculated that if a good-sized hurricane came along those boxes would be airborne, as would their inhabitants. Not pretty.

On the positive side, they were shaded by trees, and at least some of the people who lived in the trailers had done their best to beautify the place. A few had fresh paint jobs in bright colors—pastel pinks, yellows—with small herb gardens next to them. It was clear that whole families inhabited those units. Clotheslines sagged here and there, hung with garments of all sizes, for both sexes. He saw some small Latino kids running around in a clearing and cheap toys strewn about. This was entry-level America in the early 21st century.

Willie found #47, the address he had for Andrés Colón, and knocked on the front door. Red hibiscus bushes grew on both sides of the front steps. He heard a baby crying inside, and moments later a woman of about thirty answered, carrying a diapered infant. Mother and child were the same color, a beautiful mahogany brown. The mother sported a cascade of gleaming black hair; the baby was bald.

They both looked at Willie with trepidation. So he broke into Spanish to try to put them at ease, explaining to the woman that he was not an immigration agent or policeman.

"I'm trying to help a Mexican family find missing relatives. I'm looking for a man called Andrés Colón because I think he can help me. Does he live here? Is he your husband?"

The woman nodded, but only barely.

"Is he here?"

She shook her head.

"I assume he's working," Willie said. "How can I reach him?"

That gave her pause, and he thought she might close the door.

"It's very important," Willie said. "It's a friend of his I'm looking for, a man called Ernesto Pérez. His family sent me."

Her eyes flared, and he could tell that she recognized the name. She asked him to wait, closed the door, and he heard her talking. Her conversation was brief. When she opened the door again, she was holding a cellphone as well as the baby.

"He says for you to come in. He will be here soon."

The old tin can featured a faded linoleum floor that curled up at the edges. The metal roof had rusted through in a couple of spots and been patched. The place was badly worn, but efforts had been made at decorating. On the wall above a Formica dining table hung a depiction of the Last Supper on red velvet. The table was covered in a bright, flowered tablecloth and propped on it was a plaster vase holding wildflowers. The refrigerator door displayed children's drawings, and there was a very small, very old TV in one corner, Spanish language cartoons playing on the screen.

The lady of the house—Willie discovered her name was Natalia—served him coffee. He was halfway through the cup, when Andrés Colón arrived. He was a very small man, no more than five-foot two, in a baseball cap. He wore work clothes that were in good shape but covered in soot. His face was also discolored by it, and he brought with him the distinct aroma of smoke. His wife frowned at him.

"My God, you look like you've been working in hell," she said in Spanish.

"They were burning out a field when the wind shifted," he said pinching his nose as if he were still engulfed in smoke. He turned to Willie. "Before they send the harvesting machines into the fields to cut cane, they burn off all the undergrowth. You can get caught in the smoke."

He took off his shirt and hat, so that his face, still coated in soot, now looked like a dark mask. He didn't clean up right away. Instead, he sat across the table from Willie, and his wife served him coffee.

"You are here looking for Ernesto Pérez," he said, speaking in a near whisper.

Willie wasn't sure why the man was speaking so low, but he did the same. "Yes, his sister, Cecilia Pérez, sent me." Willie took out his investigator's credential.

The other man nodded. "I've spoken to Cecilia. I've tried to tell her what I know."

"Just what was that?"

He shrugged. "I wasn't here in town when he disappeared. I was working a harvest farther north. But sometimes we talked by telephone. Ernesto had an excellent situation with his employer here and he knew it. He could stay here all year. No more having to work one harvest after another. No more moving every few weeks, being afraid that some policeman along the way who doesn't like Mexicans will stop you for no reason and hand you over to immigration agents. No more living like rats stuffed into the same small trailers by crew leaders trying to save a few dollars."

He paused, glanced at the door as if someone might be listening outside the trailer. Above them hung the religious painting. It seemed to Willie that the twelve apostles might be listening, if no one else. Andrés Colón turned back to him.

"That's why anyone who tells you that Ernesto just walked away from his job here, that he quit and just disappeared, I don't believe that. You shouldn't believe it either."

"Who is saying that?"

"The people he worked for. That's what they say."

"You think something happened to him?"

The small man nodded gravely. "Somebody did something to him."

It was clear that the "something" he was talking about was very bad, possibly fatal. The black mask of soot he wore only served to emphasize his pessimism.

"Who would want to harm or kill Ernesto Pérez?"

Cecilia Pérez had told Willie about her brother's tendency to involve himself in other people's problems, but he didn't want to put words in the mouth of Andrés Colón. As it turned out, he didn't have to. Andrés had the same assessment of Ernesto Pérez.

"Ernesto was a serious, hard-working man who had achieved a certain position here. He also attended the local Catholic Church every Sunday." He paused. "I don't want to make him sound like a saint. He liked a beer after work as well. But because of his seniority, Mexicans working here were always going to him with their problems, problems they had with crew leaders in the fields, with local residents or with other workers."

"For example?"

Colón squinted into the past until he found an incident.

"A few months ago, before he disappeared, he tried to help a woman who was being badly treated by the coyotes."

The "coyotes" were the guys who smuggled people illegally across the Mexican border and across the country. They came in all categories—good, bad, ugly and really ugly. The nastiest ones were famous for abandoning people in the middle of the Arizona desert because they couldn't keep up. The skeletons were later found by the Border Patrol. Some coyotes had been known to molest their female clients. No, they were not Rotary Club material.

"What happened between Ernesto and these coyotes?"

"They smuggled the teenage daughter of a local woman from Mexico. The fee had been paid in advance. But they arrived here and suddenly insisted on hundreds of dollars more in order to release the girl. Of course the mother worried that if she didn't pay, they might *mistreat* the girl."

Colón was speaking delicately, but they both knew what he meant. In this case, it was rape.

"She spoke to Ernesto?"

"This woman, her name is Elena, she works in the packing house at Eccles Farm, where Ernesto worked. She asked him to help her find the money to pay these monsters. Instead, Ernesto went to the head coyote around here who supplies most of the labor, a man named Narciso Cruz. Ernesto told him if the girl wasn't released, he would go to the sheriff."

"That took some guts."

"Yes, and Ernesto would have done exactly that, but they released the girl. He also intervened when one of the foremen working the harvest kept money that had been earned by workers. He went to speak with that person's boss, and the problem was resolved."

Willie saw that the relationship between undocumented workers and law enforcement there in Cane City was no different than it was anywhere else in the state. People without papers didn't call the cops when they were being victimized, afraid that they would end up being deported. But in this case, they turned to Ernesto Pérez, who had served as a sort of local public defender. Willie recalled Cecilia Pérez's dismay with her brother's tendency to take on that role, but he liked the missing man already.

"Ernesto sounds like a good man and a good man often makes enemies," Willie said.

Colón nodded. "The last time we talked, which was about two weeks before he disappeared, he told me he had discovered an even worse problem."

Willie's eyebrows rose. That was what Ernesto Pérez had said to his sister Cecilia during their last conversation, the one that had frightened her.

"What was the problem?"

He started to answer just as the baby began to cry, loud enough to interrupt them.

"Let's talk outside," Colón said.

He led Willie out the back door of the trailer to a pair of folding chairs that overlooked a field of wildflowers, and beyond that, cane. They still could not be seen by the neighbors, which seemed to be the idea.

"So, Ernesto told you about a problem," Willie said.

Colón nodded. "Yes, but he didn't tell me more than that. He couldn't talk for long. He said only that he had heard about something very worrisome and he was looking into it. I told him he had to be careful, that he couldn't keep pissing people off who have power around here. But he said, if it were true, he would go to the sheriff. He never communicated with me after that, and when I tried to call him, he didn't answer."

He fell silent, gazing out of his hellish mask. Willie had seen that gaze many times in the past. That was the look people got when they thought about death. Willie realized Colón had been speaking of Ernesto Pérez exclusively in the past tense. He didn't seem to have much hope.

That didn't change the job Willie was being paid to do. He had no way of knowing where the kid, Pedro, might be, but if he followed the trail of the father, he might cross paths with the son.

"This man, Narciso Cruz, the coyote who Ernesto had trouble with, where can I find him?"

The other man's head came up. He was clearly scared, and Willie hurried to reassure him.

"Don't worry, I won't mention your name."

Colón told him where Cruz lived and a bit more about him. Willie wrote it down.

"And this other man, the one he went to see about the stolen wages?"

"It isn't a man. It's a woman who is the crew leader. Her name is Loretta Turk."

Willie frowned. "Loretta Turk doesn't sound very Mexican."

"She's not. She's a black woman from here who speaks some Spanish. It wasn't her who kept the money, it was a foreman, but she was in charge of that crew. Right now, her crew is working Eccles Farm."

At that point, Willie reached into his coat pocket for the photo of the boy. He had waited until then in order to get all the information he could on the father; the whole "backstory," the same as you did in police work. Now he held up the snapshot.

"This is Ernesto's son, Pedro. Cecilia Pérez told me that he came here to see you."

The other man nodded. "Yes. He was here several days ago. He asked me the same questions you have asked."

"And you answered them the same way."

Colón shook his head hard. "No, I didn't. I told him I didn't know what had happened to his father and that he should go back to Miami. He left and I haven't seen him again. I didn't tell him about the problems his father had with Narciso Cruz and Loretta Turk. I didn't want him accusing anyone, getting himself hurt. You look like a man who can take care of himself, so I told you, but I didn't tell him."

Willie got up and left Andrés his card with his cell number on it. He asked him to call if he saw the kid, or if anything else came up Willie should know. He went back into the trailer briefly to thank Natalia and headed for his car.

He was glad that Colón thought he could take care of himself. In Miami, that might be so. Up in farm country, which apparently featured its own variety of bad guys, both homegrown and imported, he wasn't quite so sure.

CHAPTER SIX

illie followed the instructions Colón had given him to Narciso Cruz's house. They led him one stoplight south, then west on a local two-lane road. He drove past scenic fields where sweetcorn grew. Scarecrows were propped here and there amid the stalks. These were scarecrows made of straw, not the human ones—the pickers he had seen in the fields. They watched him pass by with their fixed, button eyes and frowns on their faces, as if they weren't happy to see him.

He found the housing development Colón had mentioned—The Bountiful Harvest Estates. Willie stopped at the entrance. The houses were all newish Mediterranean manses surrounded by generous yards, the whole shebang flanked by cane fields. Whatever your business was, your harvest had to be fairly bountiful to afford one of these joints. Willie figured the local gentry lived on their farms, and this was where the relatively few professionals in the county had put down stakes—doctors, attorneys, agricultural engineers, whoever. It might seem a surprising place for a "coyote" to reside, but Andrés Colón had told Willie that Cruz did not do the actual smuggling himself these days. He was the head of the local labor supply operation—a sort of "executive coyote." Since the county's main industry was agriculture and it depended on undocumented workers, Narciso Cruz was a big wheel in those parts.

Willie followed the directions, drove to the very back of the complex and stopped outside the last house. It was a two-story, umber-colored, stucco villa with a red tile roof and matching shutters. A tall, black, wrought iron fence penned in the property. Two large royal palms grew in the front yard, about as tall as the house. Flower beds surrounded the building, bursting with tropical flowers, ferns and vines that crawled up the walls. It looked like nature was trying to pull the house back into the ground from which it had grown.

As Willie drove up, the lush front lawn was just getting finishing touches from a landscaping crew. He wondered if the laborers were among the immigrants Cruz had helped import across the Mexican border. Given what Cruz did for a living, he probably had little trouble finding help around the house.

Willie got out and took advantage of the open gate to access the front door. He smiled at the lawn crew as if he belonged there and rang the bell. Moments later a Latina in a black maid's uniform answered. Willie addressed her in Spanish.

"I'm here to see Mr. Narciso Cruz. Is he at home?"

She nodded. "Who should I say is here?"

"Tell him former Police Sergeant Cuesta is here to talk to him."

Willie put in a reference to his former position figuring that by the time the maid relayed the message, it would be, "There's somebody from the police here." That was a better way to get in than saying he was a private investigator.

It worked very well. The maid disappeared for about a minute, returned and led Willie through the house. The spread featured beautiful hardwood floors and pale blue walls where large landscape paintings hung. They looked to Willie like different views of Mexico; some were of the dry but gorgeous canyons of northern Mexico and others celebrated the green, tropical mountains of the South. The furniture consisted of knockoff antiques meant to evoke the Spanish Colonial era. Traditional Mexican weavings and rugs were placed all around. Cruz was obviously protecting himself against homesickness. He had brought Mexico with him to Florida.

The maid led Willie onto a shaded patio at the rear of the house. It overlooked a spacious backyard where numerous fruit trees grew—mango, orange, papaya. The owner sat in a canvas chair overlooking them, as if he were planning his next fruit salad.

Narciso Cruz looked like he had eaten a lot more than fruit salad in his life. He was a man of medium height, but wide, three hundred pounds or so. He looked to be about sixty, with bristly gray hair and gray stubble on his chubby cheeks. His eyelids were so puffy they were almost shut, the muddy brown eyes behind them barely visible.

Andrés Colón had told Willie that Cruz himself had once smuggled people into the country across the Arizona desert. These days he hired others to do the actual smuggling, which was good because at his size Cruz would have melted in the desert, like an extremely large pad of butter.

He didn't move but simply gazed up at Willie. He was a heavy breather.

"I am told you are from the police," he said in accented English. Given that he was an "executive coyote," one might expect him to be worried, but he wasn't.

"I was once with the police," Willie said.

He handed Cruz a card, and the big man read it.

"Private investigator. I see. What is it I can do for you?"

He motioned Willie into a canvas chair next to his. As he did, a loud screeching noise erupted from the far end of the patio. Willie turned and saw two large cages hanging there, holding macaws—one bright red, the other an electric green.

"They are Tarzan and Juanita," Cruz said. "They came from back home to keep me company. Now tell me what it is you need."

"I am looking for two people. I am told you know one of them."

Willie handed him the photo of Ernesto and his kids.

"This is Ernesto Pérez. He is—or was—an employee at a local farm owned by the Eccles family. He has been missing for several months now. I am told that not long before he disappeared, he came to talk to you about a certain problem he had with your organization."

Cruz stared at Willie several beats, his breath even more audible. Then he reached to the table next to him, retrieved a half-smoked cigar, lit it and puffed a plume of smoke into the still air. From the sound of him, smoke was the last thing Mr. Cruz needed, but that wasn't Willie's business.

"Are you saying that I had something to do with this man disappearing, mister detective?"

The coyote trade was a rough business. In his time, Cruz had probably seen his share of despair, violence, death. The fat man carried that kind of gravity in his gaze. It was fixed on Willie, and it wasn't fun.

"I'm not accusing you of anything," Willie said. "I just want to know what happened when he came to see you. I'm told he tried to intercede for a female friend of his. She had some trouble concerning a child of hers your operation brought from Mexico."

Cruz's irritation subsided. He studied Willie's words through a cloud of smoke.

"I don't know what it is you have been told about me, Mr. Cuesta. I am a labor contractor, the most successful labor contractor in this county. I came here thirty years ago and have been a legal American resident for some time. Growers here depend on me to make sure they have the workers they need to plant and harvest their crops. They leave that to me. I don't disappoint them."

Willie figured those growers asked few questions. In fact, they probably asked none at all. Agriculture was an enormous industry in Florida. But picking crops was the lowest and worst paid rung on the American labor ladder, not considered suitable work for anyone who was legal. Thus, the need for an illegally imported labor force. Cruz was explaining why dealing with a former policeman—or even a current policeman—didn't worry him. When you were a necessary cog in the local economy, the authorities weren't about to mess with you. He puffed his cigar and proceeded.

"I also have good relations with workers, since it is often I who helped them find jobs. That being the case, workers sometimes come to me with problems. Yes, Ernesto Pérez approached me at one point. He, like me, has been here in Florida for some time and we know each other. The problem his friend had was not with me. I had never met this woman or her relative. The problem was with an employee of mine. I told that employee to meet with him and straighten it out. The employee later told me the matter had been settled, and Pérez was pleased. That was the last time I saw Pérez."

"Who was this employee?"

Cruz hesitated. "He is not someone who would harm Ernesto Pérez."

"Then he should be willing to talk to me, Mr. Cruz. I am not interested in your business dealings or his. I am not an immigration agent. I am only trying to locate a man for his family. His loved ones are very worried about him. That is my mission, nothing else."

Cruz considered that. "Where are you staying here in town?"

"I have no idea."

"You should check in to the Planters Inn, on the other side of the state road. It's the only decent place in town." He waved Willie's business card. "I'll have my employee call you. His name is Víctor."

"Víctor what?"

"Let's just call him Víctor Coyote. Don't worry, he'll make contact with you."

Cruz used a brass bell sitting on the table to summon the maid. As he waited, a question occurred to Willie.

"You've been here a long time. What is it with this Sovereign Rights Movement and all these weapons? Does it affect the Mexicans here?"

The fat man shrugged. "It has all happened recently. Suddenly, some of them want to live in the Wild West. They can't live here without us, the Mexicans and Central Americans. No one else will pick their products. The demand for my service doesn't end. Maybe the fact that there are so many of us here now has made the locals nervous. I think that sometimes." He shrugged. "But so far no big trouble that I know of." He went back to chewing his cigar.

The maid arrived. Willie followed her back through the house. Next to the front door stood a table where several of Cruz's business cards were strewn. Willie nabbed one. Just then, one of the macaws screeched again. It made Willie flinch as he ducked out.

CHAPTER SEVEN

Willie drove back into town looking for a place to eat. His search led him onto side streets just off the main drag. It was there he discovered what amounted to the Latino shopping district that had sprung up in Cane City to serve the large migrant population. A number of the old groceries now called themselves *bodegas* and advertised food products from Mexico and Central America. A coin laundry was now a *lavandería*. On those streets, they were peddling cellphones—*teléfonos celulares*—and calling cards that made connections to Latin America a lot cheaper than usual. The local Catholic Church had posted an announcement on one corner, advertising a schedule for Masses on Sunday, although in this instance they were called *misas*. Jesus was still Jesus, you just pronounced his name differently.

Willie spotted a couple of Latinos and noticed they didn't have guns laced to their thighs. He wondered what the Latino migrant workers made of all the weapons in their midst. Cecilia Pérez hadn't mentioned the peculiarities of the place, but maybe she thought all the interior of Florida was like that. The mixture of the two populations worried Willie from the get-go.

He found a taco joint next to a bodega and had a late lunch. It was a tiny stucco shack with a half dozen dented tin tables squeezed in. It featured loud mariachi music and blinking red Christmas lights strung along the rafters. It was Christmas all year round in that eatery. Willie's present from the cook was some extremely tasty steak tacos served with rice and perfectly refried beans, accompanied by an ice-cold Tecate beer. The Mexicans in Cane County had apparently brought with them their genuine cuisine. It was definitely one of the perks of working in the sticks, Willie decided.

He finished eating and headed north out of town. Farther up the road, off to the east, he saw what looked like a factory, several stories tall, much bigger than any other building around. It was surrounded by cane. At that distance, it appeared unreal—as if it were made from Legos or an old-fashioned erector set, except it belched very real steam, or smoke, or both. Willie realized it had to be a sugar refinery. Rising out of all that cane, it was strange, imposing, a bit diabolical. He left it in his rearview mirror.

Soon the cane gave way again to tomatoes and other row crops. Then he reached the entrance to Eccles Farm, a wide dirt road cutting through fields. A sign hanging from a post decreed, NO TRESPASSING BY ORDER OF THE DEPARTMENT OF HOMELAND SECURITY. Willie had seen the same sign outside other farms on the way north from Alligator Alley. He figured it had something to do with protecting the national food supply, a legacy of 9/11. He had just eaten, so he figured he didn't pose a threat to the tomatoes and drove in.

Most of the year, farms offered long, peaceful views to distant horizons, uncluttered by humanity. But this was harvest season, and Eccles Farm was a hive of activity. On both sides of the entrance road, dozens of pickers worked narrow rows of tomatoes. The colorfully dressed workers were both men and women, of all ages, moving steadily, methodically up the rows of plants heavy with green tomatoes. Willie knew they were picked green and ripened later. One picker worked each plant, his or her hands moving with incredible quickness, letting the tomatoes fall into a bright, oversized bucket on the ground. The movement of the hands reminded Willie of cops frisking perps during arrests, except the farm workers were faster. They had the fingers of magicians.

Willie stopped and watched. When the bucket was full, the picker hoisted it to a shoulder and ran to a nearby flatbed trailer on the road. A collector standing there emptied the plastic bucket into a deep wire bin and dropped a red chit into the picker's bucket. The pickers pocketed their chits, ran back and frisked more plants. Under the gaze of their foremen on the truck, they always ran. Willie thought about one of the problems Ernesto Pérez had tried to fix, some foreman filching the money of pickers. You had to be a particularly callous creep to steal from people who worked that hard. He understood why the missing man had gotten angry.

The bins filled, the flatbed cranked up and sped up the road. Willie followed and, about a half mile ahead, found the farm buildings. The first was a double-wide trailer with a sign announcing that it was the "Main Office." Air conditioners were wedged inside the windows, buzzing away. Beyond that was a much larger cement block building about a size of a warehouse. It was topped with a corrugated metal roof, and Willie figured it had to be very hot inside. No air conditioners there. The flatbed drove up to a loading dock. Forklifts were lined up there to unload the brimming wire bins and disappear with them into the building—like pronged insects spearing food and returning into their nests.

As Willie stood watching, a short, white man in gray work clothes emerged from the office trailer. He was in a hurry, but Willie cut him off.

"Can I help you?" the man asked.

"I'm looking for Mr. Homer Eccles. I'm told he owns all this."

"Yes, he does. He's in the packing house. Can I ask what this is about?"

"It's a personal matter."

The other man didn't have time to argue. "Okay then. This way."

Willie followed him at a fast clip into the large building. As Willie had suspected, it was stifling hot and filled with the din of machinery. Above that cacophony, from somewhere farther in the complex, came the sound of someone yelling in Spanish. The guide grabbed a couple of hardhats off a long peg and handed one to Willie, as if they might need them when they finally encountered whoever was yelling.

Willie saw the forklifts empty the bins into tall metal vats. Machinery blocked his view of the tomatoes until he saw them again, now dripping water, being swept by conveyor belts farther into the plant. No workers were in view; it was all done by automation.

The man in gray led Willie between the conveyors into the next room. Here the process was considerably different, except for the intense heat. The speeding belts were now flanked by dozens of workers in long aprons and hairnets. They were all Latinos, as far as

Willie could tell. They plucked out undersized and otherwise unde-sirable tomatoes, tossing them into disposal bins. Like the pickers in the fields, their hands moved at lightning speed. Willie noticed that most of the workers were women. Casino owners in Vegas knew that women made the best dealers because of their smaller, quicker hands. Apparently, tomato farmers had discovered the same thing.

Willie pulled a handkerchief from his pocket and wiped his wet face. The workers wore bandanas around their brows to soak up the sweat. Someone had tied bunches of green bananas to posts near the conveyor belts, to take advantage of the ambient heat and make them ripen. On the wall nearby hung a poster of the Virgin of Guadalupe, the patron saint of Mexico, who was apparently impervious to the temperature. From somewhere in the room a radio or boom box sounded, playing Mexican ranchero music.

The faces, the heat, the Virgin, the bananas, the music made Willie feel as if he weren't in Central Florida at all, but in a Mexican factory that had been picked up by a tornado and dropped in Cane County. He was getting an inside view of contemporary agriculture in his state, a combination of US technology and lots of cheap Mex-ican labor.

Suddenly, he heard the clamor of voices. It was at the back of that room that they found the cause of the commotion. One of the sorters, a woman, had fainted from the heat. It had caused the con-veyor she was working to be stopped. Willie and his guide passed through a circle of other worried female workers. Willie saw the woman in question—actually a girl, no older than eighteen—lying on the floor next to the belt, her head propped on the lap of a Latino foreman. Her complexion was bronzed, but strangely pallid as a result of the heatstroke. The foreman tried to feed her water from a plastic bottle. She blinked vacantly as if she didn't know where she was.

Standing above them was a tall, elderly, white man dressed in work clothes. In a sea of buzzing concern, he was composed, stolid. He wasn't sweating and seemed impervious to the heat, the noise.

"Tell her we're taking her to the clinic downtown," he said in English to the foreman. "You stay with her there and make sure she gets home. Everybody else get back to work. We've wasted enough time. No sense spending months growing these tomatoes if we're going to let them rot here on the farm."

He whirled around and stopped just before colliding with Willie.

"Mr. Eccles, this fella is looking for you," the guide said.

Eccles was no happier to see them than he had been to find one of his workers fainted dead away. He indicated the girl. "Make sure they get her to the clinic," he told the guide.

Then he turned to Willie. "Follow me."

He set off back across the warehouse, with Willie in his wake. Willie noticed a telltale round, flat shape in Eccles' back pocket that signaled he chewed tobacco They passed outside and then across the yard to the "Main Office" trailer. Just before he stepped inside, Eccles deposited a squirt of tobacco juice in the dirt.

Cool air hit Willie in the face as they entered. A desk sat facing the door, and next to it stood a woman of about forty with short, blond hair. She wore tight jeans, a black western style shirt and black cowboy boots. Her large, clear plastic glasses hung from a chain around her neck, and she looked over the top of them at Willie. A placard on the desk identified her as "Myra Roth—Office Manager."

She called out something to Eccles as he passed by her. The older man didn't stop, leading Willie into a glassed-in office. He hung his silver hardhat on an old hat tree, and Willie did the same with his white one. Eccles fell into a high-backed leather chair behind a computer.

"Okay. Who are you, sir, and what can I do for you?" he asked in the same flat, hard, toneless voice Willie had heard in the plant.

Willie handed him a business card. Eccles glanced at it, but before he could speak, his phone rang. He grimaced and grabbed it. That gave Willie a chance to take the man in. Eccles was a string bean, about six-five and thin. His tanned face was deeply furrowed, probably from the sun. Maybe he had spent a lot of time standing in the rain as well. That's how deep the furrows were. Not only his hair but his eyebrows were a silvery white. Willie figured he was well into his seventies, although he had a cowlick that seemed to defy age. His eyes were brown, the gaze in them as fixed and flat as the tone of his voice. He wore beige work clothes with dark brown suspenders—no gun. Willie figured a painter could have used Eccles as a model for a portrait of an old-time farmer. All that was missing was the denim overalls and a blade of hay in the corner of his mouth.

Behind him on the wall were two calendars. Neither of them pictured a bull like Captain Camp's 4-H calendar. One of them came from an institution called the International Agriculture Bank. It featured illustrations of financial towers and super-sized cargo ships. The other was from an agrochemical company called BioMaster. Willie had seen a building with that logo in town. The poster depicted a diagram of the molecular structure of some chemical or other. Such was the modern agriculture business.

Eccles hung up and looked over Willie's card. It was only then that Willie noticed the gold Rolex on the old man's wrist. With all that land and all those employees, it shouldn't have surprised Willie that Eccles would wear one. Again, such was the modern agriculture business.

He fixed on Willie. "What could a Miami private investigator possibly want with me?"

"I'm representing the family of a man who once worked here—Ernesto Pérez. He has disappeared, and his loved ones are trying to find him."

Eccles pursed his thin lips. "The family contacted me all those months ago when he took off. I told them I didn't know where he was."

"You think he simply took off? Left town?"

Eccles shrugged. "What else could I think? That's usually what happens when a worker suddenly stops showing up. I mean, it's why they call them migrant workers, isn't it? They *migrate.* Maybe to another job, or maybe they get word from home that someone is sick and they leave from one moment to the next. People come, people go."

"That didn't happen in this case. He didn't go home. His family members fear something happened to him right here in Cane County."

"The relatives who contacted me told me that too. But his belongings were missing from his trailer here on the property. It looked like he'd packed up and left. Nothing else."

"He lived here?"

"That's right," he said, pointing farther down the dirt road. "Since he worked here year-round and had various duties at different times of the day and night, it was better for him to live on the property."

"What were those duties?"

"He oversaw the plowing, the seeding, the maintenance of machinery, turned irrigation pumps on and off." He shrugged. "Lots of stuff. I haven't been able to find anybody else to do all those different things competently, so the job is still open."

Eccles wasn't happy about that either.

Willie gazed into the distance. "Is his trailer still there? Can I get a look at it?"

The old farmer hesitated and Willie hastened to put him at ease.

"I just need a quick look. I want to be able to tell the family I covered all my bases."

The tall man grunted. "I guess so. Come with me and we'll drive down there."

Eccles led Willie to an old pickup parked just outside and they headed through the fields farther down the dirt road. After about a quarter mile, they came to a clearing. In it stood a tool shed and a small, aging travel trailer. Between them was a tractor attached to a wide plow with sharp metal teeth, and next to that sat a backhoe. A short distance away stood a sugar cane harvesting machine, a contraption with several different levels of rotating blades made to mow down tall stalks of cane. You wouldn't want to run afoul of that machine when it was in action.

Willie looked them over. "Ernesto Pérez worked with this equipment?"

Eccles nodded. "He operated it all and did the maintenance too. He was a handy fella."

Willie got out, tried the door of the trailer and found it open. He stepped up into a miniature kitchen, with a thigh-high refrigerator, a two-burner stove and a half sink. To his right, a tight meal nook; to the left, a narrow bed wedged into one corner. Across from it stood an open closet, devoid of clothes, a suitcase or anything else. The door just beyond it led into a very small bathroom, with a metal shower stall. The bathroom was clean and had also been emptied. The only thing left was a very dry cake of soap.

In only one place had Ernesto Pérez left behind traces of his having lived there. On the wall above the bed hung a small cross made of a dried palm frond, the kind given out at Catholic churches on Palm Sunday. Next to it hung a calendar. This one didn't feature a bull or ocean-going freighters. It came from the local parish, St. Anthony's, right there in Cane City. It pictured a photo of the current pope blessing the faithful in Rome. If Andrés Colón was right that something bad had happened to Ernesto, the pope's presence in that trailer had not helped.

Dust had inevitably accumulated since he had disappeared, but it was clear that the former tenant had kept a tidy home. Willie lifted the mattress to make sure Pérez hadn't left anything else behind. Through the springs he saw a photograph that had fallen to the floor. He reached through and retrieved it. In his hand he held a copy of the same photo he had in his pocket, the one of Ernesto Pérez with his three children. A piece of discolored Scotch tape was stuck to the top side. It had apparently once hung above the bed. Given what Willie had been told about Ernesto Pérez's devotion to his family, it did not seem like something he would have left behind voluntarily. Then again, if he had decided to abandon them after all those years, maybe he had ditched it on purpose. Out of sight, out of mind.

Eccles had stopped at the door.

"Ernesto Pérez lived here for free?" Willie asked.

Eccles expectorated a squirt of tobacco juice into the soil before he spoke. "That's right. It came with the job."

"And he left without a word?" Willie asked.

"From one day to the other. When I didn't see him one morning, I figured he was sick so I came looking for him. This is what I found."

Willie was feeling claustrophobic and headed for the exit. As he did, he noticed a dark streak on the inside of the door. Given his years as a police detective working crime scenes, Willie knew he was looking at dried blood. He pointed it out to Eccles.

The tall man shrugged. "Look at the machinery he worked with. I'm sure he sliced himself up from time to time. This isn't neat and clean city work here, Mr. Cuesta."

The two men were climbing back into the pickup when Eccles' walkie-talkie crackled.

"Daddy, you there? I need you up here at the house a minute."

Eccles picked up his unit. "I'll be there, Elizabeth." He turned to Willie. "The house is right around the bend. I'll just be a second and drive you back to your car."

He gunned the pickup. They traveled a couple of hundred yards, passing more swarming tomato pickers at work on both sides of the curving road, and then the Eccles house came into view. It was a two-story white plantation manse surrounded by lush green fields, with white wooden columns out front, a wide ground-floor porch, second-floor verandas and dark green shutters. It was shaded by a grove of centuries-old oak trees taller than the house, their twisting, tortured branches draped with Spanish moss. The place looked like something out of the Civil War era, except for the big air conditioning units on either side that hummed with cooling power.

A half-moon driveway made of loose white stones led up to that porch. That was where Eccles stopped the pickup. As he did, a young woman wearing jeans and a tight white T-shirt emerged from the front door. She held papers in her hand and approached the passenger window. As beautiful as the mansion, oaks and fields were, she put them all in the shade. She looked to be in her late twenties, skin as white as cream, thick hair the color of orange blossom honey and eyes that were a startling sky blue. She was tall and narrow-shouldered like her father, but full-breasted and standing close enough so that Willie could smell the scent of jasmine coming off of her. All he could do was stare. He hadn't seen a woman this naturally beautiful in many harvests.

She was surprised to find him in the truck with Eccles and did her own share of staring.

Then her eyes lit up and she laughed. "Well, who do we have here?" she asked with just a hint of her father's Southern accent.

"This is Mr. Cuesta. He's here from Miami. This is my daughter EJ. She handles accounts payable around here right now."

The lady leaned against the truck. "What brings Mr. Cuesta all the way here from Miami? I love Miami. I wouldn't leave it if I lived there."

"Mr. Cuesta is here trying to track down Ernesto Pérez," Eccles said. "The family is still looking for him."

The woman frowned. "Oh yes, Ernesto. That was strange the way he just picked up and went. I liked him a lot. He used to show me photos of his wife and kids and talk to me about them."

"He didn't mention any plans to push off, try somewhere else?" Willie asked.

She shook her head so that her honey-colored hair swayed. "No, not a word. Like I said, I was surprised that he left."

Willie handed her a business card. "If you remember anything that might help me, please give a call."

She plucked it from him. That made her remember the papers in her other hand and she passed them to her father.

"Make sure we got all this stuff because I'm about to pay all of these."

Eccles rifled through the pages and handed them back. "Go 'head and pay them."

"Yes, boss."

He put the pickup in gear and they headed back down the road. Willie glanced back and found the young lady looking at him over her lovely shoulder as she strolled back into the house.

They arrived back at the administration trailer and found a late-model dark green pickup parked outside with the logo "BioMaster" stenciled on it, like the calendar inside and the storefront downtown. A Sovereign Rights Movement decal was displayed on the front bumper. Standing next to the truck was a mid-sized man about fifty, with a very pale, hatchet-shaped face, sparse black hair slicked back, long sideburns and wire-rimmed glasses filled by unusually thick lenses. The eyes behind them were small and blinked a lot. He wore a steel gray suit, a white shirt and a string tie held by a silver clasp with what appeared to be a real, large diamond glinting from it. The ensemble was completed by a handgun in a tooled black leather holster on his right hip. The gun wasn't unusual in Cane County, but men in suits were rare—an endangered species like the Florida panther

"This is Mr. Cuesta from Miami," Eccles said. "This here is Quincy Vetter, chairman of the county commission, local landowner, also the owner of BioMaster, the agrochemical company."

Willie extended his hand. "I see the name of your company all over Cane City. The insects don't have much of a chance in this town."

He was exaggerating a bit, but it was always good to be on positive terms with the local strongman, especially if he wore a gun on his hip.

Vetter took Willie's hand very tepidly. His expression didn't change. He studied Willie through his thick lenses as if he were inspecting an insect under a microscope. Maybe that came from owning a pesticide company, killing bugs for a living.

"Miami. Lots of New York people down in those parts," he said with a reedy voice.

Willie shrugged. "Some. Not all of us."

Willie knew that to some folks in central and north Florida, the term "New York people" had a connotation. Sometimes it just meant Jews. Other times it referred to people of more liberal political persuasion in general, including gays and lesbians. Either way, it wasn't a compliment. Vetter was poking Willie a bit with the comment. Willie just smiled.

Eccles then gestured towards the pickup truck. It was only at that point that Willie noticed an older man sitting in the passenger seat.

"This is Quincy's father, Merton Vetter. Retired grower and former municipal leader."

Merton Vetter, a man of about eighty, had the same face as his son, but much more worn. His white hair was longer and unkempt. He wore old-fashioned overalls with a work shirt underneath. His eyes were green and blazed with an inexplicable glee. He greeted Willie with a smile as toothy as an alligator's. Willie had to wonder if the old man was still all there.

Quincy Vetter turned his attention to Eccles. "We have to talk, Homer. It's important."

Eccles turned to Willie.

"Let me know if you find Pérez. I owe him a week's pay. I'd like to know where to send it."

Willie said he would. He headed for his car, hoping that Ernesto Pérez's forwarding address was not in the next world.

CHAPTER EIGHT

illie started back down the dirt road to leave the farm, but had
to stop because the thoroughfare was blocked. It was the end
of the workday, and old retired school buses had pulled up next to
the fields to pick up the field hands and take them back to town. The
men and women filed onto the buses, sweaty, spent, each carrying
his or her big plastic harvest bucket.

Willie waited patiently, watching them. Then a face jumped out
of the crowd at him from under the peak of a black baseball cap.
Willie fixed on it because, out of a sea of other workers, that face
looked familiar. But the only farm worker he knew in Cane City was
Andrés Colón, and it wasn't him. It was a much younger man.

Willie reached for the inside pocket of his sports jacket, pulled
out the photo of the boy holding books he'd been given by Abbie
LeGrange. He glanced from the snapshot back to the kid standing in
line. Yes, it was Pedro Pérez, the person he was being paid to find.
He had no doubt. His left hand reached for the door latch, then he
stopped himself. He didn't want to approach the kid in front of the
other farm workers.

The buses pulled out when the last workers had boarded. Willie
fell right behind the bus Pedro was on and followed it to the center
of town, to a side street just off the main drag. There, next to a Mexican convenience store, named Juárez Grocery, it disgorged its pas-
sengers. Some entered the store, maybe to grab a cold drink to wash
down the dust of the day. Others simply walked away, headed home,
dangling their empty buckets. Pedro Pérez was among the latter.

Willie waited for him to get almost to the end of the block, and
then followed him in the car. Three blocks later, the kid crossed a
street and entered a collection of about a dozen very small brick huts

47

with corrugated metal roofs. A sign at the entrance announced that the property was called Sunset Cabins and just beneath that it said, "Proprietor: Narciso Cruz." Cruz had quite a business going, charging large amounts of money to smuggle workers in and then collecting part of their earnings in rent. He was a one-man conglomerate.

Willie sped up and saw Pedro enter cabin number two. The kid came out again without the bucket but with a can of soda in his hand. He sat down on a plastic chair, took a long swig from the soda and began to remove his work boots.

Willie saw no one else in sight and decided there was no time like the present. He pulled into the cabin complex, got out and walked right up to the young man. Pedro Pérez watched him warily, probably afraid he was an immigration agent, looking like he would bolt. Willie didn't give him a chance. He pulled out the photo of Ernesto Pérez with his children and held it up so the kid could see it clearly.

"This is your father, isn't it?" he asked in Spanish.

Pedro Pérez stared at the photo like a nocturnal creature in the headlights. Willie held up the other photo of the kid himself.

"And this is you. I am not an immigration agent or a policeman. Your family in Miami gave me these. They are worried about you."

The kid was frozen with one boot dangling from his fingers. Willie took the opportunity to hand him a business card.

"This is who I am. Your Aunt Cecilia sent me. I need to talk to you."

The kid read the card. Willie looked beyond him into the living space. The one room held two narrow cots and four bedrolls spaced around the concrete floor. Someone had hung incongruous supermarket art on one wall, a painting on velvet of snow-covered mountains. Maybe it was there to help the inhabitants deal with the heat. At the rear was a tiny kitchen where Willie saw large sacks of rice and beans propped on a counter next to old, dented pots that sat on a two-burner stove. From the looks of the place, there wasn't a woman in residence and the male tenants did their own cooking

The kid snapped out of his shock. "The others will be back soon so we can't talk here."

Moments later, they were in Willie's car driving down the road away from town. They pulled into a side street of single-family homes and stopped. Many years earlier, someone had planted the entire block with bright orange *flamboyán* trees. Now they were tall and in flower on each side of the street, so that it appeared the neighborhood was in flames.

Willie turned to the kid. He looked pretty much like he did in the photo, but now dressed as a field hand. What struck Willie most were the eyes. They were deep brown and invested with an intelligent, somber, steely gaze way beyond their years. They resembled the eyes of his father, which Willie had seen in the photo, except now the kid was angry at Willie for finding him.

"You shouldn't have come here," he said. "My aunt shouldn't have sent you."

"She and everyone else in your family is extremely worried about you. Come back with me to Miami. Let the authorities here handle this."

The kid shook his head hard. "First of all, I need to make money to help my mother. And second, the authorities here will do absolutely nothing to find my father. They told my aunt that he went to live and work somewhere else. Basically, that he had abandoned us. My father would never do that. Never. Something has happened to him."

Willie sifted through that. In a way, the possibility that something had happened to his father might be wishful thinking on the kid's part. The alternative was that Ernesto Pérez had, in fact, abandoned the family, betrayed his loved ones. That might be even more painful. To Willie it seemed like a no-win situation. The kid obviously knew that, but he was still there. He needed to know the truth so bad it was worth crossing the Arizona desert, risking his life to find the answer. Some people were like that. Willie knew, because he was like that too.

"You're working for the same farm your father worked for. What are you trying to do?"

Pedro shrugged. "If I came here asking a lot of questions about him, I could just get myself in trouble, like my aunt told me. Someone would probably call the *Migra*," he said, using the slang for immigration agents. "I decided to get a job on that farm so I could talk with people who know my father. Maybe they can tell me where he is, what happened to him. I'm not leaving here until I find out."

Willie appreciated the kid's chutzpah and his investigative instinct, going undercover.

"So, you're picking tomatoes for the Eccles family."

"That's right. The harvest crews always need people. It was easy to get hired. Almost everyone working here is illegal and uses phony Social Security documents issued under made-up names. I got mine in a matter of minutes in a flea market near here. I look more like my mother than my father, so no one here makes the connection. I mention to some people that I'm from the same town in Mexico as Ernesto Pérez and ask casually if they happen to know him. They don't suspect I am his son."

"And what have they told you?"

The kid hesitated, staring hard at Willie, trying to decide whether to trust him any more than he already had. Willie realized right then that he was going to have to help the kid, work with him, or go home empty handed. He had to take on the twofer.

"I'm on your side," Willie said. "I want to help you figure out what has happened to your father. I see that's probably the only way I can take you back safely to your aunt. And since I'm a former policeman here in Florida and a licensed investigator, I can do things you can't do."

Pedro Pérez took that in. He was a smart kid and probably understood that he could use help. Besides, Willie wasn't going away.

"No one has been able to tell me anything specifically about my father. But just a week before he disappeared, he told my mother over the phone that he had discovered some trouble here, something happening to workers."

"He told your aunt and Andrés Colón the same thing. Have you heard what that might have been?"

"No. I have asked some people as quietly as I can if there might be problems on the Eccles Farm. Or anywhere in this town. A few of them get nervous when I ask them. They look away, they walk away. Some don't talk to me again."

Willie considered what Andrés Colón had told him about Ernesto Pérez's run-ins around town. Andrés hadn't told the kid, but Willie had a feeling about Pedro Pérez. He figured the boy was smart enough to process the information without flying off the handle. In fact, having the kid on the inside at Eccles Farm could prove to be very advantageous.

"Has anybody mentioned to you trouble with a crew leader named Loretta Turk. A foreman of hers was robbing some workers and your father said something about it to her."

The kid glowered. "No, nobody has said anything to me. But I've been cheated out of some of the buckets I have picked by those same foremen. The other workers tell me that it happens to everyone when you begin."

"You stay away from this Turk woman. I'll find her and talk to her. She can't cause me the trouble she can cause you. I assume I can find her in the fields."

"Yes, part of the time, but she often disappears around noon. The workers have told me she goes up to the Indian's place to have lunch."

"The Seminole casino?"

"Yes, that's the place."

"I know where it is. I'll try to track her down there. What does she look like?"

"Oh, you won't miss her. She's a big black woman, as tall as you, and strong."

Pedro wasn't very big. The lady's size had clearly impressed him, and scared him a bit too.

"I'm also told your father helped a woman who had trouble with the coyotes," Willie said. "Her name is Elena and she works in the packing house at Eccles Farm. Do you have any contact with those women?"

The kid nodded. "They ride the same buses we do, to and from the farm. They always sit together. Don't worry, I can find out who she is, where she lives. I can wait for her to get off the bus and follow her home."

Willie winced. "Okay, but don't do more than that. If you contact her alone, she'll probably feel there is nothing you can do to protect her. If I am with you, she may look at things differently."

Just then, a Sheriff's Office patrol car turned the corner up the street and started towards them. The kid froze, fear gripping his face.

"Calma," Willie whispered. He smiled as if he were telling the kid a joke. "Stay calm. It's just a patrol and we're just two friends talking, sharing a laugh."

Pedro feigned a smile, but the fear didn't leave his eyes.

One male deputy manned the car. He was speaking into his radio microphone as he passed, apparently about some other matter, and didn't even glance at them. The kid craned around to watch him drive off and, only after the car was out of sight, let out his breath.

"I better be getting back now," he said.

They drove back to within a block of the Sunset Cabins. Willie gave Pedro his card with his cell number on it, and they agreed to be in touch the next day.

Willie watched the kid shuffle back towards his secret life. They were now co-conspirators, searching for his father and whoever might have harmed him. The kid had good reason to be wary. They were in the sticks, although these were very wealthy sticks. Growers like Homer Eccles and his neighbors owned hundreds if not thousands of acres and employed armies of people. They were millionaires, some of them many times over. Anywhere there was that much concentrated money, there were people with lots to lose. And Cane County was a place, it was clear, where some folks felt free to live by their own rules. Outsiders, like he and the kid, had to be careful.

Willie sat for a while and considered calling Abbie LeGrange. He had found the kid, but that wasn't what he'd been hired to do. His job was to bring him back safely. That would be more complicated. Willie didn't need anybody down in Miami jumping the gun, coming up to Cane County, interfering with his case. For now, he would keep the good news to himself. He put the car in gear and pulled away.

CHAPTER NINE

On the way to the cabins, Willie had passed St. Anthony's Catholic Church. Ernesto Pérez was known to attend services there, and in his cramped trailer he had hung a calendar from the church. Willie pulled in to see if anyone could talk about the missing man.

It was a small church, made of sand-colored brick. It featured a steeple that rose three stories and some very vivid stained-glass windows. The Mass schedule posted in front, just like the one in the middle of town, announced various weekly Masses in Spanish and one in English. That gave Willie an idea of the ethnic makeup of the congregation. On the other hand, the sign said the pastor was Father Philip Finlay, who didn't sound Latino at all.

The doors to the church were locked. Willie went next door to a smaller building marked "Rectory." He was just about to ring the bell when the door opened. He found himself staring at a man in late middle age, wearing a black cassock, a clerical collar and horn-rimmed glasses. The priest was just as surprised to see Willie.

"I was just going to ring the bell, Father."

"Well, I must be psychic," the other man said, with the hint of an Irish brogue. "Can I help you, my friend?"

"I hope so."

Willie handed him a business card. "I'm looking for a man who was a member of your congregation and has disappeared. His family is very worried about him."

The priest was suddenly worried too—at least his face was.

"Follow me into the church, please, then we can talk."

Willie did as instructed, and they entered the church. The light filtered by the stained-glass windows gave the space the underwater atmosphere that old churches often had—bluish in color, dead still and silent. The priest dipped his fingers into the holy water, genuflected, made the sign of the cross and headed for the altar. Willie followed as dutifully as an altar boy.

The priest climbed into the pulpit and examined some papers on the lectern. He looked as if he were about to break out into a sermon, with Willie as his only congregant.

"I have a Rosary Society meeting in a little while. I need to make sure I have my notes," he said.

Willie stood next to a life-size statue of the Madonna with Child. Both mother and infant featured copper-colored skin, much like the Mexican and Central American faithful in town. The priest finished his business, descended from the pulpit and headed out the side door of the church with Willie in tow. They entered the back door of the rectory, passing into Father Finlay's office. The priest waved him to a chair. Hanging behind the wooden desk was a crucifix on which hung a dark-skinned Christ, the grown-up version of the child statue in the church. Apart from that, the other decoration in the office consisted of model airplanes. They were everywhere—old WWII-era war planes, commercial airliners, modern fighter jets, stealth bombers. The priest gave Willie time to take them in.

"When I was a boy, I wanted to pilot fighter jets," he said. "But it turned out I didn't have the eyesight for it." He tapped the horn-rimmed glasses with his forefinger. "Of course, the entire Irish Air Force didn't number more than about ten planes. That would have been another issue."

He picked up a framed photo on his desk and showed Willie. It depicted an elderly woman in a high-cut black dress who seemed to disapprove of whomever was taking the snapshot.

"My saintly mother told me that my desire to fly planes reflected my desire to be closer to God in heaven. I didn't argue. I entered the priesthood, learned Spanish, was a missionary in Latin America for a long time. Now, in my later years, you find me here. In other words, my mother redirected my lofty ambition." He had a sly smile on his very Irish face.

Willie gazed around at the planes. They all seemed to be flying around him, like the last scene in the King Kong movie when the giant ape is climbing the Empire State Building. But these planes weren't firing at him, at least not yet.

"How can I help you?" the priest asked.

Willie handed him the photo of the missing man.

"I'm looking for a member of your parish, or former member. A man named Ernesto Pérez."

The priest glanced at the photo. "Oh, yes. I know Ernesto. He used to come to church every Sunday and sometimes attended night services. He even served as an usher. I was surprised when he left town."

"Are you sure he simply left town, Father?"

The priest considered that. "Well, he stopped showing up at church. In this parish, when that happens, you assume the people have just moved on. The family contacted me soon after that and I told them the same thing."

"That was months ago," Willie said. "He still hasn't made contact with them. They and I are afraid he didn't leave town, that something happened to him."

The priest looked aggrieved. It was occurring to Willie just how easy it might be to do away with a migrant worker. Everyone was willing to assume that the person had simply "moved on," and by the time they realized he or she hadn't, the trail was cold.

"Father, did Ernesto ever mention to you that he was afraid someone wanted to harm him?"

The priest shook his head. "No, never. Why would anyone want to harm him?"

Willie told him about how Ernesto Pérez had interceded to defend fellow Mexicans, at least two times that he knew of. The case of the girl threatened by the coyote and the instance of the foreman stealing money from workers. The priest paid close attention.

"He has always been a good man, Ernesto has. A man who had concern for others. Do you really believe someone would murder him over those matters? These conflicts involving coyotes and labor crew leaders happen here all the time, I'm sure."

"I understand, but not long before he was last seen, he told his family and a friend he was looking into another problem."

The priest perked up. "What was that?"

"He didn't say, although he made it sound serious. That's all we know. Right after that, he disappeared."

The priest folded his hands on his lap, lowered his head and fell into silence. It was almost as if he was praying to find out what had happened to Ernesto Pérez, but he looked more troubled than pious.

"What is it, father?"

The other man looked up. "A few months ago, a man came here to confession. He was a local man, or at least he spoke English without an accent. He had a question for me. He asked me if it was a sin to tamper with the dead."

Willie frowned. "What did he mean by that?"

The priest shook his head. "I asked him the same question, and he didn't really answer it. He just put the same question to me again. 'Is it evil to disturb dead people in their graves? Can you commit a sin against the dead?' I asked him who these dead people were and how he had come to disturb them. At the same time, I assured him anything he said in the confessional would remain confidential. He said he still couldn't tell me all that." The priest shrugged. "I didn't know how else to help him, so I asked if he had thought of speaking to the authorities about it."

"And?"

"That was a mistake. The moment I mentioned the authorities, he got up from his knees and left. He has never come back."

"Do you have any idea who it was?"

"No, I don't. Of course, I couldn't tell you even if I did know who it was. It has been on my mind ever since."

Willie squinted at him. "There's no real reason to think the disappearance of Ernesto Pérez and that confession have anything to do with each other, Father."

"When did you say Ernesto Pérez disappeared from here?"

"About three months ago."

The priest nodded somberly. "Yes, it's about then that this individual came to confession. Ever since that day, I've been wondering who and what he was talking about." He met Willie's gaze. "Hopefully, it has nothing to do with Ernesto."

Willie thanked him, and they agreed to stay in touch. He left the older man sitting there surrounded by his miniature aircraft.

CHAPTER TEN

The sun was setting when Willie stepped out of the rectory. Somewhere to the west, a farmer was burning off cane. The last rays of sunlight turned the smoke a fulminating crimson color. It gave the landscape an otherworldly glow.

He Googled the Planters Inn on his phone and found an address just south of the town center, a block off the main drag. He headed that way, turned onto a side street and saw a white wooden house, three stories high with gables on the top floor. It looked like it had been built by the same contractor who had erected the Eccles manse. They both had that antebellum thing going on.

Willie pulled into the gravel parking lot, removed his bag from the trunk and entered the lobby. It was a cozy space, with an old-fashioned wooden front desk, hardwood floors, an antique chandelier and lights mounted on the walls that were made to look like old oil lamps. A large bouquet of wildflowers sat in a vase on the counter. Next to it stood the desk clerk, an older woman in a flowered dress and a crimson cloche hat with a red hibiscus tucked in the band. The wildflowers were her only company, and she seemed to take her style from them. She broke out in a warm smile.

"Hello, there. Are you lookin' for a place to lay your head?"

"As a matter of fact, I am," Willie said.

She held out a liver spotted hand. "I'm Iris." Even the name grew out of the garden.

Willie shook her hand and filled out a registration form. He handed her a credit card and said he wasn't sure how many days it would be.

"Here on business?" she asked.

"Yes." Although he could tell she was curious, she didn't ask what business.

"Given that the place is pretty much empty right now, I'll give you the junior suite on the second floor, facing the sunset. But I'll only charge you for a regular room."

Willie thanked her, carried his bag up a wide staircase and down a gleaming hardwood hall. For a farm town, the room was sumptuous, with a four-poster, queen-sized bed, an Oriental rug and antique furnishings that included a couple of large, stuffed chairs set before a fireplace. On the walls hung reproductions of Audubon prints, birds native to the region—egrets, herons. Willie assumed the small inn had been built to accommodate big buyers of the local agricultural products when they showed up in town. That was the only possible explanation. Cane City wasn't exactly a hot tourist destination.

He was just unpacking his toiletries bag when his cellphone sounded. The caller spoke Spanish.

"Is this Mr. Cuesta?"

"That's right."

"I'm Víctor. Narciso Cruz told me to call you."

Willie ears pricked up. Víctor was the coyote who had allegedly tried to extort extra money from a local woman before Ernesto Pérez had intervened.

"Where are you?" the other man asked.

"The Planters Inn."

"Okay. I'll be there in ten minutes."

Willie was downstairs, nestled in the small sitting room just off the lobby, when Víctor walked in. He was about thirty years old, brown-skinned, rail thin, with long, slack black hair falling to his narrow, bony shoulders. He wore tight black jeans over his pencil-thin legs, a snug black T-shirt, and shades, even though it was night. He looked all about him as he crossed the lobby, skittish as a cat. Iris frowned behind her desk, definitely not accustomed to welcoming clientele who looked like him. He reached the desk, removed the shades, asked her something and she pointed over his shoulder in the direction of the sitting room. She was already looking very sorry that she had accepted Willie as a guest.

Víctor entered the sitting room and lowered himself into the easy chair next to Willie, almost disappearing in its folds. On the walls of the sitting room hung old, framed black and white photos of people who looked like the original settlers of Cane City. They were all white. Víctor was a representative of the new wave of local settlers. It was a vivid contrast.

"You're Cuesta, no? Narciso Cruz told me to come here."

He reached into his shirt pocket, retrieved a pack of cigarettes and was about to light one, when Willie pointed to a "No Smoking" sign on the wall nearby. Víctor kept the cigarette in his long fingers, playing with it nervously, swept his hair from his face, crossed his skinny legs and squeezed his knee with his free hand. He was a bundle of barely contained jitters.

Willie had dealt with people smugglers—coyotes—while he worked as a cop. They often stayed awake for days at a time as they moved "human cargo." They tended to live on Red Bull, cocaine and little else. This guy looked like he was on the same diet.

"I want to talk to you about your encounter several months ago with Ernesto Pérez."

Víctor's face stormed over and he spoke Spanish in a seething whisper, his small eyes blinking rapidly. "That was nothing but a misunderstanding, man. A woman I did business with didn't understand how it worked. She didn't listen to what I told her. Nobody tried to rob her. She never paid me any more money. And nobody did anything to her daughter. There was no reason for her to go to Ernesto Pérez. None."

Víctor suddenly turned and looked over his shoulder, as if someone were sneaking up on him. There was no one. Willie didn't move, the picture of calm in comparison to the jitterbug before him.

"But she *did* go to Ernesto Pérez. And he went to you. What happened between you?"

Víctor's hands flew up. "What happened? Nothing happened. There was no reason for him to be there. I told him that. Nothing except this stupid woman not understanding how things work. He didn't yell at me, and I didn't shout at him. We didn't touch each other. I told him it would all be straightened out the next day and he walked away. Period."

Maybe, maybe not. Víctor didn't seem like the kind of guy who settled disputes calmly and amicably. He looked like the kind of guy who didn't know the meaning of the word calm. The chance that

Ernesto had walked away as if "nothing happened" seemed slim—as slim as Víctor himself.

"After he had accused you of trying to extort extra money out of the woman? After he interfered in your business? You did *nothing?*"

That question in itself made Víctor extra mad. He grabbed the arms of the chair as if struggling to stay in it. His lips went pale and he whispered, "You don't understand, hombre. When all this happened, I had just finished a business trip. I wasn't looking for trouble. I only wanted to rest. Do you get that?"

"You mean you had just brought a group of illegal immigrants from Mexico."

Willie had spoken to many people who had been smuggled across the Mexican border. He knew that the trek across the Arizona desert could take three to four days, with a coyote leading the way. They arrived at safe houses and then it was another two days to Florida, driving day and night. There the coyote collected his pay, usually from family members awaiting delivery of their loved ones. The main idea was to keep moving, deliver the clients in the shortest time possible before immigration agents caught your scent. That was the modus operandi.

Víctor cocked his head. "*I* did not say I brought illegal immigrants from anywhere. *You* did. Narciso Cruz told me I had to talk to you, but nothing about the business."

He brought the cigarette to his lips, drew on it, then realized it wasn't lit, frowned, and used it to jab at Willie.

"The cargo I brought in this case, I took very good care of it. Nothing bad happened to it."

He was talking about the young woman he had smuggled.

"I guess you were too tired," Willie said. "You took good care of *it*, which is why you decided to charge more at the last minute."

"I've told you that isn't true."

"Did you ever see Ernesto again after that encounter?"

The coyote shook his head hard and fast. "Never."

"Do you have any idea what might have happened to him?"

He was still shaking his head, "No."

Willie handed him a business card and told him what he told everyone else.

"If anything comes up you think I need to know, there's the number."

Víctor took it, but Willie wasn't expecting to hear from him ever again. The other man jumped up, scissored his way quickly across the room and out of the inn without shaking hands, as if some invisible being was chasing him.

When Willie walked into the lobby, Iris was partially concealed by the vase of wildflowers. She stared at Willie as if she was surprised he had emerged from the meeting alive.

"Everything all right?" she asked.

"Couldn't be better."

She gazed out the door where Víctor had disappeared.

"I've seen that fellow around, but he's never been in here before. He dates a local girl named Dusty Powell. Dusty has a reputation for being a bit of a party girl."

Iris glanced at the door through which Victor had just disappeared. "I like a man with a bit more meat on his bones myself."

She turned her gaze to Willie and made him feel like a lamb chop. He wished her good night and headed for the Planters Inn suite to plant his head on his pillow.

CHAPTER ELEVEN

Willie woke the next morning to the loud chattering of birds in the branches of the oak tree just outside his window. He lay in his four-poster bed feeling like an old Southern plantation owner from the Civil War era. This was an unusual feeling for a Cuban American.

He shaved, showered, dressed and went downstairs for breakfast, which was included in the room rate. Only one other person was in the dining room: a heavyset, well-tanned man in his thirties, neatly if casually dressed. He wore a pocket protector in his plaid shirt and had a briefcase propped up on the chair next to him. A coffee cup sat on the table before him and he sipped from it as he studied a document. Judging from his frown, the contents of the document, the coffee, or some other matter was displeasing to him. He was not a happy diner.

Willie sat a few tables away. It turned out Iris was not only the night desk clerk, but the breakfast waitress as well. She brought Willie the house breakfast, which consisted of eggs, link sausages, a large pile of grits and a stack of buttermilk pancakes on the side. The Planters Inn prepared you to spend all day tilling the back forty. Willie skipped the grits, nibbling only enough of the eggs and pancakes to till the back ten. He would eventually be going back to Miami and had to maintain his boyish figure.

Halfway through his meal, County Chairman Quincy Vetter entered the dining room, wearing the same gray suit he had worn the day before and what looked to be the same gun. He peered around briefly through his thick glasses, spotted the man with the briefcase and approached that table. They shook hands, somewhat somberly, and Vetter sat down across from the hotel guest. While Willie worked on his vittles, the heavyset man addressed Vetter, apparently about subject matter covered in the document. Vetter interrupted him repeatedly, mostly to shake his head and apparently to offer an opinion at odds with his tablemate. The heavyset fellow presented some rebuttal, but it didn't appear to do any good. Vetter continued to scowl. Finally, Vetter stood up, pushed his chair in, offered a last caustic comment, adjusted the holster holding the gun, nodded curtly, and left.

Willie now understood why the heavyset man had appeared unhappy from the start. He must have been anticipating an obviously unproductive exchange with the county chairman.

Iris came around to pour coffee refills for both of them.

"Doesn't look like Quincy Vetter's meeting with that man went very well," Willie said, speaking softly so as not to be heard across the room.

Iris glanced at the other diner and dropped her voice. "That's Mr. Anderson from the state water management office. Quincy, he doesn't get along very well with any of those state fellas. To say the least."

That wasn't surprising to Willie. A town run by the Sovereign Rights Movement would not be friendly territory for state employees.

Mr. Anderson was on his cellphone now. He delivered a brief, sober report to a person on the other end, disconnected, threw a couple of dollar bills on the table, shoved the document back in his briefcase, and left.

Willie finished his breakfast, returned to his room, unpacked his laptop, and wrote out reports of the interviews he had done with Andrés Colón, Homer Eccles, Narciso Cruz, Father Finlay and Víctor Coyote. He would need to account for his hours to Abbie LeGrange. From time to time, he glanced out at the fields. His eyes had adjusted to the lack of tall buildings, to the long views that farm country afforded. He understood how staring at the horizon tended to slow down country folks. No matter how fast you traveled and how far, the horizon would always be in the distance. He was enjoying the fresh smell of the earth in Cane County, the sight of wind moving sensuously through the cane, the vast skies, the room to roam not found in the city. He just hoped the truth of the case he was on didn't end up like that horizon, always out of reach.

By the time he finished it was almost noon, and he headed for the Seminole Outpost north of town with the idea of finding Loretta Turk. He left enough time to duck into the Sheriff's Office for a talk with Rory Camp. He found Camp standing in the lobby of the station speaking with a middle-aged couple. The woman was extremely thin, with wheat-colored hair and eyes that were reddened as if she'd been weeping. The man was huskier, wore a cowboy hat and boots and appeared stunned. Camp patted the lady on the arm, shook hands with the gentleman and watched as they left.

"Those are the parents of the kid we found dead from a heroin overdose," Camp said. "They had no idea what their son was involved in. Now he's dead."

"Any idea who sold him the heroin?"

"Working on it. How 'bout you? Any luck yet finding that fella?"

"No, not yet. Talking to lots of people but nobody knows what happened to him."

Willie decided not to tell Camp about finding Pedro Pérez. Pedro's standing with the police was still the same: an illegal with no local friends.

"I was just wondering if Ernesto Pérez ever had any contact with your department before he disappeared. We checked the missing person report and the John Doe file, but we never looked to see if *he* ever filed a complaint against anyone. I'm being told he might have had some friction with a couple of local folks."

"I believe we checked that when the family first contacted us. Let me make sure."

The receptionist's desk was momentarily unoccupied. Camp sat down at the computer. He brought up a file, typed in information, read the screen, shook his head.

"No, no one by that name made a report to us of any kind in the last several years. But folks in the immigrant community, they don't tend to come to us with complaints. They're afraid we'll detain them and turn them over to immigration agents. If they have problems, they prefer to settle them between themselves. It's an issue for us because sometimes we have some real bad guys out there taking advantage of people and no one ever lets us know. We can have a crime wave right in our midst but never hear about it."

It was a story Willie had heard before. Wherever undocumented immigrants lived, you had large numbers of unreported crimes. And sometimes people, as Camp put it, settled things among themselves. That's what worried Willie, that whatever problem Ernesto Pérez had encountered had been settled in the shadows, in a way that was fatal or at least very bad for him.

"It's the same way with missing persons," Camp continued. "In general, nobody comes to us, and even if they do, it's extremely hard to find these folks. A couple of years ago, the Mexican Consulate down in Miami put out a bulletin to law enforcement all over farm country in Florida looking for workers they said were missing. They had the real names of the men, in some cases photographs, but it did no good. The way it works in the fields is that the migrants work with phony documents, which they buy using false names. They never have cause to use their real names, so the local farmers don't have records of their true identities. On top of that we showed the photos and none of the growers around here could recognize any of them. Hundreds and hundreds of workers come through here every year, so that was no big surprise."

As a former lawman, Willie could commiserate, and he told the other man as much.

"Is there anything you've turned up that I should know?" Camp asked.

"Just a little bit of bad blood that you would find anywhere. But I'll let you know."

He thanked Camp and headed for the Seminole casino.

***

When he arrived, the parking lot was about half-full of pickups. Casinos usually featured cheap food to lure gamblers. This remote hole in the wall was no different. The place was obviously popular for lunch.

A sign next to the front door proclaimed: "No Firearms Allowed on the Premises." In their history, Willie figured, Seminoles had already had enough trouble from white men with guns. It seemed like a very wise policy.

Willie walked into a high-ceilinged room that held a few dozen slot machines, most of which featured blinking lights, flashing video screens with names like Wheel of Fortune, Lucky Spell, Golden Touch. Hunched in front of them on stools were about a dozen gamblers, mostly older folks. Some were probably locals, retired from the rigors of farm life with little to do. If you could milk a cow, you could pull the lever on a slot machine. Others had probably driven over from Gulf Coast beach cities like Naples and Sarasota, where the Seminoles didn't own land and there were no casinos. A couple of card tables sat near the back, but they were empty. These gamblers were lured by the siren song of the slot machine, not poker.

Right in front of Willie was the reception counter, with ATM machines on each side of it for extremely easy access to cash. Standing behind the counter was the man who Willie figured was the proprietor, a dyed-in-the-wool Seminole. He wore a traditional Seminole blouse—gold lightning bolts zigzagging through crimson cloth—and long black hair twisted into thick braids. In a sense, he was part of the décor. He also wore what appeared to be a gold Rolex on his wrist, just as big as the one sported by Homer Eccles. With the legalization of Indian gambling, the Seminoles had gone from being the poorest ethnic group in Florida to one of the richest. The watch was there to inform you of that, if you didn't know.

The dining area was to the right of the door and it was crowded, mostly with sunbaked, leather-faced men in work clothes. Willie noticed some empty holsters, but no guns.

Along the back of that room ran the bar. Sitting there by herself was an African-American woman who could only be Loretta Turk. Pedro Pérez had described her as very big. The lady Willie stared at was certainly that. Willie crossed the room and took the stool nearest to her. She was eating, glancing up at ESPN on the televisions above her between bites. While pretending to study the menu, Willie surreptitiously got a good look.

He figured that when she stood up, Loretta Turk would easily be six feet. She was not fat, but broad-shouldered, full-breasted and wide-hipped. On the other hand, her facial features were delicate—a smallish nose, modest cheekbones and chin, widespread eyes. She wore her hair in a short tapered Afro, and small gold earrings shaped likes sunbursts dangled from her pierced ears. It being the middle of the workday, she wore a gray work shirt and jeans, both clean, crisply laundered. On her belt dangled a leather sheath meant to hold a buck knife. It was empty, probably because the management wouldn't let her in with a blade on her hip. She also wore a bright, lavender-colored kerchief knotted around her neck. She was big enough to be the bouncer, but she wanted you to know you were dealing with a woman. It had probably been a lifelong struggle.

Willie glanced at her plate. It was covered in a shrimp and crawdad concoction, with sides of mashed potatoes, collard greens and a wedge of cornbread. A genuine Southern seafood plate. Willie ordered the same, along with an unsweetened iced tea. When his drink arrived, he sipped it and turned to her. He figured there was no sense beating around the bush.

"You're Loretta Turk, aren't you?"

She frowned, turning slowly towards him, a forkful of shrimp suspended halfway to her mouth. "What are your grounds for asking?" she said in a voice that was surprisingly feminine for a woman her size. "Do I know you?"

"No. No, you don't."

Willie reached into his coat pocket and handed her a business card. She read it, her frown deepening.

"Miami? What on earth are you doing way up here?"

"I'm looking for someone. Someone I believe you know."

She shoveled the shrimp into her mouth, chewed, then patted her lips daintily with a napkin

"I know just about everybody in these parts. Who is it you're looking for?"

"His name is Ernesto Pérez and he worked at Eccles Farms until a few months ago."

She sipped her tea and nodded. "Yes, I know Ernesto. He was a good worker. A guy with a green thumb, as they say. He made things grow, which is why he got full-time work from Eccles. Then one day he just picks up and moves on down the road. No warning, no explanation. Must have found something better."

She bit into her cornbread.

"So, he found a better job? Do you know that for a fact?"

To that point her diction had been precise. Now, she grimaced and shifted into a less rigorous grammar, a kind of country patois local folks might use with each other.

"Why else in God's name would he leave good, steady farm work, a job where he didn't have to move state to state no mo'? A job where he didn't have to break his back pickin' crops no mo'? Where he got to ride a tractor? Believe me, I done my share a pickin'. When they give you a job where you don't have to do that, you don't kick dirt on it. He musta got a better offer on some other spread."

"You're someone who moved up to better work. I'm told you're a crew leader."

"That's right. I don't get dirt under my nails these days."

She held out her right hand and showed him moderately long nails painted blood red. Her eyes smiled with self-satisfaction, then she went on. "I've put together plantin' and harvestin' crews for most the growers around here. I have people workin' all over the county. My pickers are the cream a the crop."

"Congratulations."

Willie picked up his tea and toasted her. He sipped and leaned towards her.

"I understand Ernesto Pérez went to you a few months ago with concerns he had about some of those workers. What I'm told is you or someone working for you was keeping part of their earnings. Ernesto questioned you about that."

Ms. Turk turned less feminine. The muscles in her thick neck tensed and the look in her eyes was much more linebacker than lady of the house. She leaned towards Willie so that now they were just inches apart.

"Let me explain somethin' to you, since you're from outta town. Before there were Mexican people workin' these fields, it was black people. People like my granddaddy, my daddy and then me. These fields were irrigated with Negro sweat. When you first started to work, you paid your dues. You paid a bucket or two to the foreman for doin' the paperwork it took to hire you and the time it took to train you. Because maybe you wouldn't be any good at all and he'd have to go find somebody else, which would cost him time. And if you did make the cut, your crew leader had to prepare for the day when you got hurt or sick and he needed to take you to the doctor or the hospital. He paid for that. He paid for the buses to transport you to the fields and for the porta potties where you did your business. You paid your dues in buckets you picked for all that. You paid them to a white man who ran the crew. Today, the Mexicans pay me, a black woman. My foremen collect the chits and they give them to me. If I catch a foreman takin' too much and stashin' some of it for himself, I call him on it. The money goes back to the picker. But everybody has to pay his dues. You paid yours along the way. I'll bet you did."

Willie soaked that in. Yes, he had paid his dues when he was a young police officer. Not in money, but in doing the shit work while senior officers punched out and headed home. He had been there.

"Is that what you said to Ernesto when he came to see you?"

"That's exactly what I told Ernesto. I didn't like what he was sayin'."

"Did he threaten to go to the sheriff, to charge you with theft?"

She smirked. "Are you kiddin' me? First of all, Mexicans don't go to the sheriff for nothin'. And second, most those sheriff's deputies are good ol' boys who grew up 'round here. They did some fieldwork in the summer when they were kids, and I'll bet they paid their dues to the crew leader just like everybody else. Ernesto, he wouldn't get nowhere with that at the sheriff's office, and he knew it. He knew the lay of the land that much at least."

"So, what happened between you?"

"I told him I'd check up on the foremen. I found one of them was thievin' and I got rid of him. Some chits went back to a few workers. That was the end of it."

"Did you have dealings with Ernesto after that?"

"Ernesto and me we always had dealings. He had to know where the crews were workin' so he would know where he could irrigate and where not, where pesticides could be sprayed and where not. We never had no problem except for that one time."

She fixed on him now. "You think somethin' happened to him. Is that it?"

"His family hasn't heard from him in months."

She thought that over. "A lot of these Mexican migrant people, they find somewhere else to work apart from the fields. There is no harder work than the harvest, so they move onto landscapin', restaurant work, roofin' . . . The lucky ones catch on with construction crews and make even more money. They get outta the fields as fast as they can, the smart ones. Now Ernesto, he did good for himself right here, hired year-round by Eccles. It didn't make much sense for him to move on, but maybe he just got tired of this farm town. Got tired of workin' six sometimes seven days a week. Tired of smellin' the smoke in the burnin' season, gettin' up in the middle of the night in the winter to irrigate the crop to keep it from freezin'. That's not fun, 'specially for a warm-blooded Mexican. And men, they don't even need all that much a reason to move on anyhow. Take it from me."

Loretta Turk was letting Willie know that she'd had her experiences with fellas and those, on average, hadn't been good. Willie figured that any guy who got involved with Loretta might be prey to attacks of nerves, especially if she wore the buck knife at home.

Willie's food arrived, and so did Loretta's check.

"How can I reach you if I have another question?" Willie asked.

"You can come here and sit right on that stool," she said. "I'll show up the way crows show up to eat the sweet corn."

Loretta grabbed her walkie-talkie and shades from the bar and lumbered out.

Just then, one of the old folks hit a slot machine jackpot. Bells and whistles blasted.

CHAPTER TWELVE

Willie was halfway through his shrimp and crawdads when his cellphone sounded.

He found Camp on the other end.

"Where are you now?" the big man asked

Willie told him.

"Well, can you come to Jefferson Street, off of Main just west of the gas station. You'll see the patrol cars."

Willie scowled. "Why, what's up?"

"We found a man dead. He has your business card in his pocket."

Willie froze. His first thought—first fear—was that it was young Pedro Pérez. He tried to ask Camp, but the captain had already disconnected. Willie threw money on the counter, grabbed his wedge of cornbread and hurried out the door. He headed north on Main, turned off and saw a half dozen patrol cars about a quarter of a mile down the road. They had blocked the street, roof lights whirling. Willie gunned it, pulling up right behind the last of those cruisers, next to an emergency response vehicle.

He saw Camp, several other uniformed deputies and two EMTs standing just off the street, under another wide canopy of *flamboyán* trees, next to a drainage ditch. Willie sidled up next to Camp and looked down. Lying in the ditch in a contorted position, his eyes wide open and dry as death, was the diminutive Andrés Colón, the old friend of Ernesto Pérez who Willie had spoken to just the day before. His face was no longer covered with soot. He had replaced his mask of smoke with a mask of terror. Several bright orange petals from the tree had fallen on him, looking like large, live embers. But they weren't what caused his pain.

Camp turned to him. "You met with him yesterday, I take it."

"Right after I left your office." Willie pointed down the road. "He lives in the Sunset Trailer Park right down there."

"Yes. One of the neighbors here told us. We've sent someone to notify his wife."

Willie studied the dead man. "Do you have any idea how he died?"

Camp crouched next to the ditch. It was the second dead body he'd had to stare at in as many days. Willie could see the strain.

"The EMTs say it's pretty clear he was hit by a passing vehicle and knocked into the ditch. From the state of the body, they think it happened about six or eight hours ago, early this morning. He was probably walking to catch the bus to go to the fields while it was still dark, got hit and landed right where you see him now."

Willie noticed a plastic tomato-picking bucket lying in the ditch near the body.

"And the person who hit him didn't stop?"

"Apparently not," Camp said. "Maybe they didn't even know they hit him. Or if they did, they didn't want to face the music."

Willie soaked that in. "You think it was an accident."

Camp glanced up at him. "Do you have reason to think it wasn't?"

"He was the best friend of Ernesto Pérez. Pérez is missing, now this man is dead."

Camp looked back at the corpse and then stood up. "What did this man say to you that might have cost him his life? Did he tell you that someone might have done harm to Pérez?"

"He said Pérez had a habit of standing up to people who were mistreating other Mexicans."

"Who was it doing the alleged mistreating? Who did he confront?"

Willie told him about the two cases he knew of for sure—Víctor Coyote and Loretta Turk.

The second name surprised Camp. "Loretta? I doubt very much Loretta Turk did anything to Pérez. She's born and bred here. A law-abiding citizen. Led the girls' high school basketball team to the state championship."

"I didn't say she did anything. I'm just saying she and Pérez had an issue over payments to some Mexicans. She says the disagreement wasn't with her precisely, and that it was settled."

"You talked to her?"

"I talked to both her and Víctor. As far as his dealings with Ernesto, Víctor says that didn't amount to very much either."

Camp ran his finger across his nose, maybe to stem the smell of death coming from the ditch.

"I'll contact Loretta. How do I find this Víctor fellow?"

Willie took out his cell and read him the number Víctor had called from. Camp put it in his own phone. Neither of those people would be very pleased with Willie, but he didn't much care. What he cared about right then was that Andrés Colón, who had seemed to him a decent man, was dead. He was also worried about Pedro Pérez and wanted to get away to phone him.

A pickup drove up just then. Andrés Colón's widow, Natalia, climbed out, carrying her baby. She was led towards the ditch, where Camp put a consoling hand on her shoulder. It didn't do much good. The instant she saw the body, she burst into tears. She would have fallen to the ground if Camp hadn't held her up.

With all his years as a police officer, Willie had seen enough grief to last a lifetime. He wanted to express his condolences and also talk to the woman about her husband's last day, but it wasn't the time. He took the opportunity to get back in his car and pulled away quietly. He needed to make sure that another person he'd given his card to—Pedro Pérez—was still alive.

Willie drove through the intersection at Main Street, turned and pulled into the first parking lot. It served a gun store named Cane County Ballistics. The show window featured numerous weapons, both large and small, hanging from filaments. It appeared to be raining guns behind that glass. Signs beneath them said: "Easy Credit" and "No Waiting Period." In the lower corner an SRM decal had been affixed.

Willie took out his phone, found the number Pedro Pérez had given him, and punched it in. It rang about a half dozen times as Willie stared into the downpour of guns and grew more worried. He was just about to hang up and head for Eccles Farms when the kid picked up.

"It's Cuesta. Are you all right? Where are you?"

The kid answered in a near whisper.

"I'm at work, at the farm. Hold on while I go somewhere I can talk." He was gone about ten seconds and came back speaking louder. "Listen, I spoke to that lady today, the one who had trouble with the coyote and Ernesto helped her."

Willie scowled. "I asked you not to do that."

"Yes, but I thought about what you told me yesterday. I figured if she was a friend of my father's then maybe it would be better if I spoke to her, not you. Maybe she would be scared of *you* but not of *me*."

Willie squinted. He hated to say it, but that made sense.

"And?"

"This morning on the bus I asked one of the other workers if he knew her and he pointed her out. Then at lunch, I was near the packing house and saw her sitting by herself talking on her cellphone. When she finished, I sat down next to her and asked her if she knew Ernesto Pérez. She said she did and what a good person he was. That's when I told her who I was and that I was trying to find him."

"What did she say?"

"It scared her. She said to do her a favor and stay away from her. I told her I only wanted to know what might have happened to my father, nothing else. I wouldn't tell anyone I had spoken to her. Do you know what she said?"

"What?"

"That my father isn't the only person who has disappeared. She said other men have gone missing."

Willie scowled. "Other men? How many and when?"

"I don't know how many. She said it has been going on for at least a couple of years. Men who worked on different farms in the county. From one day to the next they were gone."

"Well, maybe those others moved on to another town."

Willie realized he sounded like Homer Eccles and Father Finlay. Both had said the same thing about Ernesto Pérez. Again, it occurred to him how easy it was to explain away the disappearance of a migrant worker. Even he was doing it. But Pedro Pérez, whose father was one of those disappeared, wasn't buying it.

"She said some people around here believe that the men just found better work somewhere else, but others aren't so sure. These people disappeared just like my father, without telling anyone where they were going. One morning their trailers were empty, as if the earth had swallowed them. That's what she said."

"Did she give you their names?"

"No. At that point, she begged me to stay away from her. She said she couldn't afford to have trouble. Then she got up and left me sitting there."

Willie suddenly realized he hadn't yet told Pedro what he had called to tell him. "I'm sorry, but I have even worse news for you. Andrés Colón has been killed."

A stunned silence ensued on the other end.

"Killed?" the kid muttered.

"Yes." Willie recounted the story of the body being found and the sheriff deputies' theory that Colón had been accidentally hit by a car.

"Do you believe that?" the boy blurted.

"It's possible, but, no, I don't believe it."

"Somebody murdered him. Ran him over on purpose. You know it. I know it. And maybe nobody else."

"Except whoever killed him."

The kid fell silent again, maybe considering his own mortality.

Willie focused on the shop window again, on the floating armaments. "You need to be careful."

"What are you going to do now?"

"I want to talk to Eccles again and then to Colón's widow. I need to ask her if Andrés said anything about people who might want him dead."

"I'll go see her too, to pay my respects."

"No, don't do that. We don't know who might be watching that trailer. I will tell her that you send your condolences. She'll understand. You should go back to work now before you get in trouble. I'll call later."

Willie disconnected and headed for Eccles Farm. He thought about his own standing in the Cane County community, any possible danger he might be in. After having worked in urban settings with much higher crime rates and much scarier criminals—street gangs, the Russian mafia, Colombian and Mexican cartel operatives—the fields of Cane County could lull you to sleep. But Andrés Colón wasn't sleeping, he was dead. If something did happen to Willie, who would know and how soon would they know it?

With those thoughts in his head, he dialed Fanny Cohen's number back in Miami Beach.

She answered with her brisk bark, "Cohen here."

"It's me, *mamita*."

Willie heard the car radio in the background, but she turned it down right away.

"You on your way to the university?" Willie asked.

"On my way back. Just gave a one-hour lecture on the Russian mob. From Leningrad to Brooklyn to Miami Beach. Told those kids about those bodies we found that time in the oil barrels in the Glades, with the fingertips cut off and the teeth pulled out so they couldn't be identified. Scared the wits out of them."

Willie found the involvement of Fanny Cohen in higher education surprising and somewhat frightening, just as her students apparently did.

Fanny interrupted his thoughts. "How is our far-flung investigator in the farm fields? Have you found who you were looking for?"

Willie told her about finding Pedro Pérez, but not being able to trace his father. Then he dropped the news that Andrés Colón had been found dead.

"He was the father's closest friend here, the first person I talked to after your friend Camp."

"Dead how?"

"He was 'accidentally' hit by a car. That's what the sheriff's office is saying officially, although Camp is looking into it."

Fanny grunted. "Accident my rear end. That's all too convenient, *compadre*."

"My thoughts exactly."

"And if somebody killed this man to cover up a previous crime, then it makes you think the previous crime would have to be very serious as well. You don't commit murder to cover up jaywalking or petty theft. It doesn't bode well for the man you're searching for."

"I'm told other people have disappeared from here, too. People who vanished from one day to the next without a word to their friends and neighbors."

Willie also told her about speaking with the coyotes, Narciso Cruz and young Víctor.

"People smugglers," Fanny fumed. "Let me tell you, guys like that are often neck-deep in other nasty business. They bring in women to stock the sex trade. They deal in drugs. God knows what you've got cookin' up there and what Mr. Pérez stumbled onto."

Fanny interrupted the conversation to yell at a driver who had cut her off. The combination of Fanny and vehicles was often volatile.

"I'll tell you one last important fact about Cane County," Willie said. "The Sovereign Rights Movement . . . you know, the anti-government militia types. . . . It's not just present here, it has muscle. The sheriff and county chairman are card-carrying members."

Fanny was rarely stunned into silence. Willie managed to do it now, at least for a few seconds.

"Now you're talking very serious *bidness*, buddy boy. Guys who belong to those kinds of militia groups have shot and killed policemen from different parts of the country. They don't acknowledge established authority. They recognize only their own inbred rules. Go read up on the history of these hooligans. A lot of it comes from right after the Civil War when the government recognized black people as US citizens. Bums like these decided if that was the case, they didn't want to be US citizens. You're involved with some real sweet individuals up there, my friend. I think it's time you grab that kid you found and head home."

Part of that suggestion was Fanny shifting into maternal mode, worrying about him. The other aspect was that Fanny always wanted to be part of any interesting case. She wasn't in Cane County with him, and that ticked her off.

"Thank you for the warning, Professor Cohen, but the kid won't leave here until he finds out what happened to his father. Don't worry, I know who I'm dealing with."

"Maybe, but there are lots of places to bury people up there, Willie boy, and you're surrounded by people who plant things for a living. Don't forget it."

Willie thanked her for the concern and promised to call again. He disconnected and continued on his way to Eccles Farm, except now as he passed the vast farm fields, he couldn't help thinking of them as potential resting places.

CHAPTER THIRTEEN

W illie parked outside the administrative trailer at Eccles Farms and entered the air-conditioned metal box. Myra Roth, the office manager, was at her station. She was in a slightly different cowgirl outfit today, but still had the plastic glasses on a chain around her neck. The glasses reminded Willie of Fanny Cohen's mahjong-playing girlfriends. He wondered how many cowgirls played mahjong, if any.

"Well, howdy again," she said.

"Is Mr. Eccles in?"

She pointed vaguely over her shoulder. "He's up past the family house. They're burning off a cane field before they harvest it. Just look for the smoke."

Willie thanked her and headed that way. In the fields on both sides of the road he saw tomato pickers again. They were at least a bit closer to the horizon than they had been the day before, dwarfed by the distance and by the sky.

Willie took the bend in the road, passed the Eccles manse and spotted a smudge of smoke about a quarter mile farther on. He pulled up about a hundred yards short of it, right next to Eccles' pickup. He saw the old man standing up the road, overseeing the burning.

As Willie approached, he watched a tractor rumble along the edge of the cane field. Attached to it was a large tank on wheels, and attached to that was what appeared to be a flamethrower. It directed a fiery liquid at the base of the cane stalks, where the undergrowth and chaff quickly burst into flames. As the tractor advanced along the perimeter of the field, the flames started to move quickly through the block of cane. The sudden conflagration created a subdued roar punctuated by sharp cracks. Black clouds of smoke rose, creating low-hanging thunderheads. All that was left behind by the rushing wall of flame was slightly singed stalks ready to be cut down. The tractor was nearing where Willie now stood. That was when Homer Eccles noticed and rushed toward him.

"What are you doing there? Get away from there."

Willie stepped back a bit from the burning field. A few embers flew above, burning out harmlessly before they could ignite anything else. Meanwhile, the old man himself was burning mad. He pulled Willie away from the roar and heat of the flames.

"I thought you were being paid to find a missing man, not to be nosing around my property."

Willie seemed to have caught Eccles on a bad day. He answered calmly, trying to soothe the older man. "The lady in the office told me this was where I could find you. Yes, I'm still looking for Ernesto Pérez."

Eccles spit out some chaw juice. Luckily, he aimed at the ground not at Willie. "What is it you want now?"

The heat and his bad humor had turned his complexion more florid than usual.

"I wanted to tell you that one of your workers was killed this morning."

Eccles' jaw fell. His tobacco-stained teeth were in evidence. "Who was it? What happened?"

Willie told him about Andrés Colón, how he'd been found.

"Did you know him personally?" Willie asked.

Eccles shook his head. "No, the name doesn't ring a bell. I have dozens of workers who pass through here every year. My name is on the checks, but I employ different crew leaders who head separate crews working different properties. They're the ones who know them by name, not me."

"The police seem to think it was accidental. That he got hit by someone who didn't see him walking along the side of the road. The driver disappeared."

Eccles' green eyes narrowed in a squint. "You're not buying that, I take it."

"Andrés Colón was the best friend of Ernesto Pérez. Pérez has disappeared and now Colón is dead . . . dead less than a day after I arrived to question him."

Willie pictured Colón the day they'd met, his face covered in soot from just such a cane fire as the one now marching through the adjacent field.

"You're saying somebody ran him over on purpose because they wanted to shut him up?" Eccles said.

"I'm not saying. I'm simply posing the possibility."

Eccles scowled. "Of course, you're being paid to be here. I assume if you tell your clients there's something to investigate, they'll keep on paying you. Pérez could simply have moved away, and maybe this other man was, in fact, run over by accident. Maybe you see a way to make hay up here, but I'm not buyin' it, and I'll be damned if I help you with your racket."

Willie glanced at the billowing smoke and then back. "Mr. Eccles, I've been told that several other workers have disappeared around here over the past couple of years. Have you had any other workers leave suddenly, the way Ernesto Pérez supposedly did?"

"No, I haven't, and I don't need you going around asking questions like that, spookin' my workers. I've answered your questions about Pérez and shown you all I can show you. You go on and investigate, but you'll stay off my property from now on."

He pointed down the road to the entrance. "Read that Department of Homeland Security sign near the gate. No Trespassin'. You come here again, you can get fined thousands of dollars . . . that's *if* somebody doesn't shoot you."

Willie had been menaced many times in his career. He gave Eccles the smile he reserved especially for such occasions. It was warm and fuzzy.

"Thanks for the country hospitality, Mr. Eccles. We'll be seeing you by-and-by."

Willie climbed into his car and headed out. He was halfway to the main drag when he saw Eccles daughter, EJ, she of the creamy skin and honey-colored hair, safe from the hellfire and soot of the family business. She trotted a horse along the road, heading towards him. He stopped. She did the same.

"Hi there, Mr. Miami," she said with the same saucy twinkle she had displayed on first meeting. "How are things going for you in our fair county?"

"Well, they were going better before your father ran me off the ranch just now."

Her expression turned sour. The horse, a gorgeous chestnut color, slightly sweated, let out a snort. He, or she, didn't seem to like Willie's news either.

"Wait 'til I get ahold of him," EJ said. "We don't get charming gentlemen from Miami here every day." She cocked her head to one side. "What did you do to get him riled?"

"I asked some questions he didn't approve of."

She looked off in the direction of the house. "Daddy can get ornery. Especially since my mother died almost a year ago . . . he gets in tempers."

"I'm sorry about your mom."

"That's why I came back here. He doesn't really need me to do the books. He has high-powered accountants who do the real work, but he wanted me here after she passed. I was living up in Orlando, working in the hospitality industry, enjoying city life. That changed everything."

"You weren't planning to come back some day?"

She shook her head hard. "No siree, soldier. This town is too small, too dead for this lady. In fact, I was hoping to move to Miami at some point. That's where I'd really like to live."

"You've been there, have you?"

"Yes, a few times." She fixed on him. "Cuesta, sounds just a tad Cuban."

"Just a tad."

"You dance salsa, do you?"

"*Sí, señorita.*"

"Maybe you could teach me to dance salsa while you're here. Private lessons. If I'm going to move to Miami someday, I'll wanna fit in."

She said the words "private lessons" with an extra dose of slow Southern drawl. Willie didn't have a lot of experience with country girls, but he knew when a local girl was encouraging him to explore the cabbage patch with her, so to speak. Homer Eccles had issued a none-too-veiled threat to shoot Willie if he trespassed. If he had known what Willie was thinking just then, he would have loaded his shotgun—both barrels—and never let him leave the property.

The horse was getting antsy, pawing the ground. Ms. Eccles patted its beautifully curved neck.

"I'll talk to daddy now and see why he doesn't cotton to you. I got a feeling Quincy Vetter has put something in his craw about you. Quincy doesn't care for outsiders."

"So I gather. We met yesterday, and he wasn't exactly wild about the experience."

"Well, I'll work on Daddy. Why don't you and I meet later at the Planters Inn and have dinner together? I'll be there at eight. Maybe afterwards you can give me my first salsa lesson."

She shot him another glance—both farm fresh and provocative. Then she spurred the horse and trotted away.

CHAPTER FOURTEEN

It was now late afternoon. Several hours had passed since Andrés Colón had been found dead. Willie decided to head to the trailer park, express his condolences to the widow, and also ask her anything about her husband's last days that might help him with his case.

Pulling in, he found the residents had used a table to create a kind of altar just outside the Colón trailer. It was covered with wildflowers and the tall votive candles that could be found in any Latino grocery in Florida. Willie had some in his own house, just in case a hurricane hit and he lost electricity.

He knocked on the door of #47, but no one answered. A neighbor approached him. She was carrying the Colón baby he had met the previous day.

"Natalia's not there," she said. "She's at the hospital, where they keep the dead people. She's waiting for them to give her Pedro's body."

She was talking about the county morgue. Willie asked where he could find the hospital. It turned out to be on the same street as the Planters Inn, south of the city, on the opposite side of the main drag, about a mile down. It was a one-story, sandstone building almost a block long. He might have confused it for a school except for the two ambulances parked outside.

He entered the sun-drenched lobby. The walls were decorated with large watercolors of cane fields, Everglade vistas, luminous cloud formations over flat farmland. The smile the receptionist flashed him was also luminous. When he asked for the morgue, that smile dimmed just a bit. She directed him to take the corridor to the left and then enter the door just before the emergency room. He headed that way out.

Because of his years as a police detective, Willie had spent more time in morgues than most living people. He remembered the first time he had entered a room that had a drain in the middle of the floor, as if it were an enormous shower. Except, the drain wasn't for water; it was for blood. It had freaked him.

Willie took the indicated door and found himself in an antechamber to the morgue. Another receptionist manned a desk there; a young, pale woman sitting behind a computer. She wore a bright, blue dress, a matching ribbon in her hair, kept a vase of wildflowers next to her and smiled as he entered. She did her best, but it was hard to brighten up the morgue.

Sitting across the room from her was Colón's widow. She was accompanied by two women who were apparently friends or neighbors, there to accompany her in her grief. Her eyes were raw from tears. She clutched a soaked red bandana in one fist, rosary beads in the other. Willie sat down across from her. It took her a moment to recognize him. Once she did, she became as wary as she was grief-stricken.

"You came and asked Andrés about Ernesto Pérez. Now he's dead. Maybe they are both dead."

It was clear she did not think her husband's death was an accident. The problem was, she seemed to be putting it on Willie. His was the face she associated with her anguish. The women with her heard what she said and stared hard at him. Eccles had just run him off his farm, and now these people didn't look too fondly on him either.

He dropped his voice so that the receptionist could not hear him. "I'm very sorry about your loss, señora. But if you feel someone hurt your husband on purpose, then I need for you to tell me anything that might lead me to who did this . . . and who might have harmed Ernesto Pérez. I will do my best to help you."

She shook her head slowly, sadly. "I have no idea who did this. But I know Andrés was very worried about what had happened to Ernesto. He even talked about leaving here. He was scared."

Willie knew that. He had sensed it when he'd spoken with Colón.

"Is there anything that might have happened in the past day since I saw him that could be connected to his death?"

She stopped and thought, all the time kneading the rosary beads between her fingers as if trying to squeeze an answer out of them. She finally did. "Last night, when we were already in bed, someone called him. He talked to the person for only a minute or two. Whatever the person said disturbed him, worried him. I asked him what was wrong. He just shook his head and told me to go sleep."

"You don't know who it was who called?"

She shook her head helplessly.

"Or what that person talked about with Andrés?"

She stared off into her memory and something occurred to her. "I remember Andrés said a name, a woman's name. Carlotta."

Willie frowned. "Carlotta? Do you know a woman named Carlotta? Did he?"

She raked at her tears with the bandana. "No, we don't know anyone by that name. Whoever he spoke to, *they* talked about this Carlotta. Andrés asked who she was. That's all I heard."

"Have the police returned your husband's belongings to you, the ones found on the body? Did they find his cellphone?"

She reached into the purse next to her and handed him a phone. "That was Pedro's."

Willie brought up the calls received in the last day. The very last one had come in at 10:17 the night before and lasted two minutes. It came from a local Cane County number. Willie held the phone up so the woman could see it.

"Do you recognize this number?"

She stared hard, as if the digits themselves had caused her grief. "No, I don't."

Willie took out his notebook and wrote down the number. Just as he did, the door to the corridor opened. A woman entered wearing a white nurse's hat and uniform with a crimson "A" stitched near her left shoulder. She was a large woman, around seventy, with bright red hair, a round face, heavily rouged cheeks, bright pink lipstick and large blue eyes outlined in mascara. As she got closer, Willie read the name badge above her large breast: "Mrs. Vetter."

She approached Natalia Colón, who appeared apprehensive just at the size of the woman.

Mrs. Vetter reached down and grabbed her hands. "I just wanted to tell you how sorry we all are to hear about your husband, my dear."

Her Southern accent was the thickest Willie had heard in Cane County. It was clear to Willie that the widow didn't understand a word the woman was saying. Between that and her fear, Natalia Colón simply stared back. The large woman patted her hand, then swiveled and looked down at Willie.

She gripped his shoulder. "And you, sir. Is there any way we can help you? I'm Mrs. Vetter, president of the Cane County Nurses' Auxiliary." With her free hand, she tapped the "A" on her uniform

Willie shook his head. "No, I'm in no need of help. Thank you."

"Are you a member of the family, Mr. . . ."

"Cuesta. Willie Cuesta. No, I'm not a relative."

"A friend, then," she said.

Looming over him with her bright eyes and those heavy, rouged cheeks, she resembled a very large kewpie doll you might win at a carnival. Except right then, Willie didn't feel like he had won anything but unwanted attention.

"Yes, you might call me a friend," he said.

She stayed staring at him, gripping his shoulder longer than necessary before she let go.

"Well, it's good that she has the support of friends. Y'all let us know if there is anything we can do for you, ya hear?"

She gave him one more grave glance, turned and left. That allowed Natalia and her friends to breathe again. The girl behind the desk had also tensed up and was still staring at the door.

"Is she related to Quincy Vetter of the County Commission?" Willie asked

She nodded. "That's Posey Vetter. She's the wife of Merton Vetter, Quincy's mom. She's a big deal in this county. She runs the Nurses' Auxiliary, the Women's Club and other organizations."

Willie soaked it all in. His guess was that Mrs. Vetter had not come in to express her condolences to the widow. She had showed up in order to size up Willie, the new boy in town. He wondered if her husband and her son had reported their run-in with him at the

Eccles property, if the presence of the private investigator from Miami in Cane County had piqued her interest. He decided to get out of there before she came back for another close look.

Willie expressed his condolences to Natalia again, promising he would stay in touch.,

Back out on the street, he drove down the road towards the main drag, then pulled over to the side of a cane field. He took out his cell and punched in the number he had copied from Andrés Colón's phone. It didn't ring at all. Instead, it went straight to a generic voice mail message. It was risky. The only person he knew who had communicated with that number was Andrés, and he'd been killed. But Andrés didn't carry a concealed weapon the way Willie did. He left messages in both Spanish and English, asking for a call back.

He started the car again and, as he did, noticed that a vehicle about one block behind him also pulled out from the side of the road. Leaving the hospital, he had noticed a black pickup with tinted windows stopped near the entrance. In his rearview mirror, it looked like the same truck.

Before he reached Main Street, he pulled over once more. The truck behind him did the same. In the country it was much harder to tail someone than it was in the city. Much less traffic to hide in. Even by that standard, this performance was pretty crude. It was a tail car that could also be used to move hay or farm animals. That was also a first for Willie.

Willie started up again, drove by the side street where he had first met with Pedro and headed for the Planters Inn, his shadow sticking with him. Minutes later he pulled into the parking lot. In his rearview he saw that the driver of the truck preferred to stay out on the street. Willie waited him out, and a minute later the pickup pulled away. Willie was too far to read a tag number. What he did notice was, like almost all the pickups he'd seen since arriving in Cane City, this one had a special feature attached to the inside of the cab just over the rear window—a rifle rack. It had a rifle in it.

He waited until the truck disappeared down the road, then headed for his room.

CHAPTER FIFTEEN

B y the time the clock hit eight, Willie had showered to get the dust of the fields off him, changed into jeans and a black shirt, and stepped into the lobby with time to spare. He took a peek out the front door but didn't see the black pickup. Maybe the driver had gone off to eat, or maybe in the countryside such operatives only worked from sunup to sundown, like the farmers. Who knew, but the tail wasn't there.

He took a chair near the door to wait. Two couples arrived and filed into the dining room. Willie saw that one of the men and one woman wore guns on their hips. The lady's weapon was petite, her holster decorated with rhinestones. He wondered if she possessed different holsters for different outfits. Willie had noticed publicly displayed weapons here and there around town all day. It was still taking some getting used to.

Thank heavens that Iris, the desk clerk, was not a gunslinger. Tonight she wore long earrings made of blue glass icicles that dangled down near her shoulders and a matching ring with a glass stone the size of a golf ball. She looked like a human chandelier. She chatted away to him about other clientele that passed through the inn— farm equipment salesmen, produce company buyers, former residents returning for visits or for homecoming football games, the occasional revival preacher.

"I could tell you a thing or two about some of those revival preachers," she said, rolling her blue eyes.

"I bet you can," Willie chimed in.

"I take it you're waitin' for somebody."

"EJ Eccles and I are having dinner here."

That peaked Iris' interest. "You don't say. Gorgeous girl that EJ. I think most people would say she is the most beautiful girl to come out of this county in many years."

"She's certainly very attractive."

Iris' gaze turned grave. "It was hard on her when her mama passed."

"Yes, she told me that was why she came back."

"Muriel Eccles, that was her mom. She was a lovely, active woman. Then one day she was dead."

Willie winced. "How did she die?"

"Thrown by a horse. They found her just off a trail out some ways from town, with her head smashed and neck broken. The horse was still standing over her hours later. Riding since she was a small child, then one moment when maybe she wasn't paying attention, it cost her life. It was terribly hard on EJ."

"I saw EJ on horseback earlier today."

"Oh EJ, she's been riding her whole life too. Muriel taught her when she was just a tyke. After the accident she stopped, but friends convinced her that she had to get back up. She's a gutsy girl."

The young lady under discussion walked in just then. EJ wore a short black dress that hugged her lovely frame, low black heels, tasteful silver earrings and bracelet. She didn't look much like a farm girl at the moment.

"I thought I'd make you feel at home, Mr. Miami," she said with a sly smile. "It's my little black nightclubbing costume."

"Well, you've accomplished that. I feel as if I'm back on Ocean Drive."

She led him into the quaint, old dining room. They sat in the far corner. It was near the mounted head of a bear and a faded black and white photograph. It depicted a very old tractor pulling a plow through a field, a white man driving it, black field hands following with rakes.

"Read the written inscription at the bottom," EJ said.

In black script it said, "Jarvis Eccles, Eccles Farm, 1937."

"That was my great-grandfather, planting crops."

Willie studied the flat fields that stretched to the same unbroken horizon he had seen over the past two days, only in black and white.

"Your family has been here a long time," he said.

"Since early in the last century, planting that same land. Although my father bought out some surrounding growers and made Eccles Farm even bigger. We and the Vetters are the two families that have been here the longest."

"I met old man Vetter, at the same time I met Quincy. He looked like a feisty fellow, to say the least."

EJ nodded once, a bit like her horse did. "That's Merton Vetter. Truth is, he's slowed down a bit in his old age. In the old days, they say, he was a bad drinker and sometimes as mean as a rattlesnake. Nobody liked working for him, which is why these days the Vetters live on their farm but lease out all their fields to other growers and let them handle the labor. Quincy's not a drinker like his dad was, but he picked up his personality. He can be 'twenty miles of bad road.' My mama used to say that."

"Your mom was from here too?"

"That's right, both the folks. I'm the only fruit that came from their union. You woulda thought two farm families comin' together would have produced more littlins."

"Not a big crop, but a very beautiful one."

She had fed him a line and now laughed on cue.

"And your ancestors are from Cuba?"

"Yes, ma'am. My parents came in the first wave of exiles after Castro took power. That was in the early 60s. Eventually, my brother Tommy was born, and then yours truly. A slightly bigger crop, but not by much."

"Very tasty, I'm sure." She gave him her saucy look and laughed.

The waiter approached. She said she drank red, so Willie ordered a bottle. On her recommendation, they ordered two plates of baked ham with collard greens, black eyed peas and sweet potato soufflé.

"No Cuban cuisine here," she said.

"So I see, but I like Southern cooking."

She smiled mischievously. It was one of those conversations where everything uttered meant something else. After the wine came, she took the talk into more serious territory.

"You're here looking for this man Ernesto who worked for us. He's gone, and you think it's something more than it seems. You left a bad taste in Daddy's mouth. He says you're trying to stir up trouble with the workers."

Willie shrugged. "I'm sorry I'm not your father's cup of tea. I have a job to do. A man who was devoted to his family, who was proud of being a provider, suddenly stopped communicating with them or with anyone else. A family back in Mexico is in danger of going hungry. It's only one man and one Mexican family out of thousands who have come here, but they don't see it that way."

Willie took out the photo of Ernesto Pérez and his children and laid it on the table in front of her.

She nodded. "Yes, Ernesto showed me this."

"This is the copy he left with his children back in Mexico." He turned it over and pointed at the inscription. "So that you remember my face," Willie read. "They still do. *That's* why I'm here."

She sipped her wine, running her tongue over her lovely lips. "If he didn't just leave town, what do you think might have happened to him?"

Willie, suspicious by nature, wondered if Homer Eccles might have sent his beautiful daughter fishing for information about his investigation. He wondered if she was bait. Well, if she was, she was very delicious bait.

"Mr. Pérez had a way of interceding in the problems of his fellow Mexicans, asking questions that ticked off some people."

"Who did he tick off?"

Willie hesitated, but only barely. He was in a small town and he figured news of his meetings with the coyotes and lunch with Loretta Turk would travel fast anyhow. So he told her as she sipped.

"I've known Loretta my whole life," EJ said. "She was a few years ahead of me in elementary school. Later I transferred to private school. She went to Cane County High. She was the star of the girls' basketball team, even got a college scholarship, but she had to quit before she finished because her momma got into a bad accident and needed her. She became a crew leader in the fields. That's a good job around here. Loretta's tough, but I don't think she could seriously harm another person."

Camp had said the same thing.

"As for the coyotes," EJ said, "I don't have contact with those kinds of folks. I know all through farm country they're seen as necessary. Not very nice people, but necessary. I can't tell you what they would or wouldn't do. Who else did Ernesto tick off?"

Willie thought that over. He was about to ask her if she'd ever heard of a woman named Carlotta, but he decided against that. If she was in fact on a fishing expedition for her father, Willie didn't need to provide Homer Eccles with every bit of information he had. It was just as well, because at that moment the baked ham dinner arrived, smelling like heaven.

Over the meal she asked all about recent goings-on in Miami. She told him about nightclubs she had been to in the past, some of which were still there, but many that were long gone. Evolution was constantly eliminating venues in the entertainment and restaurant businesses in South Florida. Willie was able to fill her in on the latest hot spots, deejays, celebrity sightings. She soaked it all in avidly.

"It must really be something to live there," she said. She glanced down at his hands, obviously looking for a wedding ring, then back at him. "Especially if you aren't married."

Truth was, it had been a long time since Willie had looked for girlfriends in nightclubs, but he didn't say that. She seemed to want to think of him as a visitor from Babylon. She told him about some of the outrageous characters and behavior she had observed in clubs when she was there. At this point, Willie had spent so many nights in clubs, seen so much outrageous behavior—including some folks who didn't even bother waiting to get home to have sex—that it was as natural as drawing breath and just about as interesting. He didn't tell her that either.

They had almost finished eating when two women walked in, neither of whom was wearing a gun. They sat down, then one of them noticed EJ and Willie sitting in the corner and came over. She was about EJ's age, late-twenties, with long, black hair and a dour expression.

EJ smiled at her. "Hello, Francine. This is Mr. Cuesta visiting from Miami. Francine teaches history and civics in our middle school."

The other woman shook her head. "Not anymore I don't. I quit yesterday. I'm moving away as fast as I can."

EJ was shocked. "But that's what you always wanted to do—teach."

"And that's what I was doing until recently, when so-called county leaders started coming into my classroom, calling themselves guest lecturers, offering what they call alternative views of history. Quincy Vetter himself strolled into my room yesterday, gun on his hip, and started telling my students there is no real United States of America—no legitimate federal government or state government, for that matter. That it's all a plot to control people's lives and take their money through illegal taxes. He said all the history in the books—the history I'm teaching by the way—is a lie. Try that out on twelve- and thirteen-year-olds and then try to keep order."

Francine shook her head in amazement, then pointed to the other woman at her table. "Libby's thinking of quitting the library, too."

EJ touched Willie's arm. "Libby Rawls runs the Cane County library. Why, what happened to her?"

"The same so-called leaders are telling her she has to take certain books out of the library and put other books in. The books they're handing her are written by other political nutbags, and they're telling her they have to be displayed prominently. So instead of Steinbeck and Fitzgerald, she has to push rubbish written by some lamebrain."

She shot a poisoned look at the gun-toting dinner party across the room. Those folks were having a fine old time. Then she took a deep breath and exhaled pure frustration.

"Anyway, I'll stop by before I leave town."

She said it had been nice meeting Willie and stalked away. EJ watched her, deep in thought.

"We're going through some political problems here lately," she said.

"So I gather."

She fixed on him, getting her saucy look back. "But let's not talk about that right now. Let's talk about salsa lessons."

She lifted her wine glass and they toasted. A few minutes later, they finished eating, knocked off the rest of the wine and Willie paid the bill. He followed her through the lobby, then outside. She walked out from under the oak trees that surrounded the inn, threw her head back and stared at the clear night sky.

"You won't see this many stars back in Miami. You should take advantage of being here in Cane County. See how many you can count."

The sky over those fields was, in fact, a sea of stars. He felt her walking away and turned to her.

"No, don't bother with me," she said. "You keep counting. Next time we see each other, you can tell me how many there are."

With that she disappeared around the side of the inn towards where she'd apparently parked. Willie stayed there a few more minutes, enjoying the night. The longer he looked up, the more stars came into focus. Too many to count.

He glanced at the street, checking for the black pickup, but didn't see it. He went back inside, said goodnight to Iris and headed upstairs to his suite.

He opened the door, turned on the light and found EJ looking at him. She was in the four-poster bed, under the covers, which were pulled up almost to her bare ivory shoulders. He saw her black dress draped over the high-backed chair next to the window, along with some underthings, and her shoes lying on the rug. The window was open to the veranda outside, which told him how she'd gotten in. If you'd grown up in Cane City, sneaking into the Planters Inn for a tryst was probably a rite of passage. She gave him that same saucy smile, which now went perfectly with her state of dress.

"You enjoy the stars?" she asked demurely. "Would you be interested in seeing some more?"

She flicked her eyebrows, chuckled at her own joke and fixed on him with those blue eyes now dewy with a combination of mischief and sex. Willie stood frozen just inside the closed door. Again it occurred to him that Homer Eccles might have sent his daughter on a mission. Maybe that mission was to lure him into this very situation, then for Homer to come through the door as the outraged patriarch with a 16-gauge shotgun and turn Willie into Swiss cheese or, in this case, chitlins. Nobody in Cane County would have to worry about the investigator from Miami anymore, and in the local court it would be ruled justifiable homicide. Self-preservation had Willie rooted to the rug.

That was when she pulled the sheet down a bit and patted the bed right next to her.

"Come on over. I need a nice city boy to save me from this sleepy place, if only for a night or two. As long as it's just between you and me. Whaddya say?"

It occurred to Willie that he should say something clever about Southern hospitality, but there was a genuinely needy catch in her voice and a frank gaze in her eyes that stopped him. He walked over, sat down and she rested her head on his thigh as if she would sleep there like a child. He stroked her shoulder and the top of her beautiful back as the fertile night air ruffled the lace curtains at the window.

Willie had never before made love in a four-poster bed, or at least he couldn't recall an occasion. She lowered the mosquito netting all around, not because of bugs, but to create a gauzy cocoon around them. She was a natural beauty, and in that soft, golden light even more beautiful. It deepened the honey color of her hair, made her creamy skin glow.

At one point the rhythmic creaking of the old bed made her laugh. Perched on him, she craned her neck back to watch the swaying canopy above.

"We're gonna break this sucker," she laughed.

Later, they lay next to each other, staring up at that canopy. She held his left hand against her breast.

"You ever been married, Mr. Miami?"

"Once for a few years."

"What happened?"

"I spent too much time being a police detective, not enough time being a husband. And you? You been married?"

She shook her head. "I came close about a year ago. He was sweet. But I was growing up and I guess I lost my sweet tooth. I called it off. Then I had to come back here."

"Because your mom died."

"That's right."

She stared into her memories, obviously painful ones. Then she curled around him, and he held her until she said it was time she headed home.

"Yes, Iris is going to wonder what your car has been doing out there all this time."

"I left my car down the street in the shadow of a tree. Iris thinks I just went home."

She got up and got dressed. Willie started to rise to see her out. She pushed him back down, leaned over and kissed him.

"You stay there. I'll let myself out. Maybe we can see each other tomorrow and you can start to teach me salsa, like you promised."

Willie smiled, said he would, but figured the dance that really interested EJ wasn't salsa. She opened the door and tiptoed out. He lay there wondering what he'd done to deserve this version of the welcome wagon. He didn't think about it for long. He turned off the light and went to sleep.

CHAPTER SIXTEEN

Willie woke up the next day with morning light filtering through the mosquito netting. EJ Eccles was gone, but her scent lingered. The thought of her made it even harder than usual for him to get out of bed.

What he did instead was grab his cellphone from where it was charging on the night table and put in a call to an old friend of his. Clark Moyer was a researcher at the Florida Department of Law Enforcement in Tallahassee. Clark was a whiz at using public records and other available data to track down people who the police were looking for. Even after Willie had left the Miami PD, Clark had been willing to help him out on cases from time to time.

He punched in the number and got voicemail. So he read out the digits he had found on Andrés Colón's phone—the call he had received late the night before he died. Willie told Clark he was looking for the owner of said phone, thanked him in advance for the help and disconnected.

He was just about to finally jump from the bed, when his cellphone sounded. He thought it might be Clark, or maybe EJ, to see if he'd survived the evening's events. But the screen said only that an "Unknown Caller" was on the other end.

"Cuesta & Associates," Willie said, sounding quite formal for a naked man.

The voice on the other end was female, Southern, fuzzy, obviously disguised.

"You wanna know what happened to Ernesto Pérez?"

Willie wiped sleep from his face. "Yes, I do."

"Then go talk to Dusty Powell. Ask her about her dealings in drugs, in heroin."

Willie squinted into the bright sunlight pouring through the window. The name Dusty Powell sounded vaguely familiar. Then he remembered that two nights ago Iris had told him that Víctor Coyote was seeing a woman by that name.

"What does this have to do with the disappearance of Ernesto Pérez?"

"That Pérez man knew what was going on. Just ask her."

"Who is this?"

"It don't matter who I am. Dusty lives off the Old Sawgrass Road, first turn to the left after the 3 R's Farm. Go right away because they're fixin' to make a run for it."

Willie started to ask who "they" were, but the line went dead. He stared at the phone as if it would tell him more, but it didn't.

Ten minutes later he was showered, dressed, and in the lobby. His handgun was tucked in his back holster, just in case. The daytime desk clerk, a young bespectacled fellow named Tip, was behind the counter. Willie asked him for directions to Sawgrass road, and Tip told him to go about seven miles north up the main drag and turn left at an abandoned gas station there. Willie thanked him.

He pulled out of the parking lot and noticed that the black pickup was not behind him. He assumed the tail driver had slept in. Willie was soon tooling along the two-lane Old Sawgrass Road, which cut straight as an arrow through fields thick with cane. About two miles down, he passed the front gate of 3 R's Farm on the right. He slowed and saw a narrow dirt road cutting through cane off to the left. He turned in there and followed the curving track, reaching a clearing and a rustic house made of wide planks with a blue shingle roof. Out front, a small black SUV was parked, apparently the vehicle "they" planned to escape in. Willie stopped his car where it couldn't be seen from the house and got out. They hadn't heard him either. From inside came loud heavy metal music. He couldn't tell Iron Butterfly from Metallica from Black Sabbath. It was one of those. As far as Willie was concerned, it was very early in the day for heavy metal.

The windows were curtained, so he couldn't see in. He checked to make sure his handgun was still in place and knocked on the wooden front door. That did little good, given the din inside. He looked around nervously at the cane that surrounded him on all sides and was just about to pound again, when the decibel level of music suddenly decreased and the door opened.

Standing before him was a woman who appeared to be in her forties, tall, thin, extremely pale, with long, prematurely white hair and glassy gray eyes. She wore jeans and a faded gray t-shirt that matched the eyes. She fixed on Willie as if she'd seen a roach in the kitchen. If you were in the illicit narcotics business, you probably didn't like strangers showing up at your door.

"Yes?"

"Are you Dusty Powell?"

It took her a few moments to decide how to answer that.

"I was just going out."

She was holding a mop in her hands, so unless she was going to mop someone else's house, that probably wasn't true.

"My business won't take more than a couple of minutes," Willie said. Using an old police officer tactic, he smiled and walked right by her into her house.

Even edgier now, she didn't close the door. "Who are you and what do you want?"

Willie decided to get right down to business before he got thrown out. "I'm told you had dealings with a person named Ernesto Pérez."

She looked confused. "Who?"

"Ernesto Pérez. A Mexican man who I'm told came to you to discuss your involvement in the heroin trade."

If her hair hadn't already been white, Willie's question might have done the trick. She stayed stock still and then stammered. "N-nobody came to me to talk about nothin' like that."

Willie was about to contest her, but a voice, a male voice, sounded from an adjacent room.

"Dusty, what are you doin'? Who's there?"

Seconds later, the owner of the voice appeared in the doorway. He was a white man, about the same age as Ms. Powell, with a shaved head and a bare, barrel chest that was partially concealed by denim overalls. His arms were like hams that hung from his shoulder sockets, and were covered in gaudy tattoos. He looked like a hybrid between a local grower and a member of a biker gang—maybe Hell's Farmers.

From behind him peeked another individual—a younger, small-ish, Latin man with gelled black hair that stood straight up from his head in spikes, as if he were perpetually frightened.

"Who the hell are you?" demanded the biker dude.

Willie was about to answer, when from outside the house he heard the gunning of car engines, the squeal of tires, the screech of brakes. Both Dusty and he turned to see several Cane County sher-iff's cruisers careening into the clearing, skidding to stops behind the black SUV and armed deputies jumping out.

Dusty screamed, "The fuckin' sheriff!"

She slammed the door shut with Willie inside, running towards the rear of the house. The goon in the overalls, on the other hand, ran towards the front window, produced a gun from a back pocket of the overalls, smashed a pane of window glass and fired several shots in the direction of the posse that had just arrived.

He paused between shots and shouted back over his shoulder. "Flush everything!"

Willie saw the little Latin guy with the prophetically frightened hair go scurrying in the direction of the kitchen just as a barrage of shots shattered the front window. Willie dove for the floor, rolled across the wooden planks until he was behind a ratty armchair. He pulled his gun from the back holster. The big goon had run out of the room, so there was no heroin pusher left to shoot, at least not right in front of him. Willie heard a toilet flush, several more shots fired from inside the house at the attackers outside, followed by another barrage of shots from the sheriff's posse that shattered more windows and thudded into walls. Glass and plaster fell in the house like hail.

Willie hugged the floor feeling like a fool—an urban rube in farm country. By all appearances, he had allowed himself to be lured into a trap by an anonymous tipster. It was a trap in which the sher-iff's men would wipe him out. Why have the driver of the black pick-up risk anything by spilling Willie's blood when public employees could do it in the totally legal performance of their duties.

Willie heard Camp's voice. The captain yelled out something, followed by several moments of silence, and then came a very dis-tinctive popping sound. Willie knew it was tear gas even before the two canisters flew through the front window, clattering to the floor.

He heard Camp issuing orders, preparing his troops for an assault on the premises. Willie made a tactical decision to surrender. He slid his gun across the floor so that it disappeared under the nearby couch. Then he hugged the floor, burying his face into the crook of his arm, in an attempt to avoid the first wave of gas. Despite this impersonation of a burrowing rodent, the gas still reached him, scorching his nasal passage and burning his lungs, making his eyes water.

He lifted his head, kept his eyes closed and yelled, "Camp, it's me, Cuesta. I'm coming out."

He waited but heard nothing.

"Camp!"

The gas seeped down his throat. He coughed it out, but immediately breathed in more of it. He had a choice. He could stay there and choke until he was unconscious, or try to crawl out and pray a jumpy deputy didn't shoot him. He didn't get to choose as just then the front door splintered. He opened his eyes only enough to see SWAT deputies in gas masks come pouring in. He could hear them swarming in from the back of the house as well. Willie held his breath, pressed himself to the floor and held his empty hands in clear view. He was quickly frisked, picked up by both arms, dragged into the open air and left propped against the tire of a car. When he stopped coughing and his eyes stopped tearing, he found Camp crouched in front of him.

"What the hell are you doing here?"

Willie spoke, sounding more like a frog than a former police detective. "I got a phone call telling me to come here if I wanted to know what had happened to Ernesto Pérez."

Willie was admitting he'd been played for a sucker, but Camp had his doubts. He wore a suspicious scowl on his beefy face that boded badly for Willie. First, he'd almost been shot to death, now his word was being questioned, as if maybe he was close buddies with the residents of the house. Then again, Camp had known him for all of two days and only had Willie's word for who he was and what he was doing there.

"You can call Fanny Cohen to confirm who I am," he croaked. "I have nothing to do with your local losers." Then Willie coughed some more.

Camp took that in. Maybe the gunfire had unsettled him as much as it had Willie.

"I got a phone call too," Camp said, "telling me to raid this place if I wanted to bust a heroin ring."

"A woman?"

Camp nodded. Willie squinted.

"I assume it was the same woman who called me so I could be here when you arrived."

Camp chewed his cud. "You're saying someone doesn't like you and wanted you to get caught in the crossfire."

"It certainly seems that way, doesn't it? Somebody who doesn't like the fact I'm here asking questions about Ernesto Pérez and, now, Andrés Colón."

Camp nodded slowly, trying to accommodate that theory in his scheme of things. An ambulance arrived just then and EMTs rushed into the house. Camp stood up, helped Willie to his feet and they followed the EMTs. The tear gas had dissipated a lot due to the open doors and shattered windows. They passed through the living room, which was strewn with broken glass, and entered the kitchen. The big, bad biker type lay flat on his back in the middle of the linoleum floor, several bullet holes in him. The finisher was above his left eye. Willie's eyes were still tearing, making it seem like he was weeping over the biker. Given the looks of the guy, those might be the only tears shed for him.

Camp gazed down gravely. "This here is Marcus Morrell. He's from Sawgrass and had already done two stints in state prison for drug distribution crimes. If he took another fall, he would probably spend the rest of his natural life in prison, so I guess he decided it was worth trying to shoot his way out. He never made a good decision in his entire life, Marcus."

The EMTs were in a small bedroom just off the kitchen, ministering to the little Latin guy. The hair was still standing, but he wasn't. He was on the floor with a leg wound. He was crying in pain, but looked like he'd live.

Willie turned to Camp. "A third person was here. A woman."

"Dusty Powell. This is her house."

Camp went to the back door, which was wide open. About ten feet away stood a wall of sugar cane.

"She must have made it out before my men could come around the back. We'll send dogs in there, but she's probably long gone by now. Did you talk to her?"

Willie told him about his very brief exchange with Dusty Powell. How she had denied knowing Ernesto Pérez, or that Pérez had confronted her and her heroin smuggling colleagues.

Camp shrugged. "Of course, if the man is dead, you have to expect that she would deny having had contact with him. If Ernesto Pérez confronted Marcus Morrell, he made a very big mistake."

The EMTs had loaded the little Latin guy onto a stretcher and were just rolling him towards the ambulance. Willie asked Camp if he could talk to the prisoner before they took off, and the captain told them to hold up.

"What's your name?" Willie asked the wounded man in Spanish.

"Gilberto Vargas. They call me Enano," he said. It meant midget in Spanish.

"You ever meet a man here called Ernesto Pérez?"

The other man thought, grimaced in pain, and then shook his head. Willie took out the photo.. "Ever see this face, Enano?"

The little man was perturbed that his trip to the hospital was being delayed. "No, I never saw him. Now let them take me before I bleed to death."

Willie and Camp watched as he was loaded into the ambulance.

"Of course, maybe he's lying," Camp said.

Willie remembered his gun and got permission from Camp to retrieve it from under the furniture. A deputy with a clipboard then sat Willie in a cruiser and debriefed him on everything that had happened. While they were at it, the sheriff arrived, the political appointee who annoyed Camp. He was a slight, white-haired man, with a narrow, silver moustache over thin lips. He was dressed in civilian clothes—white shirt, gray dress slacks—with a gold badge pinned to his chest and a pearl-colored ten-gallon hat. The deputy informed Willie that the sheriff's name was Nathan Pope. Pope gave Willie one flinty glance and without a word disappeared into the damaged house. He came out minutes later and drove away just as the deputy was finishing his debriefing.

Camp pulled Willie off to one side. "My boss, Sheriff Pope, does not like the fact that you are in our county."

"That doesn't surprise me. He didn't look real friendly. This is the same sheriff, the sovereign rights type, you have problems with."

"Exactly."

"Tell me something. Was he appointed by Quincy Vetter?"

Camp nodded. "Quincy and his allies on the county commission. Why?"

"Because Mr. Vetter doesn't want me here very much either. That's my impression. In fact, I'm told he doesn't want any outsiders showing up in Cane County. You're going to have to explain this to me. Why is this happening here all of a sudden?"

Camp looked around, obviously uneasy speaking to Willie with his deputies within earshot.

"Drive out to the road towards town. Turn into the entrance to 3 R's Farm and pull in under the trees so your car isn't visible from the road. Let me make sure everything is getting done here and I'll meet you there. Make sure to wait for me. You need to know what you're up against here before you get yourself killed."

Willie followed those directions, pulled off the road, parked and watched bees and butterflies flutter around the wall of sugar cane just feet away. After a long while he saw the EMT van drive by, heading back to town, almost certainly carrying the corpse of Marcus Morrell. A few minutes later, Camp pulled up right next to him in his cruiser. Willie climbed in.

"What's the scoop?"

Camp grimaced. "First of all, Sheriff Pope told me to run you out of town. I told him I had no grounds to do that. But that doesn't mean he won't have someone under me pull you over for some trumped up offense and make it so you'll want to go back to Miami."

Willie frowned. "People underneath you in the department will do that sort of thing?"

Camp was obviously embarrassed by what he had just admitted. "Let me explain to you what has gone on here over the past couple of years." He pointed vaguely to the east. "Over on that edge of the county, we have some rocky, fallow land that borders the Everglades. It's about two hundred acres. The state and federal governments came in here a while back and said they wanted that land to do some Everglades restoration work. They wanted to dredge it and create storage pools where they could filter out bad water that has too many fertilizers in it. They offered to exchange that land for some perfectly good land the state owns over west of here. Ya with me?"

Willie nodded once. If you lived in Florida and followed the news at all, you knew the government wanted to clean up the polluted Everglades.

Camp continued. "The problem was that the land they wanted is owned by the Vetters, and Quincy Vetter said he wasn't selling or swapping. He said he didn't want the government as a neighbor."

Willie told Camp about witnessing Vetter's very brief, very unfriendly meeting at the Planter's Inn with a man from the state water agency. "I take it this aversion to the government comes from his allegiance to the Sovereign Rights Movement."

Camp wagged a finger at Willie. "Not exactly. When all this started, Quincy wasn't part of that movement, as far as anybody knows. That came later. First came this land dispute. The next thing you know, Quincy is running for county commission chairman. It happened that we had an election coming up, and truth is nobody much wants to take the time to run that commission. Quincy, being from an old local family, knowing everybody, he got himself elected easy. Next thing we know, our county becomes a stronghold of that Sovereign Rights Movement. There are just enough people here who swallow that sovereign rights hogwash that Quincy was able to start changing things."

"Like letting people prance around with guns on their hips."

Camp stared into the cane. "He didn't have much trouble getting folks here to go along with that. They're hunters and like their guns. But in order to allow open carry we had to violate state law. The sheriff at the time, Bob Vincent, was a real law enforcement veteran and said no way it was happening on his watch. Quincy then drummed up a majority on the commission and they canned Bob Vincent. Just like that." Camp snapped his fingers. "Quincy riled them up by spouting a whole bunch of bull about local rights—'home rule' he called it—not being slaves of the government who want to take away our guns."

Willie nodded. "This all sounds right out of the SRM handbook."

"Not only did Bob Vincent leave, several other veteran deputies also bailed out. Bob was replaced by this guy Nathan Pope, who was once a patrol officer for a small force in north Florida. He's pure SRM, and the other new deputies brought in also belong to it."

Camp was shaking his head in disbelief. "This is all crazy. It makes no sense, and it's all about two hundred acres of land that nobody was using for anything anyway. Quincy says, instead of trading it to the state, he's planning to set up a shooting range there for SRM members and other militia types from surrounding counties."

Frustration was all over Camp's face and in the white-knuckled way he was still gripping the wheel.

"How is it you're still on the force?" Willie asked. "Why haven't they run you out of town on a rail?"

"Oh, I think that's coming any day. Truth is, they've needed at least one person in law enforcement here who has some real knowledge of the locals, but that won't last long if Quincy keeps calling the shots."

"Is there any reason to think he's going anywhere?"

"There are still some sane people in this county, and they have friends at the capital in Tallahassee and in Washington. They are sending reports north about what's happening here. Meanwhile, you should be careful. Some of these new guys in uniform could consider you fair game."

Somebody had, in fact, tried to have him shot up a short time ago. Whoever that whispering lady tipster had been on the phone was no friend of his. Willie flashed back to his conversation with Narciso Cruz and how he figured the number of Mexicans in Cane County made some of the locals nervous about their future. That wasn't good for people who looked like Ernesto and Pedro Pérez. Willie, a Cuban American from Miami, apparently also made them edgy.

"Your sheriff wants to have me run out of town," he said. "What I would tell him is this. If I have trouble here, what I'll do is drive back to Miami and go right to the Mexican Consulate. I'll tell them several Mexicans, not just one, are missing in Cane County, and there is a chance they met with foul play. The consulate will file a complaint with the State Department, which will be diplomatically obligated to respond. The next thing you know, the FBI will be knocking on doors here. In other words, Mr. Pope and Mr. Quincy Vetter can cope with me or with a number of guys in suits with federal shields. Willie Cuesta or guys who look like Tommy Lee Jones, if you know what I mean."

Camp considered all that. "And how about if someone decides to just shoot you?"

Willie gave that a moment's thought. "I have a lot of friends in law enforcement, Captain Camp. Including you, I hope. Fanny Cohen alone will make sure that FBI agents are all over your sheriff if anything happens to me."

Of course, Willie wouldn't be around to thank her.

"I'd still be careful if I were you," Camp said.

"Always."

Willie got out. Camp called out to him.

"By the way, that coyote whose number you gave me, Víctor, isn't answering his phone, and I can't find him."

"I'll see what I can do."

Camp pulled away back in the direction of Dusty Powell's house. Willie wiped a last gas tear from his eyes, as if he was sad to see him go. Then he headed back to town.

CHAPTER SEVENTEEN

As Willie entered Cane City, he noticed that Clark Moyer, his crime researcher friend, had called him back from Tallahassee. He hit the return icon and soon heard the always chipper Clark on the other end.

"How's swinging South Beach, Willie?"

"The last I heard it was still swinging, Clark. But I'm not there right now. I'm in Cane County."

"You've opted for the quiet life of the cane fields?"

"Well, not exactly. I haven't moved to these parts. I'm here on a case. So far it isn't quiet at all."

"Do tell."

Willie decided to spare Clark a description of the past couple of hours. "Oh, it's just a missing person, but he's proving hard to find."

"Well, the phone number you left me is a Cane County number, as you probably already know."

Willie pulled over to the side of the road and took out his notebook. "Who's it registered to and where is it right now?"

"That number is registered to a Ricardo Ramírez. The address is 211 Davis Street. Cane City. Now let's plot where he is at this precise moment."

Willie jotted down the information, while Clark pecked at his keyboard on the other end. People like Clark had access to cellphone service tracking systems—GPS coordinates—that could locate a phone. It took him a full minute to reach a conclusion.

"He's nowhere at the moment."

"Come again."

"The phone isn't issuing a signal. He has shut down the GPS function and blocked other sensors in the phone. Possibly he has it in a protective case that blocks emission of signals. Then again, maybe it fell in a lake. I'm seeing nothing."

"Got it." Willie knew people could eliminate the emissions used to track a cellphone when they didn't want police, or anyone else, knowing where they were.

"Looks like this particular person wants to stay missing," Clark said. "Good luck, lad."

Willie thanked him and disconnected. He used his phone to plot the Davis Street address, which was just a few blocks away. He was heading that way when he noticed an old school bus dropping workers off from the fields. The workers were arriving back in town earlier than usual. Willie parked, eyed the people getting off the bus and soon spotted Pedro. The kid headed off down the street towards his cabin.

Willie waited until no one else was in sight, pulled up close and motioned him into the car. They drove towards the same secluded spot where they had talked before, but a road crew was working there. Willie kept going until he found a place to pull over under an oak tree next to a long field planted with lettuce. In the distance, a small crop duster plane swooped down parallel to the earth, emitted a cloud of whatever it emitted, ascended, turned and swopped down again. The kid watched it warily.

"Short day for you," Willie said.

"We finished the section we were working and the foreman sent us home early. Somebody said it was because he has a girlfriend he wants to see. It made all the workers angry because they won't make as much."

If Willie had a job as hard as tomato picking, he would have welcomed hours off. But he didn't have hungry mouths to feed down in Mexico.

The kid clutched his empty bucket on his lap. He looked away from the plane. "Have you learned anything new on who killed Andrés Colón? Do the police have any idea who did this to him?"

Willie could see the kid was still shocked and scared by what had happened to his father's friend.

"The sheriff's people are still calling it an accident. I've told them about Andrés' connection to your father and the fact that

Ernesto disappeared. So far, I'm not getting anywhere with that, but I have another lead on what may have happened with your dad."

The kid's eyes got big. "What is it?"

Willie told him about the anonymous phone call, the female tipster who said Ernesto had knowledge of heroin dealing in Cane City and how that might have gotten him in trouble.

Pedro's face contorted. "Why would my father get involved with such people?"

"Maybe they were trying to hook young farmworkers on heroin. Maybe it was something else. I don't know for sure. Given your father's record of getting involved in other people's problems, he might have gotten in the faces of those heroin dealers."

That made sense to Ernesto's son. "What are you doing with that information?"

Willie told Pedro about going to Dusty Powell's house, encountering her and Marcus Morrell, a known drug dealer and walking tattoo gallery. Willie also recounted for him the arrival of the police and the shootout that had left one dead, one missing and one wounded.

The kid took it all in through eyes wide with fear. Then he pointed at the sky. "We were working and saw the sheriff's helicopter fly over."

"They were looking for Dusty Powell. She's the one that got away."

"Maybe she knows what happened to my father."

"Maybe. Then again, maybe I was only told that to lure me to her house so I'd get killed. Either way, it demonstrates that some very dangerous people are operating here. Which is why I think you should get out of here and go back to Miami, to your family. It isn't safe for you to be here. I can handle this by myself. I promise you I'll do everything possible to find out what happened to your father."

The kid shook his head. "No, I'm not going anywhere. I'll keep working on Eccles Farm until I know what happened to him. If you try to make me leave, that will only draw attention to me and make it more dangerous for me."

He was obviously prepared for Willie's plea. It would do no good to argue. And, of course, he was right that any public contact between them would be dangerous, just as it had apparently been for Andrés.

He told Pedro about his abbreviated meeting with Homer Eccles that afternoon and his eventual expulsion.

"He threw you off the property? He wouldn't do that if he wasn't worried about something." The look on his face hardened. "I don't like this man Eccles. He looks evil to me."

"Let's not leap to conclusions about who is evil, who might have done what."

Willie also told him about meeting with Colón's widow, Natalia, the call to Andrés the night before and the name she overheard. Carlotta.

"I wonder who made that call to Andrés," Pedro said.

Willie told him how Clark in Tallahassee had traced the call. "The phone is registered to a man named Ricardo Ramírez from here in Cane City."

The kid's eyes went big. "That's the name of one of the other men who is missing."

Willie frowned. "I thought that woman you work with wouldn't tell you the names. She was too scared."

"She didn't, but I had mentioned to one of the men I work with that I was from the same town as Ernesto Pérez. He doesn't know I'm his son, but he did say that Ernesto had suddenly disappeared. I told him I'd heard that some other Mexicans had gone missing from around here in recent months. He was cautious at first. Then he mentioned one other man—Ricardo Ramírez."

"What else did this man tell you about Ramírez?"

"Nothing. He caught himself, got up and hurried away."

"Why would Ramírez call Andrés?" Pedro asked. "Maybe *he* knows where my father is."

Willie could only shake his head. "I don't know, but I'll try to find him."

The crop duster was working its way over the lettuce field, now much closer to them. They could hear the keening engine now every time it swooped. Willie could now read the company name on the fuselage: BioMaster. Quincy Vetter was everywhere in Cane County, including the skies. The kid didn't know Vetter from Adam, but he didn't like the plane overlooking their clandestine meeting. Willie didn't like it either. He drove back to a safe spot near the cabins.

Pedro paused before getting out. "I'll ask around among the workers about Ramírez."

Willie knew he could control the kid only so far. "Be careful who you ask, what you ask. As I said, there are dangerous people in and around these fields."

The kid shuffled off, and Willie cranked up the car. He was only a few short blocks from the address he had for Ricardo Ramírez. He drove there and found a neat, narrow lot, on a short side street with one trailer on it. It was in good shape, but looked abandoned; its front door was chained shut. Willie peeked inside through a plastic window and saw it was clean and empty, just as Ernesto Pérez's trailer had been. The big difference between the two trailers was the decorations on the walls. Ernesto had hung a church calendar and cross made of palm. Ramírez was a fan of pinups, photos of young, creamy-skinned, naked women in alluring poses on several walls, all of whom were now smiling provocatively at Willie.

In the yard across the street, Willie saw an older white woman in shorts watering some new grass outside another trailer. He approached her with a smile.

"I'm wondering if you can tell me where I might find Mr. Ramírez from across the street."

She shook her head. "I haven't seen him in weeks. He's a foreman in the fields and usually when he left town for work, he would ask me to keep an eye on his place. This time, he disappeared from one day to the next without a word. Who knows where he is?"

Willie thanked her, climbed back in his car and shot a last glance at the trailer. Ernesto Pérez and Ricardo Ramírez seemed to be very different men. One was into God, the other into girls. What they had in common is that they had both disappeared.

CHAPTER EIGHTEEN

Willie hadn't eaten all day, and his stomach was growling. He stopped at the same Mexican restaurant he'd eaten at his first day in town, the place that featured the mariachi music and the Christmas lights.

Over a chicken and cheese burrito he decided that the person he needed to track down was Víctor Coyote. If Iris the desk clerk was correct, Víctor kept company with Dusty Powell. Maybe their relationship was also a business accommodation. Maybe Fanny had put her finger on it. It could very well be Víctor who brought the heroin on his trips north from the Mexican border. In general, human traffickers didn't mess with drug smuggling because the penalties for moving drugs had always been much tougher than those for smuggling people. But Willie knew exceptions existed, and some smugglers had used illegals to move drugs. Maybe that was why Ernesto Pérez had gone to see Víctor, to object to desperate Mexican migrants being placed in the line of fire, the kind of fire Willie had just experienced.

Willie took out his phone and found the number Víctor Coyote had called him from two nights ago. He pressed, waited and listened as it went right to voicemail. Camp had said the same thing, that Víctor wasn't answering. Willie tried to leave a message, but the mailbox was full. For a coyote who was often in charge of lots of clients, it seemed that Víctor was not very well organized.

Next, he tried Víctor's boss, Narciso Cruz. The executive coyote didn't answer his cellphone either. Willie dialed the landline number, and the maid answered. She said her boss wasn't home. Maybe she was telling the truth, maybe not. Willie thought of driving to the fat man's house, but given that the sheriff was looking for Víctor, the coyote's connection to Dusty Powell and the mayhem of that very morning, Willie sensed that Narciso might not be helpful at the moment. The question would inevitably arise: Could skinny Víctor have been involved in drug smuggling without the knowledge and possible participation of Narciso? Willie had a hunch the fat man wouldn't want to even hear that question, let alone answer it.

He decided to pay another visit to Father Finlay. Víctor didn't look much like a church-goer, but the priest probably had pretty good sources of information in town, especially among the Mexicans.

Willie paid his tab and headed for the door. As he did, he noticed that a man had his face pressed against the window, staring in his direction. The face was obscured by the lettering on the glass, but when he stepped out, he realized it was Merton Vetter. The old man was dressed just as he had been the day before, in overalls, and his white hair was just as windblown. He wore rubber boots that were muddy, as if he'd just come from working the fields.

He stood staring at Willie with the same fiery gaze he had worn on their first acquaintance. It was gleeful and ferocious at the same time, so that you couldn't be sure if he wanted to hug you or strangle you. For all his excitement, it appeared he was struggling to remember who Willie was.

"I'm Willie Cuesta, Mr. Vetter. We met yesterday at Eccles Farm."

The old man's stare didn't waver, as if he were still trying to remember.

"Have you seen my son, Quincy?" he muttered finally.

"No, I haven't, sir. He's not in the restaurant, I can tell you that."

Again, what Willie said didn't seem to register.

"He's a good son, Quincy. Always lookin' out for me."

"I'm sure he is, Mr. Vetter."

The other man processed that, as if he had to translate it into some language he could understand before responding, "If you see him, tell him I need to talk to him right away."

"I will certainly do that, sir."

Merton Vetter took keys from his pocket and walked a short distance down the block to an old, black pickup truck. Willie wondered if it was the same truck that had followed him yesterday. He couldn't be sure, but he thought it might be. Was the old man really looking for his son, or was he stalking Willie yet again? Why would an old man like Merton Vetter choose to follow him around? Did he understand what he was doing? Was he just acting on his son's obvious distrust of outsiders? A rifle was locked to the rack at the back of the cab. Could Merton Vetter be dangerous? As Willie watched, Merton Vetter pulled away from the curb and headed up the street, staring with all his ferocity through the windshield.

Willie climbed into his own car and minutes later parked in front of the church. The front door was locked, but a white Toyota he had noticed the other day was parked outside. It bore a small chrome crucifix glued on the license plate next to the number. A medal depicting the Virgin Mary hung from the rearview mirror. It appeared the priest was on the premises. Willie heard a buzzing noise coming from behind the building, looped around the side and found the older man in white shirtsleeves running a trimmer over a hedge. It surrounded a colorful garden, full of red hibiscus plants, hydrangeas and various other flowering bushes that Willie didn't know the names of. The priest had apparently plugged into the local pastime—planting.

He saw Willie and turned off the tool.

"This is my miniature Garden of Eden," he said in his mild brogue. "I doubt that the one in the Scriptures required maintenance, but alas we're not in Eden." He squinted at Willie. "In your line of work, I assume you're aware of that."

Willie admitted that he reached the same conclusion. The priest placed the trimmer on the table nearby.

"Still searching for Ernesto Pérez, are you?"

"Yes, although at the moment I'm looking more specifically for a young man who may know what happened to Ernesto."

The other man grimaced. "I don't like the sound of that word, 'happened.' You believe something grave may have befallen Ernesto, I take it."

"I'm afraid that may be the case. He seems to have ticked off numerous nasty people with interests to protect. Some of those people play very rough."

Willie told him what had happened not long before at Dusty Powell's house and the possibility that Ernesto Pérez, in an attempt to help fellow Mexicans, had run afoul of the heroin ring. The priest flinched with pain.

"You come to a place this far off the main highways and you think you'll be spared at least some of the sins and afflictions of the modern world, but no such hope. The devil has all the maps."

"Or a GPS," Willie said.

The priest nodded his balding head. "Who is it you are searching for now?"

Willie told him about Víctor Coyote, his connection to Ernesto, his possible link to Dusty Powell and a heroin operation. He also described the jumpy smuggler for him.

The priest shook his head. "No, he doesn't ring a bell. He hasn't showed up in church, which isn't much of a surprise, given how busy he is committing crimes."

"I figure people in your parish probably know this guy. Can you make some calls, father, and help me find him?"

The priest crossed the yard. Willie followed him through the back door of the rectory. Moments later, Willie was sitting in the office, again surrounded by the priest's model planes, a couple of the fighter planes pointing their machine guns at him. Given the experience of the morning, having more guns trained on him, even toy guns, was no fun. Over the next few minutes, the priest flipped through his old-fashioned Rolodex—just like the one Fanny had— and made several calls in Spanish to local residents. Willie eavesdropped, and it became clear that the people knew who Víctor was, but they weren't able to tell the priest where to find him.

After the third call, the priest turned to Willie. "It seems like this young fellow has smuggled a lot of local loved ones into this country," he said. "Because of that, my sources aren't very enthusiastic about telling even me where he might be found. They're being very protective of him."

Willie made a face. "It could be that, and they may also be afraid of him. I've heard he can get rough."

They thought it over.

Willie looked up. "Maybe they have doubts about why you're looking for him. It's not like you have loved ones you want smuggled from Mexico, Father. Maybe you could tell a small white lie.

Maybe you could say you know someone who needs Víctor's serv-ices to smuggle a relative here. You need to find him right away."

The priest liked that proposition. He dove back into his Rolodex. Two calls later, he hit pay dirt, thanked the woman on the other end and hung up.

"This Víctor smuggled his own grandmother to Cane County a couple of years ago, along with a cousin. When he's here, he lives with them in a yellow house at the very end of the street down from the high school. The old woman takes care of his house here and does the cooking for him."

"Grandma Coyote."

The priest shrugged. "You can take the boy out of Mexico, but you can't take Mexico out of the boy."

Willie thanked him and got away from those plastic machine guns as fast as he could.

***

In his travels around town, Willie had seen Cane County High School. He found the street again, passed the buildings, the full park-ing lot and, across the street, the football field with bleachers and a scoreboard several stories tall. At the very end of the street, he found a wooden house painted bright yellow, with a carefully tended lawn and flower beds out front, all of it neatly fenced in. Víctor was a coy-ote with a white picket fence. He, like his boss Narciso Cruz, was a necessary cog in the local economy, an accepted member of society. Or at least he had been before getting mixed up with Dusty Powell & Company.

Willie parked out front and walked up the path. The door was open, and through the screen door he caught the delicious scent of a Mexican mid-day *comida* being prepared. He knocked, and a woman who appeared to be in her seventies came trudging out of the kitchen. She was white-haired, big-breasted, comfortably plump. Víctor, all skin and bones, had obviously not inherited her genes, at least not the ones that determined his physique. She wore a long white apron over a flowered dress, all very traditional, but on her feet were strapped bright red, high-cut basketball sneakers, the expensive kind many teenagers coveted. Willie figured her grandson had purchased them for her to ease the long hours she spent standing at the stove. Despite that, she also wore a deep scowl; Grandma was distinctly unhappy about something. Willie smiled, trying his best to look as little like an immigration agent as possible.

"What can I help you with?" she asked in Spanish, inspecting him up and down.

Willie spoke quickly, trying to include familiar references to put her at ease. "I'm looking for Víctor, señora. Mr. Cruz, Narciso Cruz, put me in touch with him. We spoke two days ago at the Planters Inn, and he is helping me find someone I'm searching for. I was hoping I'd find Víctor here."

Her scowl deepened. "Well, he's not here. His lunch is ready for him and he isn't here to eat it." She plucked a cellphone out of the pocket of her apron. "I tried to call him, but he doesn't answer. He's been gone since last night. This isn't like him. Lately he's nothing but an ungrateful grandson."

Whatever trouble Víctor might be in with the authorities, he was in a worse fix with grandma.

"Do you think he might be with Dusty Powell?" Willie asked. "Not at her house—I went there. Maybe somewhere else?"

That made the woman even unhappier.

"I don't like that Dusty person. She looks like trouble to me. He should be with a Mexican woman."

Well, she certainly seemed to be right when it came to Dusty Powell. A grandmother's instincts at work. He didn't tell her the events that had transpired at Dusty Powell's house that morning. That could only scare the wits out of her and, anyway, in this small town she would probably find out soon enough.

She was inspecting Willie again. "You look skinny, like Víctor. Maybe you should come in and eat this meal before it goes to waste."

Willie had just eaten breakfast. That said, he was seriously tempted by the aromas wafting from the kitchen. But as he spoke to her, his cellphone vibrated and he decided he'd better stick to business. He thanked her, left another business card for Víctor and walked away from her with his mouth watering.

CHAPTER NINETEEN

Willie went to the car, pulled out his phone again and saw a voicemail message from a number he didn't recognize. He found the dry drawl of Homer Eccles on the other end.

"Mr. Cuesta, I want to speak to you about Ernesto Pérez and what might have happened to him. County Chairman Quincy Vetter is also here with me. Why don't you come to the farm and see us?" He hesitated. "And don't worry, no one will shoot you."

Willie considered that last statement. The possibility existed that the old man had somehow found out about his daughter's extended stay at the Planters Inn the night before and was luring Willie to an untimely end. Again, maybe that was considered a fatherly duty in Cane County. Willie thought that over but didn't think it was likely and decided to take his chances.

He headed up a side street in the direction of Eccles Farm. He had driven no more than a block when he heard the whoop of a siren behind him, glanced into the rear-view mirror and saw a sheriff's cruiser not far from his back bumper. Its roof lights were spinning.

He pulled over onto the edge of a vacant lot and turned the car off. He also reached slowly towards the small of his back, removed the handgun from the holster there and let it slip smoothly down between the front seat and the console, out of sight. Camp had warned him he might draw the unwanted attention of Sheriff Nathan Pope's patrol deputies, and Willie had been waiting for it to happen. His glancing contact with the sheriff at Dusty Powell's place had probably provoked it. Willie hadn't been speeding or violating any other motor vehicle regulation. At this stage in his case, just being Willie Cuesta was a violation in Cane County.

In the rearview he watched two deputies climb out of the cruiser in their dark green uniforms, Glocks strapped to their thighs. They were both a bit younger than Willie. One had a blonde crewcut, a neck like a tree trunk, biceps bursting his short sleeves and a gut that arrived a full second before he did. His partner was slimmer, taller. He wore his sheriff's hat and shades. Willie right away labeled them Fat and Skinny.

It was Skinny who leaned down just outside Willie's driver-side window. Willie noticed the man had once suffered a bad case of acne. Maybe from eating too much sugar cane.

"Can you please locate your license and registration and step from the car?" His Southern accent was downright syrupy.

"My registration is in the glove compartment. I'm going to grab it."

The other man nodded. This was why Willie hadn't stuck the gun in there. Motorists reaching into glove compartments where a gun happened to be stashed had provoked enough police shootings. Willie didn't need to contribute to that statistic. He found his registration and stepped from the car.

"My license is in my wallet," he said to Skinny. "I'm going to take it out."

"You go 'head and do that."

Willie handed over both documents. He noticed that neither man wore a name plaque on his shirt. The other deputies he had seen since arriving in town all wore them. He assumed they had taken them off especially for this occasion. Skinny studied the documents through his shades, then handed them to Fat.

"Miami," Fat muttered. "Lots of foreigners living down there."

Quincy Vetter had focused on "New York people." For Fat, people of foreign extraction seemed to pique his suspicions.

"Cuesta," he said, "now that's a foreign name, ain't it?"

Willie gave him his best all-American smile.

"I was born right in Miami, Jackson Hospital. Played football and baseball for Miami Senior High School."

Fat frowned. "You look a bit scrawny for football."

"I played wide receiver. I was known for my hands, not my blocking."

Fat had his doubts. "You sure you're not a gay boy? You look more like a gay Latin boy than a football player."

"As a matter of fact, I'm not, but some of my fellow officers and friends on the Miami Police Department were. Fine officers."

They both shook their heads in disbelief.

"Then what are you?" Fat asked. "Bisexual? I understand a lot of you South Beach boys swing both ways."

"No, not even that. What can I say? I just don't have much imagination in that area."

"We must've heard wrong," Skinny said.

Willie flashed his sunniest smile again. "Yes, well down in Miami, we're told that all you good ol' boys up here spend your days humping sheep. Is that true?"

They didn't like the question and didn't answer.

"See, I don't believe that myself, mainly because I haven't seen even one sheep up here," Willie said. "Of course, maybe guys keep their sheep hidden away, ready for intimate moments. I don't know. Maybe you fellas could tell me."

Fat had lost his smirk. Willie saw the muscles in his neck tense, his thick jaws clench. The cars were stopped at the edge of an empty lot. Houses stood across the street, but Willie saw nobody in sight. If the deputies wanted to get rough with him, no witnesses would be available to testify in his defense. Willie decided the traffic stop had lasted long enough. He addressed Skinny, who appeared to be the more thoughtful of the two, although only marginally.

"Before you gentlemen do something you may come to regret, I strongly suggest you listen to something."

Willie reached slowly into his shirt pocket and plucked his cellphone out with two fingers. He brought up his messages, tapped the most recent one, from Homer Eccles, put the phone on speaker and let it play.

"Mr. Cuesta, I want to speak to you about Ernesto Pérez and what might have happened to him. County Chairman Quincy Vetter is also here with me. Why don't you come to the farm and see us?" He hesitated. "And don't worry, no one will shoot you."

Willie closed his message queue. The two men stared at the phone as if it had just relayed a message from another dimension.

They looked dumbfounded at first, then betrayed. They glanced at each other in extreme discomfort.

Willie smiled. "As you've just heard, not only Mr. Eccles but County Chairman Vetter are waiting for me at this very second. If I don't arrive soon, they will be unhappy. And if I arrive with any variety of injury or even bruising, they, I'm sure, will be even more upset. As you heard, Mr. Eccles assured that no one would harm me."

Willie held out his hand. Fat returned his documents.

"It's been a genuine pleasure, gentlemen."

He pulled away. In the rearview mirror he saw them standing forlorn next to their cruiser. They were still there when he turned onto the main drag.

He drove in through the front gate of Eccles Farm and slowly up the dirt road, keeping an eye out for anyone who might take a pot-shot at him. Part of it was his run in with the good deputies, but most of it was having been on the receiving end of a barrage by sheriff's deputies just that morning. The echoes of the shots were still in his ears—and his mind. But he reached the administration trailer unscathed, parked and entered that long tin can.

Myra Roth shooed him into the adjoining office. Eccles was at his desk, and sitting in a chair in the far corner was Quincy Vetter. From behind his thick lenses he directed the same caustic gaze at Willie that he had exhibited during their first meeting.

"Sorry it took me a while to arrive," Willie said. "I just had a very pleasant visit with a couple of your local deputies. Not long before that, I had an unexpected run-in with your father, Mr. Vetter. It was downtown outside a Mexican restaurant. I thought he might have been looking for me for some reason, but he told me he was looking for you."

Vetter didn't like this news at all. His already icy gaze grew a bit icier. "Is that so?"

"Yes, it is. You might get in touch with him when you can. It seemed important."

Vetter nodded only slightly and left it at that.

Eccles waved Willie into a chair. "Everybody in town is talkin' about this heroin bust. I called the sheriff's office earlier, soon as I heard about it and the shootout up near Sawgrass. Rory Camp told me what happened. He says you were there?"

"Unfortunately, yes." Willie told him about the anonymous tip. "I got there just before SWAT did. I would have preferred to get there just *after.* Bad timing."

Eccles didn't seem too concerned about the fact that Willie had been on the wrong end of blazing assault rifles. Vetter looked even less vexed about it. Willie still wondered who the woman was that had called him with the hot tip. He wondered if Vetter, in particular, had anything to do with it.

"This person on the phone told you Dusty Powell might have been involved in Ernesto Pérez disappearing?" Eccles asked. "She said that outright?"

"That was the gist of it. Given the people I found there, if Ernesto had *any* contact with that crew, it could have proved fatal."

Eccles glanced at Vetter, who continued staring at Willie. Willie got the distinct impression that it had been Vetter's idea to arrange the meeting, but Vetter was letting Eccles carry the ball. Eccles chewed his cud and looked like it left a sour taste in his mouth.

"All this business with these drug dealers is very bad for the growers around here," he said. "Not just for the obvious reasons, Mr. Cuesta. Not just because it's illegal and not just because heroin is a horrible, addictive drug, sometimes fatal."

He glanced out the window in the direction of Dusty Powell's place and then back.

"I'm not going to tell you anything that Rory Camp and everyone else around here doesn't already know. Dusty Powell has a boyfriend who works as a coyote, a smuggler of Mexican farm workers. His name is Víctor."

Willie nodded. "He works for Narciso Cruz."

"That's right. All the growers around here depend on the coyotes to bring us our workers from Mexico and Central America. Americans won't do this work. It's that simple. It's backbreaking, and you need to pick up and move hundreds of miles north every few weeks during the harvest season. Sometimes you go days without work waiting for crops to mature and by the time you reach the end of the year, you haven't made much money. But for the Mexicans and Central Americans who have to struggle just to eat back home, it's worth taking the risks to get here and worth working hard to keep the jobs. That's why immigration agents don't bother us farmers. Because no matter which party is in the White House, nobody wants to interfere with the harvests and send the price of food through the roof."

Eccles was giving him the spiel he might have given an immigration agent who decided to target farms. Or what he might have testified to before a congressional committee, if he ever got hauled before one for employing illegal labor. He had it down.

Willie picked up the train of thought. "But if Dusty Powell is involved in smuggling heroin, and her boyfriend is Víctor the coyote, then there's a chance that the Mexican is hauling heroin with him when he transports the workers. And that would adversely affect the labor supply."

"That's exactly what worries all of us," Eccles said. He glanced at Vetter. "Isn't it, Quincy?"

Vetter squinted at Willie. "If federal drug enforcement agents get wind that heroin is entering this county, that the drugs are being moved by human traffickers who also transport farm laborers, they won't care whose business they disrupt. So far, we haven't seen federal immigration agents of any kind around here. We don't want them or need them," Vetter said through his clenched jaws, "and we don't want to give them a reason to think otherwise."

"The heroin smugglers could kill the illegal goose that lays the golden egg each harvest," Willie said.

"Precisely."

Eccles took up the conversation again. "If Ernesto Pérez knew about this heroin business, he should have told the sheriff, or me or for sure Frank Alvarez.

Willie frowned. "Who's Frank Alvarez?"

Eccles pointed vaguely into the distance. "Frank and his family own the sugar refinery you see just north of town. Their company is called Florida Sweet."

Willie had seen the smokestacks of the refinery a good distance off the road. Everybody in South Florida had heard of the brand. In fact, Willie probably had a bag of Florida Sweet in his cupboard back home.

"The Alvarezes are exile sugar growers from Cuba," Eccles said. "They have been here about fifty years, ever since Castro drove them out. All that land around the Powell house belongs to the Alvarez clan. They bought it from the Powell family. When they did, they cut a deal that the family could stay in the one small house until the day they wanted to sell that, too. Then they would have to sell it to the sugar company at a fair price. Let me tell you, Frank Alvarez won't be too happy when he hears what Dusty has been doing in his cane field."

"You think Ernesto might have threatened to tell him?"

Eccles shrugged. "I don't know, but Ernesto Pérez knows the Alvarez family because they all belong to the Catholic church here. He's told me about conversations he had with Frank. They all speak Spanish, and Ernesto would have felt more comfortable talking to Frank than to the sheriff, or to me, for example."

Willie studied Eccles' words as if he could see them floating before him.

"Both Víctor and Narciso Cruz told me that the issue with Ernesto had to do with a smuggling payment, that it was nothing more than a misunderstanding. And that nothing would have happened to Ernesto over such small potatoes. But the heroin trade is much bigger business. If this kid Víctor was mixed up in it, does that mean that Narciso Cruz must also have been involved?"

That speculation obviously caused Eccles acute discomfort.

"Narciso has lived here many years. He has been important to the agriculture industry here by supplying us with workers. He's done very well for himself—he's even a legal resident now. I don't think he would risk it all to smuggle drugs."

Eccles glanced at Vetter for support, but the exterminator was staring balefully as if he'd just discovered an unexpected insect infestation in the surrounding fields. "Lots of people have risked it all to make the kind of money that heroin brings in," he said flatly.

Vetter, the county chairman, was throwing big Narciso Cruz under the bus, or that was certainly what it sounded like. Given Cruz's role in the local economy, that surprised Willie. Did Vetter really believe what he was saying? Did he believe Cruz could be a heroin smuggler? Was he angry because the heroin smuggling, whoever was doing it, might make his county a target for the feds he hated so much? Or could it be a business decision? Did Vetter see an opportunity to cut himself in on Cruz's lucrative human trafficking

business, if he could get the executive coyote out of the way? Vetter
had the cold-blooded manner of a person who might make that kind
of quick calculation. Who knew? Either way, Willie wouldn't want
to be Cruz with a friend like Quincy Vetter.

Old man Eccles, meanwhile, had a weary expression on his
weathered face, as if a freeze had hit and he'd lost his entire crop.
Willie felt for him.

"We don't know who did what," Willie said. "I wouldn't leap to
conclusions. I'm going to talk to Cruz. Maybe he can tell me where
to look for young Víctor."

Willie left them sitting there, Eccles looking angry at the world,
Vetter with the wheels turning behind his thick, microscope lenses.

On his way out, Myra Roth, cowgirl turned secretary, waved him
down. "Have they tracked down Dusty Powell yet?" she asked.

"No, not yet."

Willie took a close look at Myra. He figured that she and Dusty
were about the same age—fortyish.

"You have any idea where she might go to hide, Myra?"

She shook her head resolutely. "No, I was never close to Dusty."
She paused and an idea occurred to her. "I'll tell you who once knew
her well. Who was good friends with her in high school. That's
Loretta Turk. Not that Loretta would ever be mixed up in anything
like drug smuggling. Her momma would kill her. But Loretta might
be able to tell you where Dusty would try to hide out even all these
years later."

"Where do I find Loretta at this time of day?"

Myra pointed off towards the north. "One of her crews is still
picking a parcel just off the state road, that way. You'll see the flat
bed. Just don't tell her I sent you."

Willie promised he would keep their secret and headed out.

He turned left onto the state road and drove until he saw the
pickers working their way up the rows of tomatoes. Moving slowly
on the dirt road that ran parallel to the rows was the flatbed holding
the big wire bins. Standing next to those large bins was Loretta Turk.
You couldn't miss her. She was a head taller, much broader and darker than the men and women working for her. Willie turned onto that
dirt road and parked not far from the truck. It crawled along as workers crossed the fields, balancing the buckets of tomatoes on their

shoulders, handing them up to the attendants on the flatbeds. Loretta dropped a red plastic chit into each empty bucket. The sound of plastic hitting plastic was the local version of a cash register's *ka-CHING* sound. The worker stored the chit in a pocket to be cashed-in later and went running back into his or her row. They were like ants, and Loretta was the queen, bigger than the rest.

Willie hoisted himself up onto the flatbed and stood next to her. She wore a kerchief around her neck again; this time it was pink. She shot him a sardonic glance.

"You come to do some tomato pickin'? If you did, you forgot your bucket."

Willie gazed over the fields, watching the workers "frisk" the plants for tomatoes. They had to bend deep to get to the lowest ones, just as Willie had once checked suspects for knives concealed in their socks or shoes. But the farm workers had to do it all day.

"This job looks too tough for me," he said to Ms. Turk. "I'm here on other business."

Two workers ran to the truck with full buckets. Loretta dropped chits into them once they were empty.

"What kind of business could you have with me?" she asked without looking at him.

"I was wondering if you had heard from Dusty Powell?"

That made her freeze just as she was about to drop a chit. She shot Willie an angry glance, fired the chit into the empty bucket and turned on him.

"Who told you I had anything to do with Dusty Powell?"

"I know you were friends with her in high school."

"High school was a helluva long time ago. Almost twenty years. And I'm not the only one still here who knew Dusty Powell back then."

A worker was waiting for his chit, gazing up at Loretta with pleading eyes. She winged one into the bucket and turned on Willie again.

"Listen, sucker, anyone who told you I have anything to do with drug smugglin' needs to eat some dirt. I'll arrange that for them."

Willie held up his empty hands. "I'm not accusing you of anything, and nobody else did either. I just figured someone who's known Dusty a long time might know where I can find her, who might hide her."

"Well, it isn't me. Dusty and I hung out some in school only because she lived right down the street from me. When I was in high school, white kids still hung out with white kids and black with blacks. Dusty was different. She and her momma were white, but they couldn't afford to live on the white side of Cane City. Her momma had a drug habit, that's why Dusty ended up the way she has. It started in high school, and my parents made me stop hangin' with her. I see her on the street from time to time. She waves hello, but we don't talk. That's it."

"When was the last time you saw her?"

Loretta dropped a couple of chits in buckets and thought that over. "I saw her . . . maybe it was ten days ago."

"Where was that?"

"She was at the convenience store up across from the sugar refinery. She was with that skinny guy smuggles people in from Mexico."

"Víctor Coyote."

"She was with him and another guy."

Willie squinted at her. "Marcus Morrell?"

She shook her head hard. "No, not Marcus." Her gaze grew even darker. "They say he got killed this morning."

Willie said that was true.

"Marcus is another one I've known all my life," Loretta said. "Marcus was big trouble even before Dusty was. He was doin' drugs when he was still in middle school."

"Amazing. And here in God's country."

Loretta rolled her angry black eyes. "You city boys don't understand what's goin' on up here and you never will. You think everybody around here belongs to the 4-H club and that we all spend our time milkin' cows, ridin' tractors, goin' to hoedowns."

She swept an arm before her and across those flat fields.

"Do you know what this land produces more of than anything else?"

Willie shrugged. "Sugar. Maybe tomatoes."

Loretta shook her head hard. "No, it's boredom. That's the principle product of this county. Boredom. There isn't much to do here but work and go to church. That's why so many kids pull up roots and make for the cities. Some of the ones who don't leave, they bring the city here to us."

"In the form of drugs," Willie said.

"You got it. Marijuana, cocaine, methamphetamines, oxycodone. You name it, it came here. When I heard people sayin' on TV that heroin was the new big thing, I knew we'd have that here, too. And the fact that Dusty and Marcus were involved doesn't surprise me at all."

Willie glanced at the workers wending their way up the narrow rows of tomatoes and then back at Loretta.

"You said the other guy you saw with Dusty wasn't Marcus Morrell. Who was that then?"

"I don't know his name. He's Hispanic and he was speakin' Spanish to the skinny guy. I heard him. I think I've seen him around before, but I don't know his name."

"What did he look like?"

She shrugged. "Thin, black hair, like lots of Hispanic guys, but not Mexican. Lighter skin."

"Did you ever hear of a guy named Ricardo Ramírez, a Mexican migrant worker?"

She retrieved more chits from a sack sitting next to her and dropped three into empty buckets.

"Yes, I know who that is. He worked as part of my crew at one point. Later, he got promoted. He had the same kind of year-round job Ernesto had but on another farm owned by Quincy Vetter. They say he disappeared just like Ernesto. I know him, but the other guy with Dusty wasn't him. It was somebody else. That's about all I can tell you. Dusty's mother died a few years back. She has no other kin here. I can't tell you anybody else she hangs with. I don't want to know."

Loretta shot a chit into a bucket, punctuating the end of the conversation. Willie jumped off the flatbed and made his way back to his car.

Before he could drive off the farm, his cell buzzed with a text message. It was from Abbie LeGrange, who had also called and left a message while he'd been speaking with Father Finlay. He hadn't listened to it, but now she was demanding immediate attention.

"CALL ME NOW!!!" That didn't leave much room for interpretation.

He pulled over, punched in her number, and she came on halfway through the first ring. She didn't sound happy.

"Mr. Cuesta, this is your employer establishing contact, even though *you're* the one who is supposed to be keeping in touch."

Willie winced. He had promised her either a phone call or an email every day. The night before, he had forgotten to fulfill that promise. But he couldn't very well tell her that he had been distracted by EJ Eccles. "Distracted," to say the least.

Abbie wasn't finished. "My client phoned this morning to tell me she had called Cane City last night to speak to Andrés Colón. She found out that he had been run over by a car and killed. Did you know that?"

"Yes, I know that," Willie hurried to say, so that he wouldn't sound totally out of it.

That didn't make Abbie any happier. "Then why didn't you notify me? Don't you think that was something I might need to know?"

Willie heard the truthful answer in his own head. Because I suspect Andrés was murdered, that maybe Ernesto Pérez was also killed, and I didn't want to tell you that. Instead, he gave her the details of the accident, how Andrés was walking along the side of a dark road, and that the police were investigating it as a hit-and-run accident.

At that point, he decided to distract her from the Colón killing and onto the good news he had. "I've located young Pedro Pérez."

She liked the sound of that. "Where is he?"

"He's here in Cane City."

"And you're bringing him back?"

"Well, not quite yet."

"Why not?"

He told her about Pedro's refusal to leave until he had discovered what had happened to his father.

"But I'm coming closer to an answer on that issue."

"Exactly how are you coming closer?"

Willie didn't want to tell her about the shootout at Dusty Powell's place and a possible connection to Ernesto Pérez. A report of gunplay would surely not sound like progress to her.

"I'm looking for a man who may have the answers. His name is Ricardo Ramírez . . . and a woman named Carlotta, apparently connected to Ramírez. I'm searching for them."

"Where are those people? How long will it take you to track them down?"

Willie was about to answer that he didn't know exactly. She cut him off.

"I would much rather that you simply convince Pedro to come back to Miami."

"I've tried that, and he won't do it. If I don't find out what happened to his father, then he will try to do it, and a much greater chance exists that he'll get hurt."

As he said it, Willie realized that he had also become committed to solving the disappearance of Ernesto Pérez. Even if Pedro agreed to abandon his mission and return to Miami, Willie would have trouble letting go of the case now. Ernesto had built a reputation as a good man. If something bad had happened to him, Willie wanted to know who was responsible. It was personal with him, just as the cases he had handled as a police detective had become personal.

"I'm sure the family members in Miami want to know what happened to Ernesto," he said to her. "Be patient, and hopefully we can provide them that answer, too."

Patience was not a virtue that star-spangled Abbie LeGrange often practiced. That was the sense Willie got, but right then she had no choice.

"Be in touch," she said. It was an order. Then the line went dead.

CHAPTER TWENTY

Willie reached the main gate of the Eccles Farm. Across the vast cane fields, just to the north, stood the Alvarez family sugar refinery that he had seen before and that Homer Eccles had recently referred to. Willie decided he would try to meet first with Frank Alvarez before talking to executive coyote Narciso Cruz. If Ernesto Pérez had spoken to someone in the Alvarez family about the connection between the people smugglers and heroin, Willie needed to know.

He turned north onto the main road and drove until he saw a sign:

FLORIDA SWEET
THE SWEETEST SUGAR UNDER THE SUN
PROPRIETOR: FRANK ALVAREZ

Unlike the other side roads around, this one was a full two lanes wide and paved. The refinery seemed to grow as he approached it through the cane field. About a block long, it was a massive assemblage of pipes, conveyor belts, vats, furnaces, motors, catwalks, metal ladders, elevators and more conveyor belts. Willie could see a truck dumping cut cane stalks into bins at the end closest to him, where the entire process began. Along the way, the refinery emitted plumes of hellish steam through various vents and smokestacks, creating a cacophony of sounds in the otherwise quiet landscape.

Willie reached a guardhouse and asked the uniformed agent there for Frank Alvarez. The other man pointed in the opposite direction, down a paved road that ran away from the refinery through the cane fields.

"He's not here. He's at the corporate offices about half mile down that way. You can't miss it."

Willie thanked him, followed the directions and soon reached said offices. Unlike Eccles Farm, Florida Sweet's administrative center was not housed in a trailer. Instead, nestled amid the cane, Willie found a large stucco building, off-white in color, with a Spanish tile roof. It looked like a large, tasteful, comfortable hacienda. He saw that the thick, varnished wooden doors, ten-feet high, were open at the moment. Willie parked right outside, next to pickup trucks bearing the company logo—a bright sun beaming down on a cane stalk.

The spacious central patio was covered in red Saltillo tile, to match the roof. A covered walkway, supported by white pillars, surrounded the patio and led to offices all the way around. The office just inside the gates said "Reception." Willie walked in to be received.

The young receptionist had long, raven-black hair. When she asked what she could do to help him, it was with a thick Cuban accent. He said he wanted to see Frank Alvarez.

"Can I tell him who is here to see him?"

Willie handed her a card. "You can tell him I'm here because one of the members of his church is missing, and I'm hoping he can help me find him."

The receptionist looked alarmed and picked up the inter-office phone. She explained emotionally, in Spanish, that someone from St. Anthony's Church was missing and a gentleman was there looking for him. God only knew what Alvarez made of that, but when she hung up, she said the boss would see him. She pointed him directly across the courtyard to the "executive suite."

Willie entered a large office with three secretaries working at desks and walls hung with oil paintings of the Cuban countryside. He recognized the distinctive topography found in parts of Cuba, where jungle-covered mountains jutted up dramatically right in the middle of otherwise flat, tilled valleys. Narciso Cruz collected Mexican landscapes, while Frank Alvarez favored Cuban vistas. Everybody missed home.

The secretary farthest back pointed him through a door in the corner. Willie stepped into the spacious room and saw a big mahogany desk sitting just in front of a luxurious potted palm and a long mahogany conference table surrounded by high-backed wicker chairs. More Cuban landscape art hung on the walls. What he didn't see was Frank Alvarez. Then a voice came from the direction of French doors that were open to the outside.

"I'm out here."

Willie followed the voice and found Frank Alvarez lying in an intricately woven hammock strung between the cement columns of a covered walkway overlooking the cane fields. A telephone sat on a stool next to it. Ensconced in his cocoon, Alvarez was slim and swarthy, with a shaved head that was as shiny as a café au lait cue ball and a black goatee, long and pointed. It gave him a satanic aspect at first glance that seemed to go with the factory down the road that belched smoke and not with the church he attended.

He wore a white guayabera shirt embroidered with gold filigree, a style favored by Cuban businessmen in South Florida. He was drinking coffee out of a demitasse cup. Given his age—he looked to be in his forties—Frank Alvarez was probably a second-generation Cuban exile, just as Willie was. When he spoke, it was in unaccented English, but with the guttural sound that regular doses of rum and cigar smoke deposited in the throats of Cuban men.

"Excuse me, I'm taking a break for Cuban coffee." He pointed to a small table holding a pot. "Can I offer you one?"

Willie handed Alvarez his business card, poured himself a coffee, and sat down in a hand-carved rocking chair facing the hammock. Alvarez read the card.

"Cuesta? Are you Cuban?"

"*Sí, señor.*" Willie sipped the aromatic brew and glanced out at the fields in the direction of the refinery. "This is quite the operation you have here. Very impressive."

Alvarez shrugged. "Nobody knows more about sugar than we Cubans."

He sipped his coffee. "So, what do you think of Cane County?"

"Well, I must say I'm finding the politics of the place a bit strange."

Alvarez rolled his eyes. "Yes, that's the work of my neighbor to the south, Quincy Vetter."

"I'm told he has some problem with the federal government becoming his neighbor," Willie said.

"That's right." He pointed to the southeast. "The Everglades begin at the edge of Vetter's land over that way. You follow the Sawgrass road right up the street and you get there. The far end of Vetter's property is a rocky, worthless piece of real estate, less than a square mile, that's never been planted by anyone. The government wants to take that and give him in exchange a better, more valuable piece of state land over this way. Quincy says only over his dead body."

"Just because he doesn't want the feds for neighbors."

"Crazy, isn't it? But that is his position, and he has turned it into a political movement around here. Quincy's father, Merton, I always believed he was crazy, always a bit of mad man. Quincy, I thought he was different until all this started a couple of years ago. Now I'm convinced he inherited his father's madness."

"Turning Cane County into the Wild West."

"Just about. This county is going backwards in time, in history."

"Has he tried to mess with you?" Willie asked.

Alvarez shook his shaved head. "Not yet, but who knows? He doesn't like me, because neither I nor anyone from my family or staff have joined his party."

"The Sovereign Rights Movement."

"That's right, and we won't join it in the future either. Like other Cuban sugar cane growers in this country, I have friends in state government and in Congress. Politicians who don't want this nation importing sugar from communist Cuba. Quincy knows that. I own this one small corner of the county, and so far, he has let me alone. I'm hoping all this blows over. But it may be just a matter of time before what he's doing here in Cane County interferes with my operation. Then we'll see what happens."

Willie recalled Camp mentioning influential local citizens who were in touch with officials up in Tallahassee and Washington regarding the local political looniness. He assumed Alvarez was one of them.

The sugar producer sipped his coffee. "What is this about somebody from my church being missing?"

Willie explained how he had come to be hired by the family of Ernesto Pérez.

"Do you know Ernesto?"

Alvarez nodded. "Yes, of course, I know him. A Mexican man, a bit older than me. He's been part of the parish for some time. He even does readings from the pulpit sometimes on Sundays. Now that you mention it, I haven't seen him in a while. What happened to him?"

"We don't know what happened to him. That's the issue. His family suddenly stopped hearing from him."

Alvarez frowned as if the coffee had suddenly turned bitter. "Did you ask Father Finlay?"

"Yes, and he has no idea either. Ernesto never told him he was leaving town."

Alvarez shrugged. "Well, if you're here to ask me if he said anything to me, no, he didn't."

"Since he saw you at church regularly before he disappeared, I'm wondering if he ever spoke to you about any problems he had discovered here in town."

"What kind of problems?"

Willie leaned forward in his chair, as if there was someone who might overhear him, although there wasn't.

"To be specific, the possibility that the coyotes bringing workers here were also carrying drugs, heroin . . . that would put the workers being smuggled in great danger."

Alvarez froze with the cup halfway to his frowning mouth. "Is that going on here?"

The other man had obviously not heard of that morning's mayhem in Sawgrass, so Willie filled him in. Alvarez used the palm of his hand to wipe a thin film of sweat from his shiny pate.

"My God. Ernesto never spoke to me about anything like that. If he had told me that was going on here, I would have gone right to the sheriff."

"He never came to you with any other issue, an issue that might have gotten him in trouble with bad guys around here? People who might have threatened him?"

Alvarez shook his head. "I don't know what bad guys you're talking about, and, no, he never talked to me about threats." He paused, stroked his pointed goatee and remembered something. "There's another guy who works for me who knows Ernesto. His name is Oscar Blanco. We can go ask him."

He drained his coffee, got up and led Willie out of the building. Outside, he climbed into a company pickup and told Willie to follow him in his own car. They drove back to the refinery, were waved through the gate and parked. Alvarez handed Willie a bright yellow hardhat along with a set of goggles to match the ones he himself now wore. They walked into an outside elevator cage made of thick wire mesh. Alvarez threw a control lever and took them up three stories into air that smelled increasingly of molasses. They got out and walked on narrow metal catwalks right through the heart of the raucous refining process. Willie looked down at metal rollers several feet thick that squeezed the juice out of cane stalks. You didn't want to slip and fall into those. You would end up about as thick as a business card.

They went on, and soon Willie was gazing down into a vat where a molasses-like substance was boiling. The rising steam misted his goggles. You didn't want to take a dive into that concoction either. You would very quickly turn into a sweet, well-done dumpling. They reached a glass-walled control booth, and Alvarez led Willie in. Sitting there—the outside noise now mostly muffled—was a man lighter-skinned than Alvarez, bearded, dressed in jeans, a long-sleeved denim work shirt and a red hardhat. His clothes looked too big for him, as if the steam rising all around had sweated many pounds from him. He sat stock still, facing a control board made of numerous dials and two computer screens. Temperatures, volumes, chemical components of the sugar were apparently measured at various points of the process and could be controlled from the booth. From outside, the refinery looked like a relic of the industrial age, but it was clearly being controlled by twenty-first century technology. Willie noticed that on his wrist the man wore a bulky, stainless steel watch that had lots more dials on it and appeared very expensive. It made him look like an extension of the control board.

The man suddenly came to life, typed in a command and then looked up. Alvarez made the introductions.

"This is Oscar Blanco. He is a senior lab technician here. He's also personally acquainted with Ernesto Pérez."

Alvarez explained that Ernesto was missing. He also asked if Ernesto had ever mentioned to Blanco that he was aware of heroin smugglers in Cane City. That made Blanco wince just as it had

Alvarez. He shook his head as if he was trying to the get the idea off him, the way he might want an insect off him.

"No. Mr. Alvarez here asked me to help with repairs at the church. Ernesto and I worked together a couple of weekends. That was a few months back. I don't really go to church, but after that, if we bumped into each other at the store or on the street, we always stopped to say hello. We had a couple of beers together at one point. He never talked to me about anything like that. I never heard of anything like that around here."

"The kid they found dead up in Sawgrass two days ago, he died from a heroin overdose," Willie said. "He was the second drug death in the last couple of months around here. And this morning, sheriff's deputies raided a distribution point."

Blanco looked from Willie to Alvarez and back to Willie. All around the sealed glass room, clouds of steam roiled and rose, as if they were in a control booth in hell.

"You don't think Ernesto got involved in something like that, do you?" Blanco asked. "He didn't seem to me to be that kind of person at all."

Willie shook his head. "No, I don't think he was mixed up with them. If anything, they were afraid he would tell the sheriff about them. They might have done something to him."

Blanco scowled as he took that in.

Seconds later an alarm went off on the control board, and he flinched. Just thinking about what might have happened to Ernesto Pérez made him jumpy. He turned and adjusted a dial to stop it before the whole place blew up.

Willie handed Blanco a card and asked him to be in touch if he heard from or about Ernesto. Then they headed farther along the metal walkway, through more billowing steam, and took an elevator cage down into a warehouse, where the processed sugar finally poured out of a funnel, forming an enormous pile several stories high. It was a version of the Big Rock Candy Mountain.

At that point, Alvarez led him back to his car.

"I'm going to talk to the sheriff about this heroin business and also ask him what he knows about Ernesto Pérez," he said to Willie.

Willie said he would appreciate that, since the sheriff was not wild about him being in Cane County. He glanced over the cane field to the east. "I think maybe I'll drive out to the Everglades and get the lay of the land."

"As I said, right out the Sawgrass road," Alvarez reminded him. "But don't get off that road. The Sovereign Rights types have talked about setting up a shooting range out there. I think they're preparing for the invasion from Washington. If they don't like you, you don't want to give them an opportunity to accidentally shoot you."

Willie thanked him for the heads-up. He got into his car just as the refinery released another cloud of satanic steam.

CHAPTER TWENTY-ONE

Willie headed north out the main drag and a few miles up caught the Sawgrass road to the east. It was a two-lane black ribbon slicing through the endless cane. He passed the entrance to the Triple R Farm and then the cutoff to Dusty Powell's. He wasn't about to take that turn again.

At the ten-mile mark, he passed the town of Sawgrass. It wasn't much more than a whistle stop, with a small grocery store, a laundromat, a few houses. He was through it in an instant.

A few miles farther along, the cane gave way to row crops on both sides of the road. He passed an entranceway, a sign that said "Vetter Farms" and the obligatory Homeland Security warning. Off to the south he saw farm buildings and a couple of houses, the Vetter homestead. He didn't stop there either, figuring that the welcome would not be particularly warm.

After a while, the crops ended and he entered rocky scrub land fenced off with barbed wire. The property sloped up a bit from the road. Between that and the scrub, you couldn't see very far. Several dirt roads cut off. They were gated, padlocked, and again posted by Homeland Security. Willie assumed that was the land in dispute. He rolled down a window and listened, heard no shooting, but kept moving anyway. No need to tempt any of the local gunslingers.

A green state-government placard announced that he was entering the "Greater Everglades Ecosystem." The scrub gave way quickly to greener undergrowth—reeds, clumps of bushes—then the road suddenly ended at a yellow-and-black-striped metal barrier. Just beyond it was a short, dilapidated wooden dock stretching into shallow water with more reeds growing out of it and grass growing just below the surface. The Everglades was called the River of Grass, and right there it was clear why.

Willie pulled up next to an SUV parked at the barrier. It was empty, but an airboat was tied up at the end of the dock, and someone was onboard. When he walked up, he found the same Seminole man he had seen serving as proprietor at the casino the day before. He was dressed as he had been, the same ceremonial blouse in the pattern of lightning bolts, but now he had his long raven black hair tied in a ponytail. He was pouring gas into the tank of the boat from a red can.

He glanced up at Willie and squinted as if he recognized him. "Hello," he said. "You were in the casino yesterday, I think."

"That's right. You have a good memory."

He smiled. "We Indians have good, long memories."

"You going for a ride?"

"Yes, I am. I like to take a break in the afternoon. Do you want to ride with me?"

Willie climbed aboard and introduced himself.

"I'm Nathan Osceola," the other man said, offering his hand.

Willie had heard of the Osceola family. They were leaders in the Seminole community, even down in the Miami area.

The airboat was a small, two-seater. Willie climbed up into the passenger seat right next to Nathan. He had ridden airboats in the Everglades further south, including the time he and Fanny had gone hunting for those missing Russian mobsters, figuring correctly that their bodies had been dumped out there.

Nathan hit the starter and the airplane propeller right behind them came to life. He shifted into gear, pulled the long throttle stick back, the nose of the airboat came up and they were off.

The patch of water right before them was open, and they were soon skimming over it so fast that Willie was pinned to his seat. Nathan tilted the throttle stick to one side and they swerved into a narrow channel bordered by mangrove plants. That channel twisted and twisted again until they flew into a tunnel shaded by trees growing right out of the water, long falls of Spanish moss dangling from the limbs. A blue heron feeding ahead of them took flight, soaring into the sky on its broad wings, out of range.

They emerged from that tunnel, and Nathan tilted the stick the other way so that they skidded on the surface of a large open pond of water. On the edge of that water, on the shore of a small spit of land, Willie saw an alligator sunning itself. The boat came within twenty feet of it before straightening out. Willie held on extra tight, making the Seminole next to him laugh with delight.

Ahead of them stretched a wide field of leafy water plants. They approached going at least fifty miles per hour and skimmed right through them without touching the land beneath. Willie turned to see the plume of water behind them rain down on those plants like a deluge.

Over the next fifteen minutes they speeded, swerved and skidded through open water and narrow byways. Along the way, they saw wading birds—egrets and herons mostly—turtles, racoons, one falcon, more alligators. They saw flowering air plants and at one point skirted a beautiful field of white flowers that Nathan identified as hyacinths. They made almost a complete circle, then Nathan drifted to a stop under a moss-draped tree that offered them shade.

"Beautiful," Willie said.

"Yes, it's still beautiful," Nathan said, "but it won't be that way much longer if we don't stop pumping poisons into it."

"Fertilizers in the water," Willie said.

"That's right," the Seminole said, gazing down at the surface of the water and grasses growing right under it. "You don't see it, but those of us who grew up in this world, we have experienced the differences. Yes, we still have birds. We used to have many more. The same for racoons, otters, gators. Chemicals running off from the farms have killed many. You still see fish here, but it makes no sense to catch them because you shouldn't eat them."

"Mercury poisoning."

"Yes. Bad for everybody, especially for kids and pregnant women. And the fertilizers make things grow here that shouldn't grow here. It's green still, but some of the wrong species have taken root and will eventually kill off what does belong here. All sorts of algae that are poisoning our traditional plants." He pointed at a patch of neon green scum floating just feet away. The color itself was cautionary. It didn't look natural.

Willie gazed about. "That's why the state wants that land next to Vetter's farm. To filter out the polluted water."

Nathan pointed through the thick vegetation next to them. "It's right through there, that property just a hundred yards or so. The state could easily dig out pools there and divert water to them to let the fertilizer settle."

"But Quincy Vetter would rather turn it into a shooting range to prepare the Cane County patriots for the coming invasion."

Nathan shook his head. "Just what we need next to this water. It will frighten away the last of the birds, fish and animals here."

Willie gazed into the vegetation. "And if they miss a target, maybe they'll bag you or some other local boater."

Nathan shrugged. "During the Seminole Wars, back in the nineteenth century, the American government tried to drive us Seminoles out of these Everglades. They fired at us a lot, but never got all of us out. I haven't heard any shooting yet from Quincy Vetter's shooting range. It's been very quiet over there. When they open the range, I'll probably stay clear of this particular spot."

Nathan decided right then that he'd been taking enough of a chance just being within range. He cranked up again, and a minute later they pulled back up to the dock. Willie thanked his host for the ride. The Seminole hadn't asked Willie where he was from or what he was doing in town. As he'd said, the local Indians had strong survival instincts. In this case, the less he knew, the better.

CHAPTER TWENTY-TWO

Willie had enjoyed his brief tourist excursion, but now it was time to get back to his case. He headed back on the paved road towards Cane City. As he did, he punched Narciso Cruz's cell number into his phone. It was time to confront the executive coyote about what he knew or didn't know about local heroin peddling and any contact Ernesto Pérez might have had with the purveyors.

The phone rang several times, then went to voicemail. He left another message but decided to head towards Cruz's house anyway.

It was late afternoon as he drove down the main drag and took the turn west towards the Bountiful Harvest Estates where Cruz lived. Once again, he passed the sweetcorn fields and saw that the scarecrows—the real ones—were still on duty. He was just about to leave the corn behind, when one of those life-sized stuffed figures caught his attention. This particular scarecrow was not doing a very good job; birds were all around it. Willie took a closer look at it and found that the clothes it wore were oddly familiar.

He slowed down, pulled over to the side of the road, got out and walked between two rows of young cornstalks that reached just above his waist. About fifty feet off the road, he reached the scarecrow, which occupied a small clearing. As he approached, the birds took to the sky. These weren't just any birds, they were vultures.

The scarecrow was dressed all in black, except for the same straw hat that all his colleagues wore. Scarecrows weren't usually dressed in basic black; brighter colors were apparently better for scaring off birds. It hung crookedly from a wooden pole shoved up the back of its shirt, its arms thrown loosely over a crossbeam and its head slumped down against one shoulder. Willie reached out, lifted the head up by the chin and found himself staring into the face of

Víctor Coyote. Whether he'd been doing a good job frightening crows and other birds—before the vultures showed up—Willie didn't know, but he was certainly scaring Willie. The manic Mexican had finally stopped twitching like an exposed nerve. He was dead.

***

About a half hour later, the stretch of the road running by the cornfield was cordoned off and clogged with sheriff's cars spinning their roof lights. Willie was standing with Camp and Sheriff Nathan Pope.

Víctor Coyote had been hoisted off the wooden cross and now lay on a bed of old cornhusks on the ground. The scarecrow that had originally hung on that cross lay nearby, making a strange pairing. No one had yet covered Víctor. His slightly open eyes gazed blankly at the sky, and, beyond that, into eternity. Somehow, they seemed even more lifeless than the painted eyes of the straw man.

The coroner had yet to arrive, but a chief EMT had determined that Víctor Coyote had been strangled. The dark bruises around his neck, especially over his Adam's apple, were telltale. Sheriff Pope stared down at the dead man awhile and then turned to Willie. His tone was as flat and hard as the floor of a mausoleum.

"You spoke to a man named Colón, and the next day he was dead. I understand you believe his death was intentional. You spoke to this man here, now he's also dead. And you were there when Marcus Morrell died. We are not accustomed to homicides here in Cane County, especially not three deaths in the space of three days. You seem to have brought Miami with you, Mr. Cuesta, and I don't like it."

Pope looked ready to have Willie run out of town, no matter the consequences. It looked like he'd rather deal with the FBI than have Willie around for one more day.

Willie kept his cool and tried the best he could to commiserate. "I've been a law enforcement agent, sheriff. I was on the job for years. I understand the pressure this brings on you and your men. But whatever is going on here was already underway well before I arrived. For one thing, Ernesto Pérez disappeared months ago."

Pope's gaze narrowed. "Camp mentioned something about this to me. Finding this man Pérez is why you're here, I take it."

"That's right."

"And in trying to find him you're causing havoc in my county, leaving a trail of bloodshed behind you."

Willie wasn't making himself any more popular with Pope, that was obvious, so he didn't argue.

Pope pointed down at the dead man. "Who do you think killed this Víctor person?"

"If he was, in fact, moving heroin, I would look in that direction first. I'm told he was keeping company with a Ms. Dusty Powell, who may have some answers."

Pope got an exasperated expression on his face. "We're looking for her, Cuesta. When a person escapes a police raid and a gun battle, we look for her."

"It seems to me Narciso Cruz should be able to help you. I'm told he was Víctor's employer."

Pope looked down his narrow nose at Willie. "For somebody who just arrived here, you seem to know an awful lot about our local citizenry."

"In a small town, everybody is connected to everybody else, at least so it seems. One person leads you to the next."

"Mr. Cruz is on his way here as we speak," the sheriff said. "Now I'd like you to get off this property and allow county investigators to do their work."

Willie sauntered back to the side of the road where he and everyone else was parked. Crime scene technicians looked for footprints around the body, but hardly any were detected due to the dried cornhusks underfoot everywhere. They checked for fingerprints on the wooden crossbeams where Víctor had been hung, although that didn't look much more promising. Lifting prints off unfinished wood exposed to the elements was some trick. Willie looked up and saw vultures circling overhead, saying goodbye to Víctor.

The coroner arrived, a man who looked like he might be related to the sheriff. Trim, pale, bald, with a gray moustache, he carried an old-fashioned medical bag. He bent over the dead man a few minutes and then stood up. He, Pope and Camp conferred. A few minutes later, Camp came back to his cruiser.

"How long has it been?" Willie asked.

"He says about twelve to fifteen hours."

Given the aroma that Víctor was giving off, that sounded about right. Willie glanced at the road. It would have been risky to stop there, remove Víctor's body from a vehicle and prop it in the field during daylight. Best guess was he had been hung there in the middle of the night, not long after he was killed.

A minute later, a shiny gold Escalade pulled up, and the corpulent Narciso Cruz got out. The fat man waddled across the cornhusks to where the sheriff was standing and stared down at Víctor Coyote. If he felt any emotion at seeing his employee dead, he didn't betray it. Sheriff Pope stepped up next to him. Cruz was clearly there to do the official identification. He did it quickly, holding a red bandana over his nose as he did. He answered a couple more questions, then turned around and walked back to the road, where Willie sidled up to him.

"His grandmother lives here. Somebody should break the bad news to her."

"I've already told Camp that I'll go with them to do that," Cruz said.

Willie had been thinking about the old woman in the red sneakers and how she wondered why her grandson had not come home to eat. The answer to that was the worst thing she could have imagined. He did not envy Cruz having to convey the news to her.

"Do you have any idea who might have killed him?" Willie asked.

Cruz sneered. "I don't know, but if he was using the incoming workers to smuggle heroin, then he got what he deserved."

Cruz had righteous indignation written all over him. Of course, since Víctor had worked for him, suspicion of involvement in the heroin trade would also flow his way, and he was trying to fend it off. The question was whether Víctor could have been involved in drug smuggling without Cruz knowing. Quincy Vetter had expressed his doubts about Cruz's innocence, and Willie wondered if the sheriff shared those doubts. Was this the end of the protection they had long provided to the executive coyote?

Moments later, Sheriff Pope crossed the trampled cornhusks and answered that question. "In a few minutes, Captain Camp will drive you over to the home of the next of kin and then he'll bring you back to the station. You'll need to answer some questions about the activities of your employee . . . and your own."

Pope walked away, and Cruz trundled back towards his Escalade. He leaned up against it and faced the other direction, obviously pissed off. Willie followed and leaned next to him. In the cornfield across the road, another scarecrow hung. Willie inspected it closely to make sure that it wasn't someone else he had spoken with. But this one was really made of hay.

Cruz broke the silence. "If Víctor was involved in moving drugs, I knew nothing about it," he said, his gaze fixed on something far away. "If I had known, I would have killed him myself. I have always known that as long as farmers needed the workers, I could continue to do business with little interference. You don't get involved in moving any other kind of cargo. People in this business are all aware of that." He waved a fat hand vaguely in the direction of Sawgrass to the north. "Víctor had to get involved with that stupid bitch, Dusty Powell. That's who they should be talking to."

He spit on the ground, as if Dusty was down there. Willie gazed out over the corn.

"Do you think Ernesto Pérez could have found out about Víctor using the workers he was smuggling as cover for hauling heroin? Do you think that could be what happened to Ernesto?"

Cruz scowled at him as if Willie was somehow trying to trap him. "How can I possibly know that if I didn't know what Víctor was doing. I told you already, I don't know what happened to Ernesto Pérez."

"How about a guy named Ricardo Ramírez? Do you know him?"

Cruz's scowl deepened. "What does he have to do with all this?"

"This is someone you know?"

Cruz shrugged his massive shoulders. "I know almost everyone around here. Anyway, Ricardo Ramírez is a very common name. Maybe it isn't the same one. Who is it you're asking about?"

"Someone maybe involved in the disappearance of Ernesto Pérez and the death of Andrés Colón."

Cruz shook his head. "The Ricardo Ramírez I know doesn't live here anymore."

"The one I'm looking for is gone as well. He disappeared in the past few weeks. How about a woman who calls herself Carlotta? You know anyone by that name?"

Willie saw Cruz's eyes jitter. If he had to guess, he would say Cruz was familiar with a Carlotta but for some reason didn't want to tell Willie that.

"I don't know any woman by that name."

The sun was setting beyond the corn and the scarecrow across the road. The EMTs emerged from the field carrying the stretcher. They had put Víctor in a long, skinny body bag. It occurred to Willie how an antsy guy like Víctor Coyote would have hated being closed up in that bag. Then again, nobody liked body bags.

Willie and Cruz watched solemnly as they loaded the cadaver into the wagon headed for the morgue. Camp came to fetch Cruz and take him to Víctor's grandmother's house. As a cop, Willie'd had to tell a number of mothers and grandmothers that their young ones had been killed. It was the worst aspect of the job. It didn't matter to a mother if her kid had been a saint or a criminal. To a mother, her kid was an angel. He watched them drive away. With no scarecrow on duty, some crows alighted on the stalks. The balance of nature: bad news for Víctor, good news for the crows.

CHAPTER TWENTY-THREE

Willie headed back to the Planters Inn just as the sun disappeared beneath the horizon. A flock of doves was winging through the twilight, heading for wherever they would spend the night. They were beautiful, but not beautiful enough to offset the recent mayhem.

EJ Eccles had told him she would be back that night for her "salsa lesson." He was in no mood for such a lesson, or for any interpretation of that term that EJ might come up with. After the visit by the local SWAT team at Dusty Powell's place, looking down at the corpse of Marcus Morrell and discovering the crucified Víctor, Willie wasn't feeling exactly amorous. Three bodies in three days, including Andrés Colón's, were taking their toll.

He drove to the inn with the idea of washing off the dust of the fields and the smell of death. He walked in, greeted Iris behind the check-in counter and headed for the stairs. As he did, he glanced into the restaurant and saw Quincy Vetter in deep conversation with his mother, Posey, who was in her auxiliary nurse uniform. They both looked grim, even angry, and that drew his attention.

Willie turned to Iris. "I see Quincy's sharing a meal with his mom. I met her the other day at the hospital."

Iris nodded and whispered. "Posey Vetter, Merton's wife. Her maiden name was Nickens. That was another old landowning family here at one time." She leaned forward and dropped her voice even more. "They say all the Nickens belonged to the Knights of the White Camelia."

Willie frowned. "Never heard of those particular knights."

"Like the Ku Klux Klan, only for well-to-do types . . . landowners, professionals."

"Country club racists," Willie said.

"Sort of, except we never had no country club here."

"How about her husband Merton? He belong as well?"

Iris hesitated, glanced at the Vetters and back. "People say Merton had Klan ties way back, but we supposedly don't have that 'round here no more." She seemed to have her doubts.

Willie threw caution to the winds and walked over to them. Quincy Vetter saw him coming and stopped talking to his mother. He nodded curtly as always, blinking behind his specs.

"Mr. Cuesta. I was just telling my mother that it was you who found the body of that heroin smuggler today."

Willie didn't believe that's what their conversation had been about at all. They had clearly been arguing about something, but he went along. "Yes, unfortunately it was me, and very unpleasant it was."

"I would think that man might have been a prime suspect in the disappearance of Mr. Pérez, the Mexican you're looking for. It's too bad he died before you could question him."

Willie shrugged. "We don't know for sure Víctor Coyote was involved in the disappearance of Ernesto Pérez. Not yet at least."

Willie turned his attention to the lady. "It's a pleasure to see you again, Mrs. Vetter."

The large redhead reached a hand up to Willie, and he shook it. Problem was when he went to take his hand back, Posey Vetter didn't let it go. She weighed as much as Willie did, maybe a bit more, and was no weakling. She was considerably larger than her husband. It was the kind of difference that made you wonder about the technicalities of a couple's sex life.

She was smiling up at Willie with her puffy pink cheeks and a mad glee in her periwinkle eyes. She didn't share her husband's physique, but she did have the same wild gaze.

When she spoke, her voice was a Southern purr. "My son tells me you're a private investigator from Miami, Mr. Cuesta, and that you came up here because you think we're doin' bad things to our Mexican workers. Now is that the truth?"

Willie kept the smile in his eyes. "I came up here looking for a missing man. That's all, Mrs. Vetter."

She still had his hand. In fact, she had now reached over with her left hand and stroked the back of it with the tips of her fingers. In the nurse's uniform, it was as if she were searching for a vein to insert an IV.

She didn't respond to his answer and simply went on. "Because that's the farthest thing from the truth that we mistreat our Mexicans. In fact, we do everything in our power to keep them happy and healthy. Isn't that the truth, Quincy?"

Vetter grunted an affirmative answer.

She purred on. "I don't know where you got that idea, but you can be sure that if anything were to happen to you here, you would be well cared for."

Willie heard two things in those words. One, she seemed to think that he was one of "our Mexicans." And two, she was issuing a not very veiled threat. "If" something happened to Willie was more like "when" something happened to him. The threat being uttered in that purring feminine drawl made it that much creepier.

Quincy was apparently as uncomfortable with his mother's words as Willie was. "I'm sure Mr. Cuesta has somewhere to be, mother. So do we."

He stood up, and his mother released Willie's hand. Willie told the lady it had been nice seeing her again, which was a stretch. He watched them walk out and headed for his room. He had to wonder what the two had been speaking about so intently when he had first walked in. Willie entered his room and plugged his phone in to recharge. He showered, changed and found a maid who took his clothes to be cleaned. Then he laid down on the bed and dialed Pedro Pérez. His main job, after all, was to bring the kid back safe and sound and he wanted to make sure he was all right. Pedro answered after several rings.

"It's good that you're calling me," Pedro said. "I heard something this afternoon from a guy I work with."

"What's that?"

"He says he saw one of the other men who disappeared, Ricardo Ramírez, at a Mexican store up in the town of Sawgrass. Do you know where that is?"

"Yes, I know where it is. When was he seen there?"

"Just yesterday. The guy told me something else. He said he saw Ramírez arriving at the store, and then some men drove up in a pickup, forced him into the truck and drove away. He said Ramírez tried to resist, but they were too much for him."

Willie gazed out the window of the room, over the fields, as if watching a battle in the distance.

"Did this work mate of yours tell you anything about the men who took him away?"

"He said they were local men Gringos, not Latinos. He didn't recognize them, but he said the truck they were in had a company name on it. Something like *biología*. That's what he remembered."

Pedro was pronouncing the word biology in Spanish.

"BioMaster," Willie said

"Yes, that sounds like it," Pedro said. "He said they drove off with him going away from Cane City."

Of course, maybe it wasn't a BioMaster truck, but how many companies operating locally had a similar name. Willie hadn't seen any. Or maybe the witness was wrong altogether. Maybe it wasn't Ricardo Ramírez he had seen. And did any of it have to do with Ernesto Pérez's disappearance? Willie was still convinced that Ernesto had run afoul of Dusty Powell, Marcus Morrell, Víctor Coyote and their heroin ring. Dusty Powell was the only one of them still alive. He figured if and when she was found, she would have the answers.

He had fallen into silence, and Pedro finally piped up.

"I better get going now," the kid said. "I have to go eat."

Willie told him to be careful, and they disconnected. Moments later, he heard a knock on the French door that led to the veranda. It swung open and in stepped EJ. Tonight she wore tight blue jeans and a blue silk blouse with golden lilies woven into it, which brought out the color of her honey-blonde hair.

She cocked a hip and shot him a sultry look. "I thought I'd skip dinner and the other preliminaries and get right to the salsa lesson," she said, exaggerating her Southern drawl.

Willie didn't move. She frowned. "Are we not in the mood tonight, Miami man? I thought you boys from South Beach were always in the mood."

She crossed the room and lay down next to him on the four-poster bed. "Tell me about it."

Willie proceeded to tell her about finding Víctor Coyote in the cornfield. She propped her chin on her hand.

"I heard some guy mixed up in a drug ring showed up dead. I didn't know you were the one who found him."

"I spoke to him two nights ago right in this building. I spoke to another man when I first got here, a farmworker, and he showed up dead in a ditch about a day later. And I was in the house in Sawgrass when Marcus Morrell was killed."

He had also just been menaced by sheriff's deputies and the Vetter family. He decided not to mention all that.

"You're feelin' like you have the hex on you," she said.

"Yes, you might put it that way."

She snuggled up next to him, put her head on his shoulder.

"Well, I understand not having the urge. I was the same way after my mom died. It went on for quite a while. Truth is, you're the first man I've been with since then. It took a Cuban lover to make me feel alive again."

Willie put his arm around her, two individuals who knew what it was to be temporarily out-of-service. Willie sensed that his languor wouldn't last as long as hers had. She snuggled a bit closer.

"I never thought I could feel as bad as I did when my mom died. One moment I had her, the next she was gone. Gone for good."

"Yes, Iris told me about her being thrown by her horse. Where did it happen?"

"Over south of the Alvarez plantation."

Willie squinted. "Isn't that the Vetters' land? The section that Quincy Vetter doesn't want the federal government to take over?"

"That's right."

"That's a long way from your farm."

"Not that far, not for my mom. She loved to ride and she would range all over this side of the county. She was a great horsewoman. She taught me to ride, but I'm no way as good with horses as she was. That's why it was such a shock that she died the way she did."

"Was there any way to know what had happened? Did the horse see a snake or some other critter?"

She shrugged. "We don't know what happened, but that's what we figure. Mom had come across lots of snakes over the years. I've encountered them myself. The horse will react, and you learn how to handle that and keep your mount. Whatever it was, it must have taken her by surprise. It was Posey Vetter, the mother of Quincy Vetter, who found her. She was out riding, too, and saw her lying there, but my mother had been dead at least a couple of hours. Posey said the horse was standing over her, as if it was mourning her."

The mention of the name made Willie's eyebrows elevate. "*Mrs. Vetter?*"

"You know her?"

"I've run across her a couple of times."

"She was very upset. She had known my mom all her life."

She fell into silence, and Willie kept his arm around her. They lay in silence for several minutes. Then she propped her chin on her hand.

"I got a phone call today about you."

"About me? From who?"

"Who knows? It was from an unidentified caller. A woman."

"What did this woman say?"

"'Stay away from 'that man from Miami.' You were bad for Cane County and would only get me in trouble. Then she hung up."

Willie scowled at the bed canopy above.

"You don't know who it was?"

"No. Whoever it was disguised her voice. Must have been somebody who knows we had dinner together. Here, everybody knows almost everything about everyone else. Just some busybody."

She lay her head back on his shoulder. To EJ, it was just some busybody. To Willie, it sounded like the busybody who had almost gotten him killed at Dusty Powell's place. The phone call concerned him. He thought of telling her to leave right then for her own safety, but that would only serve to scare her as well. Instead, he wrapped his arm around her tighter. He would simply have to stay away from her, as unhappy a prospect as that was.

Willie remembered the old Willie Nelson number.

Love was a dying ember
Blue eyes cryin' in the rain

She fell into a doze. Willie stared at the bed canopy, thinking about his case. After a while, he kissed her cheek, stroked her hair until she woke and told her it was time to go home. He escorted her down the back stairs and down the street to her car. There was no sign of the black pickup or any other worrisome vehicle. He gave her a warm kiss, which he figured might be their last.

The only sign left of her in the room was a hint of her scent. He undressed, brushed his teeth, turned off the light and went to bed, hoping he wouldn't have nightmares about scarecrows.

CHAPTER TWENTY-FOUR

Willie woke up early and hungry the next morning. He got ready and went down to the dining room, where Iris served him a large stack of pancakes with two cups of strong coffee. Minutes later, he pulled up at the sheriff's station to talk to Camp. The captain was just crossing the lobby as Willie entered and ushered him into his office. Willie sat down across the desk from Camp and stared at the somber brahma bull on the calendar. Given all the local violence over the past few days, Camp no longer wore the big grin he had flashed on the first day they'd met. He looked a lot more like that bull.

"Anything new on the killing of Víctor Coyote?" Willie asked.

"It's been confirmed that he died some time the night before. The cause was strangulation, but he was also struck in the head."

"It must have been God-awful for the grandmother."

Camp shook his head dolefully. "It's always awful."

"Did she tell you anything that might help find her grandson's killer?"

"No, not really. Only that he had been spending time around Dusty Powell, and grandma didn't like the looks of Dusty. She said Víctor showed up at the house the day before with Dusty and another man, who she didn't know. She said he spoke Spanish but not like a Mexican. She said he sounded Cuban. I have the deputy nosing around the small Cuban community here."

"How about your questioning of Narciso Cruz? How did that go?"

"Narciso says he knew nothing about Víctor being involved in drug trafficking. He said if he'd known, he would have killed him himself."

"Which maybe he did," Willie said.

Then he thought that over. Narciso might have killed Víctor because the younger man was selling heroin and endangering the human trafficking enterprise. Then again, if Cruz himself were involved in the heroin trade, he might have murdered Víctor to keep him quiet. In fact, Cruz might have killed Ernesto Pérez for the same reason. He laid that all out for Camp.

Camp just shrugged. "Why would Narciso hang him up in public? Why wouldn't he just say the coyote left for Mexico and never came back? On top of that, Narciso has a housekeeper who swears he was home all night. I'll keep his file open, but I can't see it."

He fixed on Willie. "What have you been up to? Not finding anymore dead people, at least I hope not."

"No, but I did hear an interesting story."

Willie told him the tale of Ricardo Ramírez being forced into a pickup over in Sawgrass, possibly kidnapped, or at least coerced. He didn't mention that the story had been relayed by Pedro Pérez and just attributed it to a migrant worker he'd spoken with. Camp frowned when Willie told him Ramírez had been dragged into a Bio-Master truck. He didn't appear to give that much credence either.

"Why would Quincy Vetter be kidnapping some Mexican?"

"I don't know. I figured you might have some idea."

Just then, Camp's cellphone sounded. He picked it up, listened and his wiry eyebrows went up.

"Where are you now, Williams . . . ? Okay. Wait there for me while I rustle up some of the troops. Just make sure she doesn't come out that main gate and gets away from us."

He disconnected, stood up, adjusted the gun belt on his hips and reached for his cowboy hat with the sheriff's logo.

"We think we know where Dusty Powell's holed up."

Willie sprung up as well. "Where's that?"

"In one of the worker cabins on the Florida Sweet plantation. Deputy Williams was poking around there. He was told by one of the workers' wives about a young, white haired woman staying there. Ain't too many young white-haired women around here, apart from Dusty."

He started out the door, Willie followed and Camp turned.

"You wanna get yourself shot at again? Is that it?"

"I'll stay out of your way, don't worry. I still need to find out what happened to Ernesto Pérez, and Dusty Powell may know."

Camp didn't have time to argue. It was also clear to Willie that Camp didn't trust some of his own deputies, especially those hired by Pope and Vetter, but did seem to have an instinctive trust in Willie. So, Willie piled into the sheriff's cruiser with him. They took off fast, with no siren sounding. Speeding north through the fields, Camp used his radio to summon several more cruisers. A surprising variety of roads led off the Florida Sweet property. Camp dispatched a car to block each one.

When they arrived at the main entrance to Florida Sweet, three deputies were waiting for them, including Williams. He was the intense young man with a moustache Willie had seen the first time he met Camp.

"Me and Donaldson went in here about a mile," he said, pointing up the road that ran through the cane. "We stopped to speak with a lady we saw at the laundry room attached to the worker housing. I described Dusty Powell to her and she pointed farther up the road. She said there are more houses along an irrigation canal there and she saw a white-haired woman outside the last one just yesterday. We left our car where it was, walked through the cane until we could see that house, but so nobody in it could see us. A few minutes later, Dusty came to the door, dumped out a pail of water and went back in. Donaldson stayed hidden in the cane watching the place, while I came out to call you."

Camp told Williams to climb in with them, ordered the two other deputies to follow and they headed up the paved road. They passed the turnoff to the refinery, at which point the road became packed dirt. A half mile farther on, they reached about twenty small worker houses built in a circle around a central green space. The stucco houses weren't large or luxurious, but they weren't crummy tin cans either. These had to be for permanent staff, not migrant workers. At least for some of its employees, the sugar plantation had perks that tomato pickers could only envy.

Williams suggested Camp stop there and that they go the last short distance on foot. Camp got on the radio, confirmed everyone else was in place and told them his team was going in.

Willie, Camp and the other two deputies followed Williams in between rows of cane about fifty yards, parallel to the dirt road. They passed two isolated worker houses that sat just off an irrigation canal, then reached a third. There they found Donaldson, who was crouched on the edge of the cane watching the white stucco structure. From there, they could see if anyone came out of either the front or back of the house.

"Is she still in there?" Camp whispered.

"Yup. She hasn't showed herself again," Donaldson said.

"Anyone else in there with her?"

"Not that I've seen or heard. And there's no car here."

Camp pointed towards the back of the house. "Williams, Donaldson, you guys go 'round back. Make sure she doesn't decide to slip out the way she did last time. If she gets into that sugar cane again, we might never find her."

The two deputies did as ordered. Meanwhile, Camp, Willie and the other two deputies moved so that they were still concealed by the cane, but closer to the front of the house. A gap of about twenty feet existed where the stalks had been cut to create parking space. Camp stopped just at the edge of the cane. The last time he'd approached the front door of a house where Dusty Powell was staying, he'd been greeted by gunfire. This time he wasn't taking any chances, or as few as possible anyway. One of the deputies had brought along a hand-held loudspeaker. Camp called out to her, his voice crackling.

"Dusty Powell, this is Rory Camp. Come out the front door with your hands visible and empty."

They waited, but the door didn't open and no sound was heard, except for crows cawing at a distance.

Camp called out again. "Dusty, don't make us come in after you. I don't want to see you get hurt."

Again, he got no response from her.

One of the other deputies spoke up. "Should we call SWAT?"

Camp put down the speaker, squinted at the house and shook his head. "No. It ain't like we're dealing with Marcus Morrell anymore. You two guys get on each side of the door. *I'll* go in. Let's move."

The three of them burst through the stand of cane, crouched over, moving fast. The two deputies deployed to opposite sides of the door with Camp right between them. Willie pulled the handgun from his back holster and followed. Camp ran right at the front door and with one powerful kick directly on the lock splintered the door jamb with the heel of his boot. The door flew open and Camp went through it, gun held out in front of him with two hands at eye level. Willie braced for shots to be fired, but not a sound was heard. The two deputies entered behind Camp, peeling off to the left and right, guns pointed. Again, nothing.

Willie stepped in, his gun clutched in both hands at hip level. Camp was just coming out of the back bedroom. He cut through the kitchen, opened the back door, and called to Donaldson and Williams. "You didn't see her?"

The two deputies walked out from behind the cane clutching their guns.

"No, nothin'," Williams said.

They all walked back into the house. Willie saw dingy walls, old tattered furniture, a vintage TV but no Dusty. Camp entered each room of the small house again and then stood stock still in the center of the living room.

"Where the hell did she disappear to?"

Willie entered the bathroom. He noticed a small, grungy rug, which had been kicked to one side and lay bunched up next to the bathtub. The tile floor beneath where that rug belonged was uneven with the grout missing along the edges. Willie knelt down, got the tips of his fingers under one edge and lifted with one hand, while holding his gun in the other. A section of tile about eighteen inches square came loose, and Willie shoved it aside. Now, he was staring down into a hole dug out of the dark earth that was just wide enough and deep enough to hold a person, maybe two.

Crouched in that hole, both her shoulders smeared with mud due to the tight fit, staring up at him despondently, was white-haired Dusty Powell. She didn't have a weapon of any kind in her hands. Willie lowered his gun. It looked as if maybe Dusty and her cohorts had thought of building an escape tunnel, like those the notorious cartel chieftains were famous for down in Mexico. But these smugglers had run out of steam before getting very far. Most heroin addicts didn't make good tunnelers; no work ethic.

Dusty blinked up at him, her eyes glazed, almost certainly high. Willie then noticed another set of eyes near her feet. They were red, beady and belonged to a good-sized rat. Dusty craned her neck and saw it at the same time. That cracked her stupor. Issuing a blood-curdling scream, she jumped towards Willie. He managed to grab her by one bony arm and haul her out.

Camp came running and hustled her out of the bathroom. Willie glanced into the hole again and noticed a sealed plastic container. He knelt on the floor, reached in with his gun barrel, nudged the container towards him, and quickly plucked it out. He said goodbye to the rat and replaced the trap door.

Prying the container open, he found several sandwich bags of powder that could very well be heroin. Another bag contained a substance that he didn't recognize but looked like it could be used in cutting the drug. It was probably fentanyl, a popular additive used to give heroin even more kick. A miniature camp stove was also stuffed in there, which he guessed was used in the process.

Willie carried the container into the crummy living room where Dusty was cuffed. Camp read out her rights, then he had the two deputies who had helped him rush the house drive her back to the station. They took the package with them.

"No sense talking to her now," Camp said. "She's high as a kite."

Camp told Willie to get back in the cruiser, and for Williams and Donaldson to follow. When they reached the circle of worker housing again, several local women were standing together staring up the road towards them. Camp stopped the cruiser next to them.

"You speak Spanish better than I do. Ask them who lives in that last house where Dusty was holed up."

Willie spoke. The women glanced warily at the sheriff's cruiser, not real happy about getting involved.

Willie fixed on the oldest one. "The deputies aren't interested in you. The sooner they get the information they need, the sooner they'll leave."

She liked that idea. "That's the house of Oscar Blanco," she said. "He works at the refinery."

Willie's face stormed over. Blanco was the lab technician he had met through Frank Alvarez. He told Camp.

"Does anybody else live there?" Camp asked.

"Only the woman with the white hair," the spokeswoman said. Willie thanked them. The cruiser roared back in the direction of the refinery. The attendant saw them coming ahead of a cloud of dust and opened the gate. Camp and Willie skidded to a stop in front of the facility, Williams and Donaldson right behind. Willie pointed up three stories to the small control booth tucked among the vats, pipes and conveyor belts.

"That's where he works. In that booth."

Camp told Donaldson to stay down below and led Willie and Williams towards the open-air elevator. Camp closed the gate and worked the control lever so that they started to rise. A few workers on the first level glanced curiously at them as they ascended. When they reached the third level, Camp stopped the elevator and they stepped out onto the catwalk. Steam drifted up around them, smelling of burnt sugar. The entire complex hummed, vibrated, hissed.

Oscar Blanco stood outside the control booth wearing the same red hard hat he had worn the day before. He held a sheaf of papers in his hand while speaking to another worker.

"That's him on the right," Willie said.

They started towards him. Blanco looked up. He knew right away that they were coming for him, dropped the papers, shoved the other guy down so that he blocked the catwalk and ran in the opposite direction. Camp started to run, but as big as he was, he would not be able to catch the other man. Willie bolted by him on the catwalk and lit out after Blanco. He jumped over the still prostrate worker and ran down the metal grating with Blanco about forty feet ahead of him. Blanco slowed, then darted up a metal ladder leading to the next level. Willie sprinted to that point and scrambled up the same ladder, pulling himself up by the metal railings. He reached the top just in time to see Blanco turn onto another catwalk, running farther back into the steaming complex. He ran after him, just above the large metal rollers that rotated and rumbled, crushing the juice out of the cane. The catwalk ended in a T, and headed off in opposite directions. Blanco bolted to the right. As he did, his red hardhat came off, falling into the rollers where it was crushed with a shattering sound, like bones being chewed. Willie sprinted towards that metal intersection, tried to turn, but slipped on the sugar spray that coated the metal and crashed into the railing. He would have flipped over it, but he grabbed the top horizontal bar like a man clutching the top rail of a ship's deck with a hungry ocean tossing beneath him. Here, it wasn't water he would fall into. It was a mechanism that would crush his bones and squeeze all the juice out of him.

He pulled himself back onto his feet. At that point, Willie knew he should back off. Blanco couldn't escape, not with sheriff's deputies waiting below. But the killing of Andrés Colón and almost getting shot to shit by Camp's SWAT team the day before had already affected Willie's inner barometer. This was his collar—nobody else's. He was in what Fanny called his "hurricane frame of mind."

Gun in hand, Willie headed down the same catwalk, staring across a maze of pipes and smokestacks through billowing steam, searching for Blanco. They were now on the fourth level and could go no higher. Unless Blanco could fly, he had to be there. Willie advanced slowly, systematically, down one catwalk and up the next, through the labyrinth of metal and mist. He was trying to force Blanco into the far corner, where he could hold him. Willie was just passing over the wide vat of molasses that boiled two levels below, and through its rising cloud of thick, sweet steam. He couldn't see more than ten feet in front of him and reached up to wipe his eyes. That was when Blanco made his move. He had lured Willie into that blinding fog. Now, he came out of the mist from behind a vertical vent wielding a large pipe wrench over his head. He was close enough that Willie saw that his beard, his brows and his black hair glistened with liquefied sugar, turning him into a demon.

As the wrench started towards his head, Willie fell straight backward, trying to raise and point his gun. He managed to pull off two quick shots that hit Blanco in the chest. The force of the slugs knocked the other man back so that he slammed into the railing. He still clutched the heavy wrench above his head and the weight of it bent him backwards over the top rail. He rocked there momentarily on his hip and let the wrench go, but by then it was too late. He was falling. Willie rolled towards the edge of the catwalk just in time to see him land, face-up in the boiling cauldron of molasses two stories below. His mouth was open in a scream, but Willie couldn't hear it over the din. Just like hell. Moments later, Blanco had sunk beneath the roiling surface.

Willie turned and saw Williams crouched on the next catwalk, his gun raised, ready to shoot. Their eyes met. Williams looked horrified. Willie stuck his sticky gun back in its back holster, pulled himself up carefully and started back down through the sweet mist.

CHAPTER TWENTY-FIVE

Willie found two ambulances and most of the sheriff's cruisers in Cane County parked outside the refinery, roof lights spinning once again. The sheriff stood next to Camp and again wasn't happy with Willie.

"Another person dead, you in the middle of it," Pope said.

Willie explained that he had acted in self-defense. The sheriff's own deputy, Williams, could swear to that. Pope stalked away to oversee the retrieval of Blanco's body.

Willie borrowed water from an ambulance crew and washed the sticky mist from himself the best he could. Meanwhile, the refinery was shut down, the vat was drained and EMTs were lowered into it. Blanco, encrusted in brown molasses sugar, was hauled out. They covered the corpse with a blanket, strapped it to a stretcher and lowered it with ropes to ground level. There, they shoved him into an ambulance headed for the morgue.

Willie recalled the time he had met Blanco right there at the refinery. The other man had worn a long-sleeved shirt despite heat. That and the rest of his clothes hung on him as if he'd lost a lot of weight. It hadn't meant much to Willie then, but now . . .

"Tell the coroner to check him for drugs," Willie said to Camp.

"Heroin," Camp said.

"*Sí, señor.*"

When Willie turned around, Frank Alvarez was standing just behind him. He looked dazed.

"Blanco was sharing his worker housing with a woman named Dusty Powell. She's a junkie and was involved in the distribution of heroin. We found the drug and paraphernalia in the house. Blanco wouldn't have bolted the way he did if he wasn't involved himself. Did you have any idea that Blanco had a drug problem?"

Alvarez shook his head. "How could I know something like that? He always came to work. He always did his job. It's incredible."

Willie knew it wasn't all that incredible. In his days as a police officer he had come across heroin addicts who were bellboys, butchers, bankers. All walks of life. As long as they got their fix, they functioned.

Alvarez watched the ambulance drive away. "He had family in Miami. I'll have to let them know."

Alvarez headed back towards his corporate offices. Willie saw Camp making for his cruiser and climbed in with him. The big man fixed on him.

"Right after we interrogate Dusty Powell, I'm going to have to depose you again, this time about the death of this man Blanco."

Camp cranked up the cruiser and headed for the station. They found Dusty Powell already in an interrogation room, guarded by two uniformed female deputies. She had been told that Oscar Blanco was dead. Soiled and disheveled from her brief stay in the "escape tunnel," she looked scared, as if the rat had followed her.

Camp sat down across from her, a tape recorder next to him. Willie stood in the corner behind him. Officially, he was just waiting his turn to be deposed. In truth, he was eavesdropping, with Camp's tacit permission.

"You've been read your rights," Camp said to her. "You can talk to me or not talk to me."

Dusty twitched. "I'll talk, but I just want it to be clear that I didn't kill nobody."

"If you didn't, who did? Who killed your boyfriend Víctor, for example?"

She looked like she would cry. "That was Oscar who did that."

"Oscar Blanco. Where did it happen and when?"

"It happened at Oscar's place two nights ago."

"Why?"

She scraped at her forearms with her nails, as if talking about her friends made her recall shooting up.

"Oscar knew you had talked to Víctor. He said Víctor had led you and your deputies to my place, to our operation. He threatened Víctor, and Víctor said maybe he would leave an anonymous message on Frank Alvarez's phone saying his lab technician was a heroin addict. That was when Oscar lost it. Oscar hit Víctor in the head with a shovel and then grabbed him by the neck."

Her face was full of horror. "I wanted to pull him off, but I was high and couldn't do anything to stop him. You saw Víctor, didn't you? He was scrawny and high and couldn't do anything either. The next thing I knew, Víctor was flat on the floor, dead."

His killing of Víctor explained why Blanco had panicked, tried desperately to escape and had ended up dead himself. He was facing heavy time. Maybe even the big injection, the kind that you never came back from.

Camp took it all in. "How and why did the body end up in that cornfield? Why not just bury it?"

Dusty shook her head. "After he killed Víctor, Oscar freaked. He shot up again. Later, near dawn, he loaded the body in Víctor's car and took off. I think he hung it in that field to send some kind of message to anybody else who did business with us who might snitch. I guess that was it. He was out of his mind."

Given Willie's confrontation with Blanco, he couldn't argue with that assessment. Camp glanced down to confirm that the recorder was working and then looked back at her.

"How did Blanco get involved in all this to begin with?"

She was still scraping at her arms. "Oscar was from Miami and was bored by this place even more than most of us. When he first came to work here, he would buy pot from me. Later, he liked Percocet. When heroin started showing up, I needed someone who would help me cut it. He knew some chemistry and told me and Marcus that he could figure out how to do it if we gave him some. He liked it a lot. Too much."

Willie remembered what Loretta Turk had said about boredom being the principal crop they produced in Cane County. Oscar Blanco had apparently died from it.

"The heroin he processed was all brought into this country by Víctor Coyote?"

Dusty nodded. "That's right. It's gotten tougher down on the border and fewer people are coming from Mexico than used to come. Before, he made plenty just moving people, but now he was making much less. That's when he decided to bring drugs. He had people he smuggled into the country carry what he called 'medical kits.' He told them they were for emergencies, held medical supplies and would only get opened in case some accident happened along the way. He hid the heroin in there. He didn't carry any of it himself, didn't even have a trace of it on his body. When they got here, he took the kits back. The people didn't even know what they were carrying."

Camp leaned his big body towards her. "Did Narciso Cruz have anything to do with this drug business?"

That question scared Dusty more than the others. "I never dealt none with Narciso."

"That's not what I asked you. Do you know that Narciso was involved?"

Willie wanted to know that too. The others she'd named were all dead. Narciso Cruz was alive, very big and from the looks of him, probably quite dangerous. Dusty's frightened gaze jumped to him, as if she could read his thoughts, and back to Camp.

"I told you I got no reason to believe Narciso was involved, and you better not go around sayin' I did."

Camp assured her he wouldn't do that and turned off the tape recorder.

Dusty Powell had confessed to drug crimes of considerable weight, while trying to make sure she wasn't charged with murder. That was the theme. Of course, she had been neck-deep in a criminal enterprise that had resulted in people dying, so she might get charged anyway. That was probably why she was trying to be as helpful as possible. That said, so far she hadn't shed any light on the case Willie was working.

Willie cleared his throat and Camp glanced at him. Willie stood at the end of the interrogation table. "What did you, Víctor or Oscar have to do with the disappearance of Ernesto Pérez?"

Dusty flinched and turned towards him. "We didn't have nothing to do with that Pérez man."

"Pérez complained to Víctor about heroin being smuggled at the same time people were being smuggled, which put them in danger, and that's why Ernesto was eliminated. That's the information I have."

She shook her head hard. "That never happened at all. Pérez complained to Víctor 'bout some girl he had smuggled. He didn't know nothin' about the heroin. Whoever told you that was talkin' shit. That never happened."

"And Andrés Colón, the friend of Pérez' found dead on the side of the road?"

"I never even heard of him." She poked her chest with a finger. "Listen, what happened to me is bad enough. Marcus, Víctor and Oscar are all dead. But you can't connect me with every dead person around here. You can't pin *everything* on me."

Willie didn't believe for a moment that Dusty herself had harmed Ernesto Pérez or Andrés Colón. And if one of her male accomplices—Víctor, Marcus or Oscar—had done it, she had no reason to protect him now. They were all dead. She was winding down, and he left it at that.

Camp had the female deputies take Dusty Powell to a cell.

He turned to Willie. "My God, what has this county come to?"

"I'd say you have a problem."

"This is what happens when the people who run the county decide they don't have to follow the same laws as everybody else in the state and the country. Who do you think you're going to attract?"

"Other criminals," Willie said.

"Exactly. Once you tell the world that you don't want the federal government in your county, you're telling them they don't have to worry about the Drug Enforcement Administration. In the case of Quincy Vetter and his clones here, they've also turned down state help of any kind, so we don't have the Florida Department of Law Enforcement keeping track of what's happening here."

"And when the migrant workers who are being used to carry drugs, or who find out about it, are afraid to approach the local authorities, you have the perfect storm," Willie said.

"Bull's-eye."

Camp got to his feet. "I still need to depose you, but it will have to wait."

"I assume you need to pay a visit to Narciso Cruz."

"Yes."

"I'm with you."

***

Camp and Willie pulled up to Narciso Cruz's mansion in the Bountiful Harvest Estates with Williams and Donaldson in a cruiser behind them. Camp had dispatched two other deputies he trusted to guard against any escape from the rear of Cruz's spacious spread. In the end, it wasn't at all necessary.

The tall wrought iron gates out front were wide open. The two sheriff's cars drove right in. Willie saw Cruz's gold Escalade parked near the front door, its back hatch open and suitcases piled inside. The two cages that held the macaws were in the back seat. They were both squawking, not all that happy about going anywhere. A smaller car, an aging Honda, was parked behind the Escalade. Cruz's maid, not in uniform, was loading a battered suitcase into it. Camp and Willie approached her.

"What's going on here?" Camp asked.

"Mr. Cruz, he's leaving. He says he is closing the house and going back to Mexico. Me, I have to find another job."

"Is Mr. Cruz here?"

She pointed at the second floor.

Camp and Willie let themselves in and climbed the wide spiral staircase. Camp pulled his gun just in case Cruz took exception to having his escape interrupted. They reached the second floor and heard voices at the end of the long hallway. When they arrived at the master bedroom, they saw big Narciso Cruz with a man who appeared to be his gardener. Cruz was giving the other man instructions about what to carry down to the car. Beyond them, Willie saw a large, circular bed with a mirror attached to the ceiling above and bright red shag carpeting beneath it. Cruz had established quite a love nest for himself. For a fat man, he apparently saw himself as quite a Lothario.

He glanced over at them, then down at Camp's gun and went right on packing.

"Going somewhere, Narciso?" Camp asked.

"That's right. I'm going back to Mexico. I'm getting out of here."

Camp lowered his gun. "Just why is that?"

"Why? I'll tell you why . . . " He was folding a very large flowered shirt. "Because my life has been threatened, that's why."

"Threatened by who?"

"By Quincy Vetter, that's who. He accused me of being a heroin smuggler, said that I should be shot. If I stayed around, he would be glad to do it."

He tossed the shirt into an open suitcase and roughly grabbed another one as if he were strangling a man wearing it.

"He wouldn't listen to me. I told him the same thing I told both of you: I've never had anything to do with drugs of any kind. Víctor was involved in that without me knowing nothing. I'm not so stupid that I would screw up the business I had. I had a good thing. Quincy, he's known me for years. He knows I'm not stupid, but he wouldn't listen. Before I end up with a bullet in my back, I'm leaving."

Willie stepped out from behind Camp. "You still insist that Ernesto Pérez didn't come to you or Víctor to complain about workers being used as drug mules?"

Cruz's big yellow teeth flashed in a grimace. "I told you I knew nothing about the drugs; not from Víctor, not from Ernesto, not from anybody."

"Still, I don't think I can let you go anywhere, Narciso," Camp said.

The fat man growled. "What do you mean you won't let me go? I haven't done anything against the law."

He stopped himself. Of course, what he had been doing for a living for years—smuggling humans—*was* against the law. The fact that the local police hadn't enforced that particular law, the fact that the powers that be in Cane County counted on Narciso to break that law, didn't alter the fact that smuggling workers into the country was a crime.

"I'm investigating several homicides, Narciso. I'll need you here until I finish," Camp said. "Meanwhile, I can ensure that you won't be shot by anyone, and I'll do it by holding you in my jail. I'm arresting you on suspicion of human trafficking."

He holstered his gun, took a set of handcuffs off his belt and held them up. Narciso was clearly stunned by the news, but maybe also by the irony of it all. He was being arrested for a crime that everyone for miles around had wanted him to commit and he was being told that being arrested for it would save his life. Williams and Donaldson had climbed the stairs and stood behind Willie. Narciso stared at the cuffs for several seconds, but it was clear his choices were limited. He held out his fat wrists.

Once they were all downstairs, Narciso asked the maid to move back in.

"Somebody has to take care of the birds until I can come back for them."

The maid was in the process of unloading her Honda when they pulled away, with Narciso crammed into the backseat of Camp's cruiser. Back at the station, Williams and Donaldson ushered the fat man inside to be booked. Camp and Willie watched them go.

"Do you believe him, that he knew nothing about the heroin?" Willie asked

Camp shrugged. "I've told you from the beginning that I didn't think he was involved. Like he says, he had it good. I still don't believe he'd be so stupid. How 'bout you? Do you believe him?"

Willie made a face. "Problem is I do. I believe both him and Dusty. If Dusty knows what happened to Ernesto, she has no reason to conceal it. She could easily rat out one of her dead partners in crime. And I trust your instincts on Cruz. My own instincts are telling me the same thing. If they are both telling the truth, then Ernesto Pérez didn't run afoul of the heroin ring. Something else happened to him. But what?"

Camp simply shook his head.

A question occurred to Willie that he'd been meaning to ask for a day. "You said some time back you were contacted by the Mexican Consulate in Miami about missing workers up here."

"That's right."

"Can you remember who reached out to you?"

"Not off hand, but I can find out."

Willie followed Camp into his office, where the big man sat at his computer, typed, and eventually pulled up a file.

"Here it is. His name is John Acosta, attorney for the Consulate General of Mexico. There's a number here."

He swiveled the screen so Willie could copy it.

"I'll still need a statement from you on the Blanco business. Might as well do it now," he said, placing his tape recorder on the desk.

A half hour later they were done. Willie headed back to the Planters Inn to change his clothes yet again. He was still soaked with sugar water and had to move quick before the ants got to him.

CHAPTER TWENTY-SIX

Willie showered, washing the rest of the sugar off, got dressed, sat on the bed and dialed the number he had for John Acosta. A woman answered, identified herself as his secretary and told him the consulate's attorney was out of the building and would not be back until the next day. She asked what the call was about.

"I'm calling from Cane County in central Florida," Willie said. "I understand that sometime back Mr. Acosta was looking for Mexican nationals missing up here in farm country. Can you tell him I'm a private investigator and I believe at least two more have disappeared in the last few months? It may be more than that. Can you contact him and ask that he get back to me as soon as possible? It's very important."

She took his number and said she would do her best. Next, he dialed Fanny.

"Cohen here."

"It's me."

"Are you driving?"

"No."

"Okay. Neither am I. I'll call you right back for some face time."

This was Fanny's newest thing. Her granddaughters had turned her onto face-to-face phone conversations and, since she considered Willie an adopted son, she insisted on using it with him when possible. A few seconds later, his phone sounded, and he was staring at Fanny. He saw that she was out for exercise, walking down the beach near her house. Off to one side, the jade sea stretched towards the horizon, and he could hear the surf whispering near her.

She grunted into the phone. "It took you long enough to get in touch. I was starting to think they had planted you up there after all."

"Almost. It wasn't for lack of trying."

She sat down on the sand, seaside hotels and other beach denizens visible behind her. A sea breeze licked at her wavy hair.

"Do tell."

"I don't have time to run the full synopsis for you, but you were right about the labor smugglers here also moving drugs. One of them was doing exactly that. In this case it was heroin."

She whistled. "No kiddin'. It's like I told you, the economics are irresistible. Especially heroin or cocaine. High markup, and they're nice and light. The potential profit is hard to resist."

"Well, it was certainly hard for this smuggler. But that apparently has nothing to do with the Mexican man I'm looking for."

That caught her by surprise. "He had no knowledge of the drug smuggling?"

"No. Not that I can find."

She swept wind-driven hair from her face.

"Of course, it could all have to do with those sovereign citizens you were telling me about the other day. I've been thinking about them. A lot of those folks are worried sick—I mean sick—that the country is being taken over by people whose skin is darker than theirs. The changing demographics and all. You follow me?"

"Uh-huh."

"God only knows what they're afraid of. Maybe they think 'what goes around comes around,' that blacks and Latinos are going to take their revenge against the white folks for all those years of prejudice. As if black and brown folks haven't had enough trouble already. But that fear is out there. These kinda guys see themselves as General Custers surrounded by the dark-skinned enemy. Consequently, that ain't a good place for you to be, Mr. Cuesta, especially alone. I should have gone with you."

"You couldn't miss the violin concert."

"It was last night, and shock of all shocks, my granddaughter is not the next Itzhak Perlman. Don't try to distract me. You don't need to be on Maggie's farm no more, as a songsmith once put it."

"Yes, believe me. I get it. But I have to do the job I was hired to do before the attorney who hired me gives me the hook. One, I have a professional reputation to protect. And, two, I want to find the man who's missing. I need to know what happened to him. There are a couple more leads I'm looking into."

He told her about the call he'd just placed to the Mexican Consulate and the search a couple of years back for missing workers.

"That trail seems a tad cold," she said, just as a wave crashed nearby. "What else you working?"

"A woman's name—Carlotta."

He told her of the late-night phone call received by the late Andrés Colón.

"Who the hell is Carlotta?"

"Nobody seems to know. The widow says Colón didn't know anybody by that name."

"Well, if anybody can find her it's you. You do have a way with women. Find what you need to find and get out of there quick before those citizens get sovereign with you."

Speaking of ladies, one well-tanned example in a very sparse bikini passed behind her. Willie watched her sway by.

"I can see you, Willie boy," Fanny barked. "Keep your mind on your work."

"I will, *mamita*."

She waved goodbye, they disconnected and Willie stayed gazing into the silence. Apart from the name Carlotta, he did have one other lead he hadn't followed. The image that kept returning to him was that of Ricardo Ramírez being dragged into a BioMaster truck. Then there was the threat Narciso Cruz had reported. Had Vetter threatened the fat man in order to make him run, to make Cruz look guilty of all the recent mayhem? Had Vetter tried to fool Cruz into attracting all the law enforcement attention in order to keep it off of himself? Willie had a lot to ask the exterminator—the BioMaster.

***

He pulled up to Vetter's offices on the state road in the middle of town. Pasted to the glass front door was the decal of the Sovereign Rights Movement. At this point in the case, the crossed rifles seemed like less of a political statement and more of an out-and-out threat.

The front door was open, but it was just after five o'clock, and he found no one on duty. A desk near the entrance was unattended.

Several glass-walled offices at the rear were empty. He stopped and looked around. The place apparently served as BioMaster's corporate offices as well as a retail outlet. Posters for the company's products decorated the walls all around. They depicted different species of bugs, all much bigger than life size, which made them look like large, extremely dangerous prehistoric creatures. Brightly colored arrows representing the attacking BioMaster chemicals swept across the posters to obliterate the different pests. It all reminded Willie of some Japanese horror flick, like the original *Godzilla*.

Willie heard a toilet flush. Quincy Vetter stepped from a door in the corner, drying his hands on a paper towel. In shirt sleeves, he still wore his gun on his hip. He noticed Willie and frowned at first, then made an unsuccessful attempt at a smile.

"Looking for me, Mr. Cuesta?"

"Yes, I am."

"I was just about to leave, but I guess I can give you a few minutes."

He led Willie into the large corner office, and they sat facing each other across his desk. Behind him hung the obligatory calendar, this one graced by what appeared to be a boll weevil, or some such evil looking creature. Its beady eyes stared out at Willie as if it were gazing at a cotton bush—like it wanted to eat him.

"I understand the disappearance that brought you to Cane County has been solved," Vetter said. "You're probably heading back home to Miami."

Willie cocked his head. "No, not quite. I won't be heading back to all those New York people just yet."

Vetter frowned. "But I thought these individuals involved in heroin smuggling were responsible for the disappearance of the Mexican man."

"Apparently not. The one accused person still here, Dusty Powell, says Ernesto Pérez never knew about that little enterprise of theirs. Or if he did, he never mentioned it to any of them. They had no reason to do him harm."

Vetter smirked. "You believe her? A heroin dealer? Probably trying to save her own skin."

"To tell you the truth, I do believe her." Willie explained how Dusty could have implicated her dead colleagues but didn't. "She insists she knows nothing about it."

Vetter blinked through his Coke-bottle glasses.

"Well then, how about our long-time neighbor and labor smuggler Narciso Cruz? Don't tell me that scrawny coyote you found dead was smuggling heroin without his boss knowing. I just don't believe that. I'm told Rory Camp arrested Cruz just before he could skip town."

Vetter was showing off how plugged in he was. Cruz had just been arrested, and he already knew.

"Yes, that's true, but I don't believe he was leaving town because he was a heroin smuggler. If that were so, he would have been gone the moment Dusty Powell's house was raided, before Víctor Coyote got crucified in that cornfield. No, I think Narciso headed for the hills because you, the head of the Sovereign Rights Movement in this county, threatened his life."

Vetter's gaze narrowed. "Is that what he told you, Mr. Cuesta?"

"Yes, it is."

"Well, that's another lie you have swallowed whole. I didn't threaten him at all."

Of course, it was Vetter's word against Cruz's. The county commission chairman against a known criminal. Frankly, Willie found the human trafficker more trustworthy than the politician sitting in front of him.

Just then, Vetter's cellphone sounded. He checked the screen, answered and listened briefly, all the while his gaze fixed on Willie.

"Yes, that's just fine. Don't worry . . . I have that under control."

He disconnected.

"As I said, Mr. Cuesta, Cruz lied to you. I kill insects, not people."

"That may be, Mr. Vetter, but I've been told of another incident involving another missing worker that I have no explanation for."

"What incident is that, pray tell?"

Willie repeated the account he had been told of Ricardo Ramírez being dragged into a pickup truck in Sawgrass.

Quincy Vetter squinted hard at him from his hatchet face. "Why would that interest me?"

"Because I was told it was a BioMaster truck he was dragged into that took him away."

Vetter removed the glasses from his face, revealing flush indentations on each side of his narrow nose, pulled a large blue bandanna from a pants pocket, polished the lenses and replaced them. Of course his seeing Willie clearly was not the issue, but remaining absolutely calm while being pressured by an invasive insect was the issue.

"To begin with, Mr. Cuesta, I have no idea who Ricardo Ramírez is. No one by that name works for BioMaster, of that I'm sure. I lease lots of land to tomato companies. In the course of the agricultural year, many people work on that land. But I don't manage those workers. Even if he had been employed by me, I still see no reason anyone in authority from my firm would have acted in that manner. Any such incident would have certainly been reported to me. I have never heard of the man or the incident."

"Nonetheless, workers in one of your trucks were observed doing just that."

Vetter assumed a patronizing gaze. "When did this allegedly happen?"

"Two days ago?"

"Did your alleged witnesses get a license tag number on the truck?"

"No, not that I know of. It happened quickly."

"Did they give you names of the men who conducted this alleged kidnapping?"

Willie shook his head. "No, the man who saw it said he didn't recognize the three men who manhandled Ramírez."

Vetter's scowl deepened. "So, it was only one person who saw this happen. Well, I propose to you he either made a mistake or made it up for some reason. People exist in this world who are small, powerless, and they attack the reputations of other individuals. And you have not explained, Mr. Cuesta, why any of my employees would be doing what you are suggesting they did." He stopped and stroked his chin theatrically. "Let's see . . . How much do you think kidnappers could demand in ransom for a farm worker? One hundred dollars? Maybe two, with a sack of beans thrown in for the bargain?"

Vetter's thin lips curled into a cramped version of a smile. Willie decided that Vetter had sat still for the interview simply to find out what Willie knew and didn't know about what was going on in Cane County. He was trying to determine just how dangerous Willie might be to him. So far, he didn't find him dangerous at all.

"Homer Eccles tells me that you believe something criminal happened to this man you're searching for," Vetter said.

"Ernesto Pérez."

"Yes, that's the name. Now you're talking about a kind of kidnapping in broad daylight in a small farm town, Sawgrass. This isn't Miami, Mr. Cuesta. We don't have the kind of crime you have in the metropolis."

Willie studied the man. He had expected more bluster, more ideology from the strongman, not this methodical cross examination. He had been preparing for a political extremist and instead got a prosecutor painstakingly trying to trip up a witness. Quincy Vetter was making it very difficult to read him, so Willie decided to poke him a bit.

"Yes, Cane County is clearly different from Miami. Here, you simply write your own rules. You secede from the state. You know there are people in this county who believe you've gone crazy."

Vetter's steely gaze hardened, and his tone grew more grave. He bit off his words. "To begin with, these aren't my rules. These were the laws of this land before outsiders—like you—started meddling in our business."

"Outsiders like the state and federal government? You don't think that's just a bit extreme here in the 21st century?"

"No, I don't. The theft of our freedoms proceeds day after day and will lead to our eventual enslavement."

"Like the freedom to walk around with a gun on your hip as if you're Jesse James."

Vetter's hand traveled to his belt just next to his handgun. "Our Second Amendment rights have already been ransacked by the government. Here we have simply returned to the original law of this land—home rule. It is our God-given right to defend ourselves, especially against government usurpers."

"All the government wants is a useless scrap of land and all they want to do is flood it with water. They aren't planning to build a nuclear power plant next door."

Vetter sniffed. "That's the way it begins. The next thing you know they find a reason to take your fields. If you resist, they render you harmless, which is another way of saying they shoot you down. Remember Ruby Ridge, the Branch Davidians in Waco and the Oregon wildlife refuge."

These were all places out west where local extremists had tangled with federal law enforcement. People had died.

Vetter slapped his holster. "That's why we go armed around here."

Willie rolled his eyes. "Mr. Vetter, these days, if the government decides to take you out, that pop gun you're wearing won't do you any good. Some technician at the nearest Army base will type a few codes into a computer and a smart bomb will hit you right in the belt buckle. You won't scare him much."

Vetter's hand moved away from his belt buckle onto his desk, He leaned back. "The good residents of Cane County support me and the policies of the Sovereign Rights Movement. We need to protect our heritage, our culture, our way of life. Our *bloodlines,* Mr. Cuesta."

"Yes, you certainly don't want Hispanics polluting your precious bloodlines, including outside invaders like me." Willie's mind skipped for a moment to EJ Eccles, who seemed to like his blood type just fine, but he didn't mention that.

Vetter simply smiled.

Again, Willie sensed he was being played with. Vetter was giving him the sovereign rights spiel, the same one he probably used with his fellow Cane County citizens. But something in that smile made Willie wonder if Vetter believed it all himself. From the beginning, something in Vetter's eyes had told Willie that the man was just a bit too smart to swallow that manure. Willie suddenly got the sense that the whole town had been turned into some kind of anti-government roadside attraction. But why would you take the place in such a crazed direction if you didn't believe it yourself? Was it simply a small-town power trip? He didn't know, and in the end he didn't care. He only cared about his case.

"What happened to Ernesto Pérez, Mr. Vetter?"

"I can't tell you that, Mr. Cuesta."

"Are you saying you don't know, or you choose *not* to tell me?" Vetter didn't answer. He fixed on Willie with a dead-eyed stare through the microscopes he wore for glasses and didn't bat an eye.

Willie had grown tired of the game. He stood up and headed for the door—before Vetter tried to spray him with something.

CHAPTER TWENTY-SEVEN

Willie drove out of range of Quincy Vetter and called the kid. It was already growing dark, and the crews would be in from the fields. When he dialed the cell, instead of ringing it went straight to voicemail. That was unusual. Pedro always had his phone on and almost always answered it right away. He dialed it again and the same thing happened.

Maybe it was nothing. Maybe the phone had just gone dead, but after the meeting with Vetter, Willie was on edge. He had been careful to not be seen with the kid, but Pedro was on his own most of the day, poking around, trying to find out what happened to his father. Willie's stay in Cane County was coming to a close soon and he couldn't afford to let anything happen to him now.

He stepped on it, drove to the worker cabins, pulled up to Pedro's unit and knocked on the door. No one answered, so he tried the knob. No luck. One worker sat outside the cabin next door. Just back in from the fields, his clothes were sweat-soaked, grimy, and he sipped from a water bottle. Willie spoke to him in Spanish.

"Is Pedro Pérez here?"

He shook his head. "No, he's not here. They offered him over-time work, and he went off to do it."

"Who offered him this work? Where did he go?"

The other guy shrugged. "Three Americans, local men, came. He got into a pickup truck, and they drove off."

"When did they come?"

"Just a few minutes ago."

Willie scowled. "Did you recognize them?"

The man sipped from his bottle and shook his head.

"Did you get a good look at the pickup truck? Was it green, from BioMaster, the chemical company?"

"No, it was a black truck. I didn't see a name on it."

Willie thought of the truck that had followed him and also the one Merton Vetter had driven. Maybe it was the same truck and maybe this was too. The three white men matched the general description of the team that had kidnapped Ricardo Ramírez up in Sawgrass.

Maybe Willie had been careless and was followed during one of his meetings with the kid. He winced as if he'd been stabbed in the stomach.

"If Pedro comes back, tell him to call Cuesta. Remember, Cuesta."

He didn't leave him a business card. When people carrying your card kept showing up dead, you got skittish about handing them out.

Willie climbed back in his car and started into town, his head spinning. He had just said to the man, *if* Pedro comes back, not when. He was already thinking the worst. He slammed the palm of his hand hard against the steering wheel. He was in Cane County with one basic task—to bring back the kid safe and sound. Now, Pedro might be in the hands of those who had killed his father.

What he couldn't understand was why the kid got in the truck. He knew Ricardo Ramírez had disappeared in just that way, a pickup truck manned by unknown locals. Maybe Pedro thought it was the only way to find out what had happened to his father. Pedro was a smart kid, but he had lost patience. Now, he would disappear just as Ernesto had. Willie saw the face of Cecilia Pérez, who had put her hopes in him. His hands tightened on the steering wheel as if he would tear it right out the car.

Willie's internal barometer had dropped to a dangerous, unstable level. He found himself speeding back in the direction of the Bio-Master offices. What he pictured was barging back in there, grabbing Quincy Vetter by the hair, shoving his pistol into the exterminator's mouth and demanding to know where the kid was. Of course, Vetter wouldn't take kindly to that, and Willie very well could get himself shot. But he was in hurricane mode, and such small concerns didn't register.

He was almost there when his cell rang. He glanced at the screen and saw the kid's number. Maybe his killers were calling to taunt Willie.

"It's me," Pedro said before Willie could speak.

Willie pulled to the side of the road and skidded to a stop on gravel. "Where the hell are you!"

He was shouting. The kid answered him in an urgent whisper. "Some guys came to the cabins to kidnap me."

"Yes, I know. I was just there. Where are you now?"

"I'm hiding in the bushes just past the Indian's place. I need you to come get me."

Willie slammed the car into gear. "I'll be there."

Two minutes later, he pulled up to the overgrown field just beyond the casino. Through the windows of the place, lights flashed and bells rang. Someone in there had gotten lucky, and Willie hoped good fortune smiled on him too. Pedro saw him and ran from the bushes to the car. Willie had him lie down in the backseat. He had lost his hat and his face was scratched, maybe from where he had thrown himself into the bushes.

"What the hell happened?"

"These three guys came to get me. They said it was to do extra work on Eccles Farm, but I've never seen them before. I knew they wanted to kidnap me, so I played dumb. I told them I needed the extra money and jumped right into the back of the pickup with my bucket. One of them got back there with me. I smiled at him a lot, like a complete fool. As we were cutting through town, the truck slowed down to make a turn. I waited, threw the bucket at him, jumped out, ran behind the buildings, through alleyways, and kept running. They were shouting, and the truck came after me. I made some turns and headed here. They never saw me, but they drove by here twice trying to find me, so we better get off the road fast."

Willie stepped on it, trying to figure out where he could stash the kid. He couldn't take him to the inn because that would certainly be a place the pursuers would look. He rummaged through his three days of contacts since arriving in Cane City. Then his eyes settled on the steeple of St. Anthony's Church, clearly visible behind the other buildings. Willie headed for it.

They pulled into the parking lot of the church. Willie saw the door open. He hustled the kid inside and found a handful of people, mostly older women, sitting or kneeling in the pews as if Mass were about to begin. The priest, now wearing vestments, stood near the altar. Willie waved at him, and Father Finlay descended the steps to the altar rail.

"I need a favor, Father."

He explained that Pedro was Ernesto Pérez's son, how he'd come from Mexico to find his father and the danger he was now in. The priest's face looked as if he'd just heard a very serious sin in the confessional.

"So, he needs sanctuary."

"That's right, father. Sheriff's deputies may even come searching for him. Can you protect him from them? Can you give him that sanctuary?"

The priest took Pedro by the arm. "Don't worry. Nothing will happen to him here with me."

Willie told Pedro he would be back for him. The kid, at least momentarily convinced of the danger he was in, didn't argue. Willie hurried out of the church, the women all watching him and wondering who he might be.

He climbed back into the car and sat stock still trying to figure out what to do. He could confront Vetter as he had impulsively set off to do. But hat would accomplish nothing other than possibly getting himself shot. He wondered if the call Vetter had received while Willie sat in front of him was about kidnapping Pedro. Vetter had responded cryptically to whoever was on the other end. Willie had no way of knowing what the call concerned, at least not yet he didn't.

Willie had kept Pedro from becoming yet another migrant who simply disappeared. Still, he didn't understand what was going on around him. Why would local agro-thugs be kidnapping Mexicans in broad daylight? What was the connection between them and the political madness that permeated Cane County?

He sat, staring at the lighted cross on top of the church steeple. Then the saints smiled on him. His cellphone sounded, he saw a Miami number he didn't recognize and answered. In the background he heard raucous voices and loud music. A man yelled on the phone:

"This is John Acosta speaking. I received a message that it was urgent to call you."

Willie yelled too. "Yes, Mr. Acosta. This is Willie Cuesta. I'm calling from Cane County."

Acosta asked him to hold on a moment. The attorney apparently moved to a different room because the other voices were no longer audible and the music was faint. His own voice was loud and precise, like most lawyers Willie had met.

"Excuse me, I'm at a bachelor party. I understand you have information on missing Mexican nationals up there, Mr. Cuesta."

Willie stared out the windshield at the lighted cross on the steeple. "That's right. Their names are Ernesto Pérez and Ricardo Ramírez. And there may be more. I can email you the contacts for Pérez's family and the details of his disappearance. I don't have much on Ramírez."

"Okay, please do. I'm very interested."

"I'm told this may not be a new problem around here."

"No, it isn't. Over the years, we've had numerous Mexican men go missing in Florida, some of them who worked harvesting crops. They disappeared from different places, but the one locale where workers more than any other were last seen was Cane County."

"How did you determine that?"

"By speaking to other workers who knew them. One day they were working the harvest in Cane County, then the harvest moved north to the tomato fields or citrus groves in another county, but certain men didn't show up."

"Did you get anywhere tracking them?"

"We stumbled over a few of them because people happened to recognize their photos. Those workers were perfectly fine. They had just decided to head off in another direction for another harvest. But we made no headway with most of them. Since the men use false names, Social Security numbers and green cards to work, we couldn't connect them to employers through their real identities."

Willie nodded at the attorney who was two hundred miles away. That was what Camp had said. The whole informal labor system on which US agriculture and the food supply depended, including the tacitly accepted use of false documents, had made it impossible to find the missing men.

Acosta continued. "We went around with photos of those other men. We couldn't find growers who could remember employing them. Maybe they were telling the truth, or maybe they were just afraid to admit they had employed workers with false papers."

"How many were you searching for at the time?"

"We had about thirty names altogether on the original list. As I said, we found a handful. The other two dozen had disappeared. Their families have never heard from them. And I'll tell you something interesting we found along the way." He hesitated. "Actually, it's much more frightening than interesting."

"What was that?"

"A couple of years before that, some other men had gone missing, but they weren't Mexican migrant workers."

"Who were they?"

"They were homeless men who had been recruited from homeless shelters in places like Tampa and West Palm Beach, recruited to harvest crops. Many of them were black. A handful of particularly bad growers went in there and offered them food, shelter and paid work. It turned out that they paid those men not in money, but in booze, drugs. Almost all of them had substance abuse problems. That was why they were on the street to begin with. The growers charged them more for the alcohol and pills than they made working and kept them there perpetually paying back their debts."

Willie's gaze narrowed. It was the old indentured servant con, practiced in the South, in one incarnation or another, for many years. It occurred to Willie that homeless men, like migrant workers, were hard to keep track of and easy to get rid of.

"Some social workers found out about it and blew the whistle," Acosta said. "But some of those men were never heard from again either. Their families are still looking for them."

"And, again, the growers didn't admit to employing them?"

"Exactly. I'm told the social workers went to the suspect farms in several counties with photos, just as I did in the case of the Mexicans, but they got nowhere."

"Can you remember what farms you went to in Cane County?"

"I went to a few. I remember one in particular because workers mentioned it as a place where some of the missing men had worked and that the owner was a mean son of a bitch."

"Who was that?"

Acosta hesitated. "It's been a long . . . "

"Was it Vetter?"

The other man reacted excitedly. "*Exactly!* His name was Merton Vetter. He denied he had employed any of them and there was nothing else I could do. Let me tell you, that's one mean old cuss."

Willie froze. The cross on the steeple went out of focus as he stared into the distance. It was as if he was trying to mentally track Merton Vetter, wherever he might be at the moment.

Acosta brought him out of his silence. "You there?"

"Yes. Listen, you need to get up here. Someone tried to kidnap another of your Mexican nationals today. He managed to escape, and I have him hidden, but who knows what else could happen. You need to bring the FBI with you. Other matters are going on here that the FBI needs to investigate."

"I'll call my contact at the bureau first thing tomorrow."

"Better yet, call him now and be here by morning. It's *that* urgent."

Acosta hesitated. "I guess I'll miss my lap dance. I'm on my way."

CHAPTER TWENTY-EIGHT

Through the screened front door of the brown stucco house came the sound of a television playing a sitcom with a laugh track. Several kids cackled and added their comments, speaking over each other. It was all loud enough that nobody heard Willie's knock, so he knocked again.

He turned, glanced at the high school football field directly across the street and then back. He was about to try again when a black boy about five years old, dressed in a faded green Nike t-shirt, came to the door and gave him a quizzical look.

"Is your mother here, son?"

The kid stayed fixed on him but shouted over his shoulder. "Mama, there's a man here."

Beyond him, Willie saw three other kids scattered on the floor and the sofa, ranging in age from about seven to fifteen. The furniture around them was worn and had never been fancy, but the place was well kept.

Loretta Turk emerged, still dressed in her work clothes, now partly covered by a long, bright pink apron. She was drying her hands on a dish towel and wasn't happy to see him.

"What are you doin' here? At my *house?*"

Her son stayed next to her, clutching at the apron, staring at Willie.

"I need to ask you some questions on a certain matter."

"Don't you think you already asked me enough questions? I don't know nothin' about Dusty Powell, except what I told you. And I don't know where that man Ernesto disappeared to."

"My questions aren't about them. They are about some black men who disappeared from around here a few years back."

Those words penetrated her aggressive attitude. Willie could see them touch thoughts behind Loretta Turk's tough veneer. She knew, or at least suspected, what Willie was talking about. She studied him for a few beats in silence.

Willie looked beyond her at the kids and then back. "We probably shouldn't have this discussion in front of the children."

She pointed over his shoulder. "Meet me over there on the field. I'll be a few minutes."

Willie crossed the street, walked through an open chain link gate and passed under a scoreboard that read: "Cane County High School Fighting Gators." He sat in the first row of bleachers at about the forty-yard line. Over the stands on the other side of the field, he could see black smoke billowing into the air, somewhere in the distance where a farmer was burning off a field. He thought of Andrés Colón's soot-covered face. Andrés Colón who was now dead.

Loretta Turk, sans apron, lumbered into sight and sat down next to him. They stared out at the empty field as if they were watching ghosts play a game. Willie was there to talk to her about ghosts, but not the football playing variety.

"So why are you comin' to my house to talk about somethin' that happened years ago?" she asked

"Because I have at least one Mexican worker dead, two more missing—possibly dead—and just a while ago someone tried to kidnap another one living at the worker cabins. In fact, the one they tried to snatch was one of your workers on Eccles Farm. You didn't send anyone over there looking for workers to do overtime, did you?"

"No, I didn't. I don't know nothin' about all this."

"I'm not saying you had anything to do with any of it. I don't believe you did, but I was just told that other workers have disappeared from around here, and they weren't Mexican. They were black. I thought you might have some information about all that."

The look on her face was both angry and wary. She gazed back out at the ghosts playing football, or maybe at the ghosts Willie was asking about. She seemed to be trying to make up her mind, so Willie gave her a nudge.

"Ms. Turk, the Mexican Consulate in Miami is sending someone here to investigate all this. That person is bringing the FBI, and that could lead to immigration agents invading here as well. I think we both know that would make your workers scatter to the four winds. That wouldn't be good for you." She turned on him. "You don't need to strong arm me, mister investigator. I know all this needs to come out. I was just trying to remember when all that happened."

She took a deep breath, let it out and talked of the ghosts.

"It was about three years ago that I first found out, but it was goin' on for at least a couple of years before that. Growers were havin' trouble findin' and keepin' Mexican workers, because they didn't know how to treat those workers. Then I started hearin' that local folks had seen black men on those farms, black men they didn't recognize. Strange thing was, you never saw them in town—not in the grocery stores, not in the laundromats. Nowhere. You always see workers on the street here in their off hours, takin' care of their needs, but not those men. Some farms around here are pretty isolated. I got curious, so I went to see what was goin' on."

"You made contact with those men?"

She nodded. "I went over to a couple of different farms at night. I drove over to one farm in my truck, turned the lights off, kept a low profile. I found some old beat-up trailers set up there in a circle. I mean really old, ratty trailers. The men were livin' in those trailers, if you can call that livin'. There were at least a half-dozen of them to a small trailer, all sleepin' on dirty old mattresses on the floor— no sheets, just crummy, dirty blankets. The places were crawlin' with fleas and cockroaches."

She shook her head in disgust. "The trailers had no workin' kitchens, just Sterno stoves, and all they were gettin' to eat was canned food. Beans, spaghetti, that kind of crap. The places smelled to high heaven. But most of those men didn't pay their livin' conditions any mind."

The memory astounded her still, that was obvious.

"They didn't mind because they were high or drunk or both," Willie said.

"Uh-huh. You know about this, then. Those men had been livin' in homeless shelters over near the coast. They were alcoholics, drug addicts and they were paid in liquor and pills. I told them I was going to notify somebody in government, but they said not to. They were afraid they would get in trouble for the drugs."

"So, what did you do?"

"I went to Social Services anyway, and it was investigated. The growers claimed those workers were makin' up the part 'bout being paid in alcohol and the drugs. They said the workers had bought those substances themselves and were lyin' 'bout it."

"And the investigators believed that?"

She shrugged. "Nobody around here was goin' to act against a local grower based on the word of some addicts from out of town. There were no criminal charges, but the worker camps were broken up. Before they left town, though, some of those men told the Social Service investigators somin' else."

"What was that?"

"They said that over the past few years some of the workers in those camps had plumb disappeared. They were gone from the camps, from one day to the next, and they never showed up back at the homeless shelters where they lived in the first place. Some of them had still been in touch with family members, but that contact stopped, too."

"What did the investigators do about that?"

"What could they do? These were homeless men, shiftless, addicted men. They could have headed off anywhere. The investigators asked the growers if they knew the whereabouts of these men. They said they didn't. So, they dropped the whole matter."

The decision not to pursue the investigation had obviously left a bad taste in the mouth of Ms. Turk.

"Who were these growers that recruited in the homeless shelters?"

She pointed off into the distance above the bleachers.

"One was an old boy named Yulie Nolan. He died a couple of years ago."

"Anyone else?"

"The other was Merton Vetter, Quincy's poppa."

They both sat in silence. Willie's cellphone vibrated. He saw EJ Eccless' phone number on the screen.

He turned back to Loretta. "Do you have any idea what might have happened to those men who went missing?"

She fixed on him. "What happened to them is the same thing that happened to the Mexican men you're lookin' for. That's what I think. I hope you find out what that was . . . before it happens to you, too."

Loretta stood up.

"Don't come to my house anymore. I have nothin' left to say."

She turned and walked back, leaving him alone with all the ghosts.

CHAPTER TWENTY-NINE

B y the time Willie got back into his car and took out his phone, the sun had set. Aside from the call from EJ, he found a voicemail from Camp that had been left an hour earlier.

"The sheriff just called me. He told me to go to West Palm Beach and pick up a prisoner they're holding for us. Don't ask me why he's sending me, a captain. I don't like it, but it's his call. I won't be back until sometime tomorrow. Keep your head down, be careful."

Willie didn't like it either. He felt Quincy Vetter's hand involved in it.

He pressed EJ's number. The first thing he had to tell her was that the recreational aspect of his time in Cane City had come to a close. Any contact with him could be dangerous for her. It was unfortunate, given how gorgeous she was, but it had to be. As it turned out, that wasn't what she had in mind. She picked up on the first ring.

"I need to see you right away," she said. "Quincy Vetter just came to see my father. He said you had been to his office. He was angry and talked about a lot of things. They didn't know I was there, or maybe Quincy just didn't care, I overheard some stuff you need to know."

He had just told himself he had to stay away from her.

"Tell me now, over the phone."

"No, I can't. I'm still in the house. I need to see you, but it can't be at the inn. Vetter knows about my being there with you. Meet me behind the abandoned gas station north of the Seminole Outpost."

Willie figured that was isolated enough to see anyone approaching. "Okay. I'm heading there now."

* * *

EJ was already there when Willie pulled up, her car tucked behind the station, lights off. He doused off his own lights and she got in with him.

"Okay, tell me what went on with Vetter," he said.

"First of all, he knows that you and I spent time together at the inn . . . in private. He told my father that. I was in the next room and overheard all of it."

"How does he know that?"

"I don't know how he knows. Maybe Iris does some spying for him. Maybe he had somebody following you and watching the place. Maybe that woman who called me told him. But he said he knew right away from the first day you showed up asking about Ernesto Pérez that you would be trouble."

Willie didn't suspect Iris. He figured it was much more likely that Merton Vetter, or whoever had followed him in that black truck, had spotted EJ making her surreptitious entrances.

"Did he say why exactly I would be a problem for him?"

"No, but he told my poppa that he should keep me away from you, because if he didn't, I was going to get hurt."

Willie winced as if someone were already hurting her. The implication was crystal clear. He didn't have to say it out loud. She did it for him.

"That sounds like he's sending someone after you, maybe to kill you. What reason would he have to do that? What did you do to him?"

Willie shook his head. "It isn't what I did to him. It's his father, maybe him too, what they did to other people. And the fact that I'm getting close to something they don't want anyone to know."

She was baffled, so he recounted for her his conversation with John Acosta concerning not only the disappearances of Mexicans but also the black workers from several years back. The more he told her, the more shocked she was.

"You think they killed those men? Why would they do that?"

"I don't know. Maybe they decided that killing them was cheaper than paying them. What I do know is the moment the government started talking about getting access to that land out there on the edge of the Everglades, Quincy Vetter suddenly turned into a political whack job, telling people only over his dead body would they get their hands on it. It makes me wonder what's out there."

"You think if they killed people, that's where they buried them?" Something else suddenly occurred to her that frightened her. "You think that's what happened to Ernesto Pérez?"

"I don't know, but I need to find out. I have two other leads, and I don't understand how they connect."

He told her about the abduction of Ricardo Ramírez from the store in Sawgrass.

That made her big, blue eyes flare. "Sawgrass is on the road to the Vetter farm and to that land out near the Glades."

"Yes, I know. I was out that way yesterday."

"What's the other lead you have?"

"Just a woman's first name: Carlotta." He told her of the phone call to Andrés Colón. "I've asked every Mexican I've talked to if they know a woman named Carlotta around here, but they don't."

That made EJ stare hard into the night, as if she were trying to find that mystery woman in the shadows.

"Maybe it isn't a woman at all. At least not a living woman."

"What does that mean?"

She pointed over at the houses to the east. "Just before you reach the Everglades on the Sawgrass road, you see some dirt roads cutting through that fallow land on the very edge of the Vetter holdings."

"Yes, I saw them."

"Well, one of those dirt roads, if you go down maybe a half mile, you come to an abandoned quarry and what's left of an old house. It was built about a hundred years ago by a man who ran the quarry. He fell in love with a local girl named Carlotta. He named the place Casa Carlotta."

"Does anybody live there?"

"No. A fire gutted the house a long time ago. When I was in high school, we went there sometimes to drink and smoke pot. Nobody was living there then, and the Vetters don't cultivate it because the land is rocky. The farm workers probably don't even know it's there."

Willie had figured Carlotta was a woman in the migrant community and had only asked Mexicans about her. It hadn't occurred to him to ask EJ or any other local. If he had, he would have solved the mystery of Carlotta much sooner.

His thoughts flashed to John Acosta, who would be heading for Cane County with FBI agents. Willie could tip them off as to where they might look for the missing men, but he knew they would keep him from the scene and freeze him out of the investigation. Even with local cops the FBI tended to be insular, takeover artists, and Willie was a private investigator. They would shove him aside as soon as they were finished milking him for information. They would also take all the credit for solving the case. Willie was being paid to bring Pedro Pérez back. The family also wanted to know what had happened to Ernesto. It was Willie's case and he wasn't going to simply hand it on a silver platter to some feds. He would have called Camp, but Camp was gone.

"What are you thinking?" EJ asked him

"I'll drop you off. I'm heading out there."

"You should wait until morning."

"I can't afford to do that."

"You'll never find the right turnoff. All sorts of dirt roads cut off there. I'm going with you."

Willie wagged a finger at her. "No, you're not. I don't want to have to worry about you."

Her expression hardened. "Here's what you need to know. It was Posey Vetter who said she found my mother's body when she was out riding her horse. It was on that land, near that quarry. Supposedly my mother was thrown by her horse, which lots of people, including me, had trouble understanding. Now you're telling me awful things, maybe murder, are going on out there. I'm thinking maybe my momma saw it. Maybe she wasn't thrown by her horse after all. Maybe someone wanted to shut her up, the same way they want to shut you up," she said, jabbing her finger into his chest. "The question isn't whether you're taking me with you. The question is: Are *you* coming with *me*?"

Willie could see she wasn't simply talking tough. From day one, she had been decisive with him, starting with her surprise appearance in his bed at the Planters Inn. Now she was talking about something much more serious, the death of her mother. She had told him what a blow that had been to her. He could only imagine what she was feeling now at the prospect that her mother had been murdered. No, there was no sense trying to argue with her. She would go without him, which would only be worse. He put the car in gear. They were headed for Casa Carlotta.

CHAPTER THIRTY

They drove north to the Sawgrass road and then headed east on the two-lane black top. They passed Triple R Farms, the turn off for Dusty Powell's cabin and then downtown Sawgrass, what there was of it. It was almost midnight now, and the few buildings were shuttered. They kept going.

No vehicles passed going in the opposite direction. It was just them and the dark sea of cane on both sides of the road.

EJ stared into that darkness. "What do you think we'll find when we get there?"

"I have no idea. Maybe nothing. Maybe whoever was speaking to Andrés on the phone that night wasn't referring to this place at all . . . but I doubt it."

Ten minutes later, they passed the entranceway to Vetter Farms. In the distance, they saw lights in the family houses.

"One or more of the Vetters has trouble sleeping," Willie said.

EJ didn't respond.

They hurried by. About half a mile later, the Vetter fields gave way to unworked land covered in scrub brush.

"This is where the old quarry land starts," she said. "Slow down, the entrance is coming up."

Over the next quarter mile, they passed a couple of gated dirt roads Willie had seen the day before. They went a bit farther and then EJ. piped up. "That's it. Stop here."

The entrance in question consisted of a rusted metal gate secured with a large padlock. The Homeland Security No Trespassing sign was posted next to it. Willie wondered if the irony of using a government sign to keep the government off the land had occurred to Quin-

cy Vetter. Those signs hadn't stopped Willie so far and wouldn't do
so now. It wasn't about to stop EJ either.

"Pull over and turn off your lights," she said. "We can walk from
here."

Willie parked the car under a tree across the road. He had his
handgun tucked into its back holster under the flap of his black
guayabera. He grabbed a small flashlight from the glove compartment. On either side of the gate, the property was protected by simple barbed-wire fencing attached to wooden posts. Willie stepped on
the middle strand and lifted the top one to let EJ squeeze through.
She did the same for him from the other side and they were in.

The dirt road ahead of them curved through the scrub brush. The
night was perfectly still, the sky clear and flooded with stars, the
same ones EJ had made him count the night they made love. Right
then, Willie wished there were fewer of them. The starlight allowed
him to see the landscape around him clearly, which meant they could
be seen as well.

EJ pointed over the scrub to the west and spoke in a whisper.
"Do you see that barbed-wire fence dividing this land from the rest
of the Vetter acreage?"

Willie said he did.

"They put that in after my mother was killed. Now you can't ride
out here. Quincy Vetter said it was necessary because of safety concerns. At the time, I believed him."

It was obvious that she no longer did.

About a quarter mile up, the rutted road was blocked by oil barrels and next to them was another No Trespassing sign. They walked
around it and kept going. On both sides of the road, they saw large
mounds of dirt, five- and six-feet high, no more than thirty feet apart.
Willie could see at least a hundred of them, so that in the dark the
place looked like some sort of pre-Colombian ceremonial ground.
Of course, those ancient archaeological sites usually turned out to be
burial grounds, a fact that made Willie's skin crawl. He needed a
closer look.

He took EJ by the elbow and steered her off the road, through
the scrub to the closest mound. They stopped there and looked down
into a narrow hole about six feet deep, ten feet long. It looked like a
backhoe had carved it and left it empty. They walked ten yards away

to the next hole and found the exact same thing. On the way back to the road, they passed two more. They were all approximately the size of graves. In the last one, a scrap of old clothing lay at the bottom of the hole, but that was all. Willie crouched down and shined the flashlight. The cloth was in tatters and looked like maybe it had been under soil for some time. The hole had apparently been someone's grave. From the look on her face, EJ had clearly reached the same conclusion, but she didn't say a word.

He got up and they walked back to the road. It made another bend, and Willie could see a structure in black silhouette about two hundred yards away

"That's the old house," EJ whispered. "That's where we'd go to drink—Casa Carlotta."

Willie stepped off the trail, silenced his phone and told her to do the same. Then they crouched and made their way to the edge of the scrub, where they could clearly see what was left of the plantation house. It had once been a two-story manse, about the size of the Eccles family house. Now, the roof was gone and much of the second floor, except for a charred beam. The first floor, made of stone, was also charred, but it still stood, although the windows were gone and all that remained were dark holes. Sitting near it were several trailers. Two were long, like ones he'd seen in the Sunset Trailer Park. A couple of others were small, like the one Ernesto Pérez had stayed in on Eccles Farm. Their front doors were all chained and padlocked. The site looked much like the one Loretta Turk had described, which had housed the black workers. Beyond the house and the trailers were more of the spooky mounds.

"Who lives in those trailers?" Willie whispered.

"I don't know. They weren't here before when we used to come to drink beer."

One trailer had a light burning inside, the others were dark. Willie stayed where he was and studied them. Then he noticed a pickup truck parked at the point where the dirt road entered the clearing. It faced the trailers and, as he watched, a person in the driver's seat struck a match, lit a cigarette or cigar and flicked the match out the open window. He was apparently a night watchman. From there he could look out over the trailers, the mounds all around and the road. *Why* a watchman was needed in such an empty, forlorn place was the question.

EJ had seen the man in the truck too and touched Willie's arm. "I need to see what's in those trailers," he whispered.

"How?"

"I don't know, but I need to get close."

Her big blue eyes gaped. The scene around them had obviously scared her. "How are you going to do that? The guy in the truck's going to see you."

Willie studied the clearing. He could wait until the watchman in the truck had to go take a leak. That might take hours and, with nobody else around, he would probably do his business right there outside the truck.

Willie sat stone still for minutes and finally turned to her. "Wait here for me. Don't move or make a sound."

He crouched, scurried back through the scrub and crossed the dirt road where he could not be seen from the pickup truck. Stooped over, he made his way through the underbrush on the far side of that road until he was about a hundred feet from where the truck was parked. He looked around for a landmark and saw a rotted tree that was taller than the others around it. He went to the base of it, took out his cellphone, turned the volume all the way up, entered his settings and turned off the voicemail function, laid it face down so that the speaker was exposed and the illuminated screen was not. Then he headed back to where EJ was waiting.

He crouched down next to her, handed her the car keys, and asked for her phone.

"Okay, I'm going to call my number and try to get him away from that truck. If he bites, I'm going across that clearing to get behind those trailers. Once I'm there, you cut the call. You give me ten minutes and then you call my number again. Hopefully he'll go look again. If he doesn't, or if anything else goes wrong, you go to the car and get out of here quick. I'll make a run for it on my own and get back somehow."

The scheme scared her, but she nodded.

He punched his own number into her pink phone, hit send and waited. He was counting on the sound being loud enough and the watchman being bored enough to react. The silence that surrounded them was profound. Moments passed, punctuated by his heartbeat, and then the phone sounded. The ringing wasn't loud, but it carried clearly through the still night. It was audible to Willie and probably even more audible to the driver, who was closer to it.

It rang again and again. Willie's eyes were trained on the driver side window. Had the watchman fallen asleep? Unlikely. Willie could still see the ember of the cigarette.

"Come on, *amigo*," Willie whispered.

One ring later, the door of the pickup creaked open and the driver got out holding a rifle. He walked to the front of the truck and stood staring into scrub brush in the direction of the ringing. Seconds later, the ringing stopped. He kept staring, then started to go back to the truck. Willie quickly punched the call button again, waited and watched as the ringing resumed. The watchman stopped, turned around and this time disappeared into the brush. Willie thrust the phone into EJ's hand.

"Remember, wait ten seconds and cut the call."

He jumped up, sprinted across the clearing and past the burnt-out house until he was behind the only trailer with a light on inside. He peered from behind the corner of the trailer towards the truck just as the ringing stopped. EJ was an efficient co-conspirator. Moments later, the watchman emerged from the scrub and took up his post again in the truck. God only knew how he explained that ringing. Maybe he thought it was his imagination. He lit another cigarette.

Willie edged along the back of the trailer and saw that the narrow back door was also chained and locked. Just beyond that door was a small, plastic window, too small for a man to fit through. It was soiled with dust from the outside and what appeared to be cooking grease from within. A grimy, white window curtain partially covered it, but a corner of it was flipped back enough to peek through. Willie could see into what were dilapidated, water-stained living quarters. They were lighted by a small electric lantern that sat on a table next to a bare mattress wedged into the far corner. Lying there, apparently asleep, was a bronze-skinned man in soiled work clothes. His face was averted, and Willie couldn't see it clearly. A single straight-back wooden chair stood next to the bed. That was all he could see from that angle.

Willie went back to the edge of the trailer, peeked around it to confirm that the watchman was still in the truck and scrambled back to the window. He scraped his fingernails on the soiled plastic pane. The man didn't react at all, his chest continuing to rise and fall in a deep sleep. Willie did it again a bit louder, longer, and the man stirred. Moments later, he sat up on the mattress, stared at the window, got up and approached.

The man swept the soiled curtain aside, and Willie found himself staring into the face of a swarthy man with hollow, grizzled cheeks, graying, tousled hair and muddy eyes that peered out full of trepidation. Willie had to make allowances for aging, weight loss, the unkempt and haggard appearance and the fear in those eyes. Once he did, he knew he was gazing at Ernesto Pérez. It was the same man whose photo he carried in his pocket. The one who had written to his children, "Remember my face."

Willie put his index finger to his lips and then pantomimed the lifting of the window. Ernesto slid it up and Willie whispered to him.

"You are Ernesto Pérez, yes?"

The other man nodded, still astounded.

"Your family sent me. I'm here to help you."

Hope battled with disbelief in the Mexican's face, leaving him speechless.

"What are you doing here?" Willie whispered.

Horror swept over Ernesto. "They've got us finding buried bodies and digging them up. When we find one, we take the bones to the old quarry." He pointed over Willie's shoulder farther into the property. "They use acid there to destroy the bones."

Willie scowled as if he were watching it happen. "How did the bodies get here? Who are the dead people?"

"They were workers from the Vetter farm. Old man Vetter, he was the one who killed them. He buried them all over the place out here. So many places he can't remember where they're buried, so we have to dig holes everywhere looking for them."

That was what the ghostly mounds of soil signified.

"How many bodies?"

The other man shook his head helplessly. "I don't know how many are here. We've dug up at least twenty so far."

"You say 'we.' Who else is here?"

Ernesto's eyes filled with sadness. "Another *compañero* was here, but they killed him."

"Ricardo Ramírez."

He was surprised that Willie knew the name. "Yes. Ricardo escaped. He had hidden his phone near here and managed to get it to call for help, but no one came. Then they caught him and shot him right in front of me. They soaked his body in the acid too."

Willie thought of the late-night call to Andrés Colón. He decided not to tell Ernesto that his old friend had been murdered before he could bring help. Ernesto was scared enough.

"I'm sure they are just waiting to finish digging up the bodies and then they will kill me."

"Does that watchman stay there all night?"

"Yes, and he drives around the property. You have to be very careful. He's dangerous. He will kill you if he sees you."

Given that Willie was probably his last hope, Ernesto was worried for both of them.

Willie was running out of time. If EJ followed the plan, his phone would ring again soon.

"Who is here during the day?" he asked. "When do they come?"

"The old man, sometimes his son, Quincy and a couple of the men who work for them. They come soon after dawn."

"You stay here for now," Willie said. "Lie back down. Say nothing to no one that I was here. I'll be back."

Willie returned to the corner of the trailer and fixed on the pickup truck. The watchman didn't move; in fact, nothing moved. Then his cell sounded, again not loud but distinctly audible. This time the watchman did not wait. He jumped out of the truck, rifle in hand and stalked into the brush.

Willie sprinted straight across the clearing, past the burnt-out mansion. He just reached the scrub on the other side when the phone stopped ringing. He crouched down next to EJ and saw the watchman re-emerge. This time before getting into the truck, he took out his own cellphone and called someone. Willie figured he might be notifying his bosses of the mysterious ringing. Any minute more bad guys might be arriving.

"Wait here," Willie whispered.

He scampered back through the brush, crossed the road, recovered his phone from beneath the rotted tree and returned to EJ.

"Let's get out of here."

Doubled over, they hurried back through the scrub towards the road. When they reached the car, he told her in shorthand what Ernesto Pérez had recounted to him. Her mouth fell open. Then he took out his phone and entered his call log.

"Put these two numbers in your phone."

He gave her the cell numbers of both Camp and John Acosta.

"I need you to head back towards Cane City as fast as you can. Along the way call Rory Camp and keep calling him until you get him. Tell him what we found and that he has to hurry back to Cane City, gather the deputies he can trust and get out here as fast as possible. Have him call me when he's close, so I can give him the lay of the land. Then I want you to call John Acosta, the attorney for the Mexican Consulate. Tell him what Ernesto told me. Let him know where I am."

The instructions weren't to her liking even a little bit. "Why am I doing the driving and the calling? Where are you going to be?"

"I'm staying here. I can't allow anything to happen to Ernesto Pérez. It took too much to find him. I can't lose him after all this."

She started to protest, but Willie opened the driver's door, kissed her quickly, and eased her in.

"Just go. The faster help gets here, the safer we'll all be."

She cranked up the car, pulled out from beneath the tree, made a U-turn, and raced back to town. Willie turned around and headed back into that prairie of graves.

CHAPTER THIRTY-ONE

Willie trotted back on the dirt road towards Casa Carlotta. He was less than halfway back when he heard the truck coming towards him. The mysterious cellphone sounds had alarmed the watchman and provoked him to make his rounds. Willie stopped dead in the middle of the road, trying to decide which way to go.

The pickup barreled around the next curve, the beams of its headlights illuminating the ghostly mounds to the right. Willie dodged off the road to the left, trying to reach the closest mound and hide himself. Just then, the truck made another curve and the lights found him spot on. It was as if he were an escaping prison inmate in a jailbreak movie. The watchman blasted his horn and fired his rifle out the window as the truck barreled towards him.

Willie hurdled over a low palmetto plant and kept running. The truck swerved and bounded off the road. With the engine racing, the watchman came right at him through the crackling scrub.

Willie made it behind the closest mound. But the truck was racing towards it, and the watchman would soon be behind it too. That would give him a clear shot. Willie waited until the truck was almost at the pile of soil, then darted for the closest mound in the opposite direction. As he did, another shot rang out. Willie heard this one buzz not far over his head.

The watchman slammed on the brakes, throwing the truck into a skidding turn. That ended with the headlights again hitting Willie just before he could duck behind the next mound. This time two shots rang out. On the run, Willie pulled out his handgun and fired back. He hit the truck, if not the driver. He heard the impact. He was going to make his pursuer think twice about getting too close. But it didn't work. This watchman wasn't given to second thoughts. The truck roared and came at him again.

Willie decided right then that playing cat and mouse at close quarters with the pickup was a losing tactic. It only gave the watchman a shorter shot to execute. He turned and sprinted into the darkness, zigzagging between the mounds. He was betting that he could maneuver the obstacle course with greater speed than the truck. If he put enough distance between him and his pursuer, he could find a place to hide until help came.

He ran, the landscape before him looking like an illustration of the end of time, when the dead all rise from their graves and ascend to the Last Judgement. Willie prayed he wouldn't get there ahead of time.

He jumped another palmetto and a small fan palm, barely breaking stride. The watchman in his wide-bodied truck braked repeatedly to keep from plunging into a grave and then gunned it again. He managed only one shot and that came nowhere near Willie.

At one point, the truck lights swung far to the left, illuminating many more grave mounds. Willie took that opportunity to cut sharply to the right, out of the watchman's path. He sprinted another fifty yards and jumped into an open grave. Gun in hand he peeked over the top of it and watched the truck speed ahead, then circle back through the mounds desperately seeking its prey. When the headlights swung his way, Willie ducked. Crouched down, he noticed something in the dirt near his foot. It was a bone. Was it animal or human? He didn't know and didn't want to know. Standing in a grave, maybe his own grave, was bad enough.

The watchman launched himself into a hectic hunt of the burial grounds. The truck looped and darted as the driver tried to catch a glimpse of Willie in his high beams. More than once the watchman jumped from the pickup and peered into a grave, rifle in hand. So many holes surrounded him, the odds were long that he would pick the right one. If the watchman were closer, Willie would have shot him. But he was at least a hundred yards away. If Willie missed, he would give away his position and accomplish nothing. He held his fire.

Then behind him he heard the sudden roar of engines. He ducked and scurried to the far end of the grave. Headlights blazing, a pickup crashed through the barbed-wire fence separating the scrub land from the rest of the Vetter property. Another one roared right behind it. Willie would wager they were Merton and Quincy Vetter. Their trucks came speeding into the burial grounds like vicious watchdogs hunting trespassers.

Willie watched them speed by his hiding place. All three trucks met at the approximate center of the burial grounds. Their headlights illuminated dozens and dozens of holes that pocked the acreage. They still needed to find the right one, but with the three of them, the odds were shorter.

Willie feared one of them might head for the trailers to kill Ernesto Pérez, to eliminate the only living witness who could testify against them. But they didn't head that way. Willie was the immediate threat. They devoted themselves to hunting him.

Moments later, they revealed their strategy. The black truck, Merton Vetter's vehicle, parked on a slight slope at the far end of the sprawling clandestine cemetery. It kept its high beams on, illuminating the mounds. The other two trucks drove to the near end, maybe a hundred yards from Willie. In the starlight, Willie saw the two men—Quincy Vetter and the watchman—climb from their trucks. They began a painstaking dragnet of all the graves, moving deliberately on foot from hole to hole, rifles at the ready. In dark silhouette, and with their silent, stark, methodical manner, it was as if they had climbed out of two of those graves themselves. Willie felt like he was being hunted by the living dead.

He froze, his eyes fixed on them. If he tried to move from where he was, he would be instantly visible to them from two directions. He could get shot in the back, the front or both at the same time. If he stayed where he was, one of them would very soon reach Willie's chosen grave. It would be a matter of shooting his pursuer before the pursuer shot him. Then he'd have to escape the other two, who would know exactly where he was.

His other hope was that help would arrive before the stalkers got too close to his burial site. That didn't happen. Instead, the two silhouettes continued to close in. Fifty yards apart, they moved from grave to grave. Willie could see that it wasn't Quincy Vetter who was

closest to him. It was the watchman. He was a big man in a cowboy
hat, much bigger than Vetter. Every minute or so he called out: "Give
it up, boy. We don't want to shoot you." But Willie knew if he
surrendered, he would quickly be dead and bathed in acid. Just the
thought made his skin burn.

The watchman came closer through the starlight. Willie could
now hear his footsteps crunching the rocky soil. Willie reached down
and grabbed the bone in the grave. Whoever it had belonged to was
long dead, but he might help save Willie's life. He waited until the
footsteps were extremely close by, just to his right. He threw the
bone high in the air, out of his own grave towards the grave on his
left. He heard it land, and so did the watchman. The other man
hurried by Willie's grave in hot pursuit without casting a glance
down. Willie lifted his gun to the edge of the grave. He waited for
the big man to be right above him and fired once, hitting him square
in the temple. Willie knew the watchman was as good as dead the
instant the slug hit him, but his body staggered forward from pure
momentum. He toppled into the grave he'd been heading for—
heading for all his life.

Willie had only seconds before the Vetters would be on top of
him. He boosted himself from the grave and rolled on the ground.
Behind him Merton Vetter's truck roared to life and headed his way.
The headlights painted him, making the target easier for Quincy.
Willie jumped up to run and began to weave. He braced for shots
from Quincy's direction, wincing in anticipation, but they didn't
come. He searched the shadows desperately, trying to spot the
exterminator. He was nowhere to be seen. Had Quincy seen the
watchman go down and made a run for it? Was he now hidden in a
grave waiting to plug Willie just as Willie had ambushed the
watchman? Willie didn't know and didn't have time to think about
it. Merton Vetter's truck was bearing down on him.

Before Willie knew it, Merton had cut the distance between
them in half. He drove like a madman, swerving through the maze
of graves much faster than the watchman had. Willie weaved, but the
high beams never left him as the truck constantly closed ground.
Merton wasn't taking a chance on a shot. He wanted to run over
Willie with the truck. That was his weapon of choice.

Willie sprinted, but there was no way he could outrun the roaring beast pursuing him. He could hear and feel the truck no more than ten yards behind him. Just then, he saw a grave longer and wider than the others, maybe where more than one victim had been buried. Without breaking stride, Willie suddenly cut to the right and launched himself into a long jump over the grave, straining to clear the hole. He reached the other side with inches to spare, lost his balance, fell and rolled.

Merton the madman, sensing an imminent kill, came right at him and the truck left the ground. For moments, it floated over the wide grave, its front wheels spinning freely as if trying to find purchase in the air. Then gravity took over. The truck nosedived into the hole with a tremendous crash and stopped dead still, as if it had hit a stone wall. Only the rear wheels kept spinning.

Silence fell over the burial ground again. Willie looked up from where he was sprawled and saw Merton Vetter's body dangling halfway through the windshield. Blood flowed in rivulets down his badly damaged face and throat. His eyes, still wild, were wide open— and very dead.

Willie scrambled up quickly, scanning the shadows for Quincy. Then he saw the BioMaster truck racing through the maze of graves, not towards him, but in the direction of the trailers. The watchman's pickup sat empty less than a hundred yards from where Willie stood. He sprinted to it, found the keys dangling from the ignition and took off after Quincy. The specter of Vetter killing Ernesto Pérez—in some vain attempt to eliminate a witness—propelled him through the night. But Quincy was far ahead, too far for Willie to stop him.

Willie tracked Vetter's tail lights as he approached the trailers, expecting him to stop. Instead the exterminator blew right by them, swerved, crashed through another section of fencing and headed in the direction of his own homestead. Willie followed, a mile behind, barging through the cloud of billowing dust kicked up by Quincy. He watched across a tomato field as the BioMaster truck skidded to halt outside the brightly lit farmhouse. Willie held the pedal to the floor, sharply braked, turned on two wheels at the entrance and stopped next to the white clapboard house. Just as he did, a shot rang out from the inside.

Willie flinched, bailed out of the truck and hugged the ground. No more shots sounded, only dead silence. Willie grabbed his handgun and hurried to the porch. The front door stood wide open, and the lighted living room was empty. Willie edged his way forward, gun leading the way.

He glanced into a bedroom and saw a large four-poster bed. It was empty, sheets in disarray. Further down the hall, he heard a faint creaking sound. Pressed against the wall of the hallway, he advanced and peeked around a door jamb into a sitting room. Posey Vetter, dressed in a white flannel nightgown, red hair streaming, rocked slowly in an old black rocking chair. She stared straight ahead as if in a trance.

Willie stepped in and followed her line of sight. Quincy Vetter sat propped in a stuffed chair, his head sharply askew, blood trickling from his right temple. A handgun lay on the carpet beside his dangling hand.

She glanced at Willie. "And Merton?"

Willie hesitated, but she seemed to know already.

"He's dead."

Her eyes settled on Quincy again. "He came to tell me the long nightmare was over. They buried lots of men. Now I'll have to bury them both."

Willie heard sirens not far away. He took out his cellphone and called Rory Camp.

CHAPTER THIRTY-TWO

The FBI arrived mid-morning. John Acosta of the Mexican Consulate was with them.

By that time, Willie had freed Ernesto Pérez from his imprisonment and he was receiving treatment by EMTs. Camp sent a deputy to St. Anthony's Church, and he brought back both Pedro Pérez and Father Finlay. Willie and the priest oversaw the emotional reunion between father and son. Unlike Willie, Pedro recognized his father instantly. The two men exchanged a long embrace, tears coursing through the grit on the father's face.

Willie then called Abbie LeGrange, who screamed with joy into the phone and soon had the two men connected to an equally joyful Cecilia Pérez. She told them she was headed to Cane County right away.

Ernesto directed the FBI investigators to the quarry pit where Merton Vetter had emulsified all the recovered bodies with hydrochloric acid. Willie and Camp tagged along. Enough bone fragments remained to constitute evidence. The sovereign rights religionists who had served as watchmen and who had tried to kidnap Pedro were rounded up. Badly outgunned, they didn't offer much resistance. They weren't true believers.

The feds were interested not only in the clandestine graveyard but also in the questionable goings on in Cane County. They pulled aside Sheriff Nathan Pope and grilled him. He swore on a stack of Farmers' Almanacs that he knew nothing about the killings on the Vetter land. That kept him tied up so that he couldn't interfere with Willie and Camp. The two of them, accompanied by a female FBI agent named Compton, drove to the Vetter homestead and interrogated Posey Vetter in the living room of her house. The body of her son had been removed and transported to the morgue.

Mrs. Vetter offered no resistance. She was determined to defend the memory of her son and in doing so provided valuable details about her husband's crimes.

"Merton, he killed them all," she said matter-of-factly.

"The black homeless men and later the Mexicans?" Camp asked.

"Oh, yes. Black ones, brown ones, you name it."

"Why did he do that?"

She shrugged. "Sometimes it was because he simply didn't want to pay them what he owed them. Other times, it was his temper. Merton, he had a terrible temper on him. He'd smack one, and that boy would threaten to go to the police. That was usually the end of him. Merton always waited 'til the harvest was ending and figured out a way to get them alone . . . one or two of them. No one ever saw them again. When people came looking for them, he just said he'd last seen them driving away. I told him it would catch up to him in the end, but he wouldn't listen to me. He said they was just colored people, and there was too many of those to begin with."

She spoke as if she had warned her husband to not eat so fast or not to drink too much. You wouldn't have known she'd been married to a serial killer.

"That was why these last years we only leased the land, so that Merton wouldn't have any business with the workers."

"And Quincy?"

Posey Vetter shook her head hard. "Quincy, he never killed any of 'em. He only tried to cover up for his father."

"Is that why he got involved in all that sovereign rights hogwash?"

Posey met Camp's gaze. "Well, we couldn't let the government dig up that land, now could we? Quincy did what he had to do to keep that from happening." For a moment she beamed. "Of course, near the end, he got carried away with it all. He convinced himself what he was saying made sense, and he convinced other people, too." She met Camp's gaze. "He was a clever boy, my Quincy."

Camp questioned her a while longer and finished, but for Willie there remained one more issue.

"Mrs. Vetter, can you tell me what happened to Muriel Eccles, EJ Eccles' mother?"

That made the widow wince. "O, poor Muriel. She went riding onto that land one day and saw Merton digging up two bodies. She rode away as fast as she could, but Merton went at her in the truck. The horse panicked and threw her. Merton said he could tell her neck was broken, so he put her out of her misery with a big rock. He considered it an act of mercy. But oh, I felt so bad about Muriel. After all, she was one of us."

Being "one of us" hadn't counted for much with Merton Vetter.

Posey Vetter was taken away on a charge of accessory to numerous murders. Camp and Willie drove back together to the trailers, where Willie gave Camp a detailed account of all that had happened during the last day. In the sunlight, the field full of graves looked just as spooky as it had the night before.

"It's as if the Rapture had come to this town," Camp said.

"Amen," said Willie.

***

It was dusk by the time he arrived back at the Planters Inn. Camp had insisted EJ stay in town, refusing to risk her safety after she had described the open graves on the edge of the Everglades. Her father had also insisted that she stay behind. She had called Willie a couple of times during the day to find out what was happening. He told her he was safe, but nothing else.

He called her from his suite. Minutes later, they were sitting next to each other on the edge of the bed. He filled her in on the deaths of Merton and Quincy, and Posey's confession of everything the family had done. He also decided he had to tell her himself the truth about her mother's death, before it came out anyway in the charges against the Vetters. She listened to him silently, her expression hardening, as if she had Merton Vetter standing before her.

"The man who killed your mother is dead," Willie said. "The man who helped him hide his crimes—Quincy—is dead. Posey Vetter will be in prison for a long time, probably as long as she lives. You helped do all that. You avenged your mother's death."

She took that in, nodding once. Tears rolled down her cheeks.

He laid her down on the bed and wrapped her in his arms. She lay quiet, and in time they fell asleep. When he awoke, she was gone. This time she left a note on the pillow next to him.

Thank you for everything you did for us, Mr. Miami. After all this passes, I will track you down. You still owe me salsa lessons.

* * *

By two p.m. the next day, Willie was back in Miami Beach, sitting on Fanny Cohen's balcony, eating an egg salad sandwich on rye and drinking a glass of Portuguese *vinho verde*. Fanny made the best egg salad in the western hemisphere.

She had just finished debriefing him on all the events that had unfolded in Cane County. When he explained to her that the whole Sovereign Rights Movement had been a device to hide the Vetters' murders, she flicked her fine eyebrows.

"Why doesn't that surprise me. People who use that kind of political language are perfectly willing to spill blood. In this case, they did their killing first and spouted their radical bilge later. But it was the same people."

The image he painted of acres pocked by empty graves also made her grimace.

"Remember, I warned you those people up there liked to plant all sorts of things. You're still lucky they didn't plant you."

"If they had, whatever grew out of me would have been very sweet."

Fanny rolled her eyes. "You're just too Cuban for words, Willie boy."

Willie didn't argue. They sipped their wines and watched the brilliant midday sun play off the dazzling surface of the aquamarine sea.

ALSO BY JOHN LANTIGUA

Burn Season

Heat Lightning

The Lady from Buenos Aires: A Willie Cuesta Mystery

On Hallowed Ground: A Willie Cuesta Mystery

Player's Vendetta: A Little Havana Mystery

Twister

The Ultimate Havana